DISTANT TELEPATHS

Distant Telepaths

Stories

Timothy Zahn

OPEN ROAD
INTEGRATED MEDIA
NEW YORK

Copyright © 2025 by Timothy Zahn

"Red Thoughts at Morning," *Analog,* copyright © 1981
"Dark Thoughts at Noon," *Analog,* copyright © 1982
"Black Thoughts at Midnight," *Distant Friends,* copyright © 1982
"Bright Thoughts at Dawn," copyright © 2024

ISBN: 978-1-5040-9693-5

This edition published in 2025 by Open Road Integrated Media, Inc
180 Maiden Lane
New York, NY 10038
www.openroadmedia.com

CONTENTS

INTRODUCTION

Forty-odd years ago I had a strange idea: a small group of tele-paths who could communicate with each other over hundreds of miles, but could never get physically closer than twenty miles or the mental pressure would kill them both. (I was probably feeling isolated that day. Writers' ideas come from the strangest places.) I liked the resulting story, so a year later I wrote a follow-up, and ten years after that I added a third.

With those stories now thirty years out of print, it seemed like a good idea to make them available again.

Unfortunately, I'd left things on a sort-of cliffhanger. Not a *real* cliffhanger, with people in horrible and imminent danger—I try not to do that to my readers. But there were certainly unpleasant consequences lurking around a corner ahead.

In such a case, the only solution is to write a new story to close off those loose ends. (I suppose you can also simply ignore the problem and hope no one notices. But if my experience is any indication, readers notice *everything*.)

So herewith is the complete and final saga of Dale Ravenhall and his distant telepath friends.

Unless, of course, another idea occurs to me. . . .

—Timothy Zahn

RED THOUGHTS AT MORNING

It had been one of those long, frustrating days, the kind that makes you feel like the dish rag at a greasy spoon, and I wasn't in any shape for the headline that jumped out at me as I opened my *Des Moines Register* that evening: TELEPATH KILLED IN HIJACKING.

I stood there, just inside my apartment door, rainwater running off my coat onto the rug, and read the first few paragraphs. Amos Potter, of Eureka, California, had been on a commuter flight from San Francisco to Los Angeles when three men at the other end of the plane produced guns and a bomb and demanded to go to Cuba. The pilot had obediently changed course, but had had to set down in Las Vegas for fuel. Police and FBI men had stormed the plane, killing all three hijackers and wounding four passengers. Amos hadn't been found until it was all over: he'd been stabbed in the heart with one of the galley's steak knives and left in one of the lavatories.

Tears welled up in my eyes and I tossed the paper aside. I'd never met Amos, of course; never even been within two hundred miles of him. But he'd been a sort of elder statesman to the rest of us, the embodiment of easy dignity and high moral character, and it was largely because of him that we had won any tolerance at all from the world.

I made my way to my couch and collapsed onto it. *Colleen,* I called.

Yes, Dale. She must have been expecting my call. *I've seen the news, darling.*

Why didn't you call and tell me? The news at noon mentioned the hijacking, but I didn't know Amos was aboard. Or . . . any of the rest of it.

Maybe I should have called you. Her thoughts wrapped soothingly around my pain, the telepathic equivalent of taking me in her arms. *But I knew you were going to have a rough day, and I didn't want to dump this on top of you at the same time. Did that go all right?*

More or less, I told her. *Both sides spent the whole day arguing legal details before the judge. I got to sit there and listen to them discuss my abilities and ethics as if I wasn't there. When I wasn't being insulted I was being bored. Hardly seems important now, though, does it?*

I know, she agreed soberly. *Did you know Amos well?*

Not really. I felt her smile, and couldn't help smiling myself. It was truly the sort of answer a telepath would give: only when you don't know how complex human beings really are do you lightly state that you "know" someone. *I couldn't reach him in Eureka, of course, but he used to come to Pittsburgh or Louisville once or twice a year, and I always talked with him for a few hours then.*

Me too. I used to feel a bit isolated up here in Regina; you remember how I used to fly to Salt Lake City a couple of times a year just to talk with him. I'm going to miss him.

Yeah. We all are.

For a few minutes we sat silently, maintaining contact without words. Colleen's presence had a warm, comforting texture to it, and slowly the tensions of the day began to fade. Finally, I stirred. *Have you discussed arrangements with any of the others yet?*

A little. I talked to Gordon in Spokane, and he thought the only fair way was to let all of us draw straws to see who'd get to go to Eureka and attend the funeral.

No, I shook my head, *it should be between those who knew Amos best. That would be Gordy and Nelson, I guess.*

Colleen shifted uncomfortably. *Do you think it would be wise to let Nelson go? I mean . . . you know how he gets sometimes.*

Oh, he'd be all right, I assured her. *He was only mildly paranoid to begin with, and living in San Diego's been good for him. Every time Amos went down to Los Angeles he improved a little; some of Amos's calmness had to rub off at that distance.*

All right. She was willing to concede the point. *Do you want me to suggest that to Gordon?*

If you would. I thought for a second. With Amos gone, Gordy was out of touch with everyone except Colleen. *I'll call Calvin in Pueblo and have him relay the message to Nelson.*

You feel up to that?

I smiled. *Yes. Thanks for always being there when I need you, Colleen.*

Thank you, she said quietly, and I knew then that she'd received as much comfort from me as she'd given.

I love you, Colleen.

I love you, Dale. Good-bye.

We broke contact. I'd loved Colleen for nearly three years now, and she'd loved me even longer. And the knowledge that we would never meet each other was a dull ache permanently lodged in my throat.

What a stinking world.

Sighing, I got to my feet and headed for the kitchen to see about some supper.

I slept poorly that night, and was back at the Des Moines

courthouse at nine sharp the next morning for another day of arguments. In one sense the question before the court was straightforward: the judge had simply to decide whether or not my testimony as a telepath could be admitted as evidence in a robbery case. In practice, however, the legal issues and ramifications surrounding the whole concept formed a jungle that made the Amazon basin look like the Pampas. My mood this morning wasn't helping a bit, either; it was dominated by depression, fatigue, and some unknown beast nagging at the back of my mind, and all I wanted to do was to crawl back into bed. I wished to heaven I'd never let the D.A. talk me into this.

Today, for the umpteenth time, Urban, the public defender, wanted to hear about my range.

"Think of it as listening to someone whispering," I told him once more. "Within two or three feet I can't help but hear someone's thoughts. Farther away, up to about twenty or twenty-five feet, I can choose whether or not to listen; beyond that, I can't hear at all."

"Except with your fellow telepaths, of course," Urban said briskly, as if I needed reminding.

"The defendant isn't a telepath," I pointed out as patiently as possible.

"Of course not. Now, you referred to this as akin to hearing whispers. We all know how easy it is to misunderstand whispers sometimes—"

"The analogy referred to range, not accuracy," I interrupted. "If I can hear the thoughts at all I hear them clearly. Always."

He started to ask something else—and right then, for no particular reason, the crucial question hit me like a Trident missile.

How the hell do you unexpectedly stab a telepath?

It *had* to have been unexpected; the lavatory door had been unlocked and the paper hadn't mentioned any signs of a struggle. But that was impossible; given the circumstances. Amos was most certainly reading out to his full range. So why hadn't he seen the killer coming?

Urban had finished his question by the time I made up my mind. "Excuse me," I said, pulling out my handkerchief and pretending to clear my sinuses. I didn't want to just go glassy-eyed on them, after all; I've learned that sort of thing can be disconcerting to people. But safely hidden behind the handkerchief, I could make my contact. *Calvin? Calvin, are you there? Calvin?*

Right here, Dale, came the calm thought. *You sound agitated.*

I'm getting there, I agreed. *Listen, you've got the location log this quarter, right? Can you clear me to Las Vegas tonight? It's important.*

From Des Moines? That was Calvin—no unnecessary questions asked. *Any direct flight would bring you too close to Pueblo, but I could move out of town for a few hours if necessary.*

No, it's not worth that. Besides, I doubt there's a direct flight, anyway.

Then if you go via Denver or Salt Lake we should be all right.

Great. I'll make some reservations and get back to you as soon as I know my schedule.

All right. Oh—and you'll have to be out of there by six tomorrow evening. Gordy's flying down to escort Amos back to Eureka.

Yeah, okay.

Calvin was getting curious. *I trust you'll tell me what all this is about sometime.*

Sure, but later. I've got to go now.

Talk to you later.

I slid my handkerchief back in my pocket. Already I felt better. "Now, what was that question again, Mr. Urban?"

I got through the rest of the morning without any real trouble. During lunch break I called a travel agent and he worked out a pair of connecting flights that would get me into Las Vegas by ten. That was later than I'd wanted, but my only other option was to wait until after Gordy had come and gone. This way I'd have at least most of tomorrow before I had to leave town.

The judge and lawyers weren't happy about my announcement that I was taking a few days off, but they accepted it with the grace of reasonable men who have no real choice in the matter. By seven-thirty that evening I was on the first leg of my flight . . . and by eight we were circling Denver, just a hundred miles from Calvin's home in Pueblo.

It's a strange sort of sensation, and more than a little scary the first time you experience it. Even a hundred miles apart. Calvin and I were now close enough that it was no longer possible to block our surface thoughts from each other: to tune each other out, so to speak. It's the same thing that happens when a telepath and human are only two or three feet apart, but with the extra complication that it's a true two-way communication. If the plane now suddenly turned due south and Calvin and I got even closer . . . but that wasn't something I wanted to think about.

Of course, as long as you didn't panic, the effortless communication provided by a close approach was a good opportunity to talk. Calvin and I spent quite some time doing just that, discussing life in general and ourselves and our fellow telepaths in particular. But he couldn't hide his curiosity about my sudden trip, just as I couldn't hide my somewhat perverse decision to make him bring up the subject first.

Calvin cracked first. *All right, you win,* he said at last. *You're not going to Vegas just to say good-bye to Amos—I can tell that much. So?*

You're right. I explained as best I could the questions I had about Amos's death—not an easy task, since a lot of my feelings hadn't really made it to verbal level yet.

6

He mulled at the problem for a bit after I finished, his thoughts an orderly flow of questions, possibility, and logic. *Interesting,* he said. *I agree; something here doesn't ring quite true. I don't know, though. Suppose one of the hijackers recognized Amos, decided to kill him to cover their trail, and threatened to kill some of the other passengers too unless Amos went quietly? He was nobler than the rest of us put together, and I could see him giving in under those circumstances.*

Maybe, I said slowly. *But I still don't like it.*

I can tell, Calvin came back dryly. *You're broadcasting uneasiness over two states. Look, I doubt that there's anything sinister going on here, but I agree it ought to be checked out right away. Let me know if I can help, okay?*

You'll be the first I call, I assured him.

Good. Oh, one other thing you may not have heard about yet: the question's been making the rounds today as to whether or not we should ban commercial air travel by our members.

I thought we settled that issue years ago.

We did, but it's getting another look. If there's going to be a resurgence of hijackings, the margin of safety's going to be all fouled up, and it may be smart to stick with trains or private planes for a while. Suppose, for instance, Amos's plane had been diverted to Pueblo or Des Moines instead of Vegas.

We both shuddered. *Yeah,* I agreed soberly. *But I think the risks can be minimized.*

Yeah, well, I'm not going to debate it with you now. Just think about it, and we'll all discuss it together in a week or so.

Okay. I'd better enjoy this trip, I thought glumly—it might be the last I could take for a while.

Fine. Well, you seem pretty tired, so I think we should break now. I'll talk to you later, Dale.

I glanced out the window in mild surprise. Our layover was

over, and we were once again airborne. Beneath the plane the ground was dark; Denver was far behind us. The close approach was over. *Good night, Calvin,* I said, and broke contact.

I dozed the rest of the trip, trying to ignore the peculiar looks and even more peculiar thoughts the stewardess kept sending my way.

Sometime during the middle of the night I decided I hated Las Vegas, and that first impression was solidified the next morning during my taxi ride to police headquarters. It wasn't just the high proportion of the criminal element roaming the streets: every city has some of that. Rather, it was the greed, goldlust, and despair I could sense all around me. This was a frantic town, a city founded on hedonism and life's more transient gains, and it simultaneously angered and depressed me. It seemed grossly unfair that Amos Potter, a man who had loved the quiet outdoors and had spent his life helping others, should have had to die here.

But the police, at least, were courteous and helpful, and I was routed to the proper officer with a minimum of delay. He was a squat, muscular man with a swarthy complexion and the unlikely but circumstantially appropriate name of Lieutenant James Bond.

"Honest," he insisted as he gave me a quick handshake. "What can I do for you?"

"My name's Dale Ravenhall," I told him. "I wanted to ask a few questions about the recent death of Amos Potter."

He recognized my name and drew back almost imperceptibly. "I see. I'm sorry about Mr. Potter. Was he a good friend of yours?"

"We are, by necessity, a somewhat tight-knit group," I said. "Are you the one who found Amos on the plane?"

He shook his head. "One of the SWAT team discovered the body." His mind flashed the man's name—Sergeant Tom Avery—which I filed away for future reference. "I was called in right away to head that part of the investigation."

"Were there any signs of a struggle? The newspapers didn't mention any."

"No, there weren't, and that's something I don't understand. You people are supposed to read minds at a pretty good distance, right? So why didn't Mr. Potter lock the door?"

I scowled. "I don't know. That's one of the things that bothers me about this."

"What are the others?"

"The lack of struggle, for one," I said, sensing even as I ticked off my list that he had many of the same questions. "The use of one of the galley knives for the murder when they had guns. How come they were clever enough to smuggle those guns aboard in the first place, and yet got themselves killed on their first stop."

"You missed two important ones," Bond said. "Why did they pick a puddle-jumping commuter plane from San Francisco, of all places, to hijack to Cuba? And why didn't Mr. Potter contact one of you people before he died?"

I frowned. That last hadn't occurred to me. "I don't know. I was too far away myself at that time, but maybe he *did* talk to one of the others. I can check on that right now, if you'd like."

Bond had never watched a telepath in action and wasn't sure he wanted to start now. But professional considerations outweighed any squeamishness. "Go ahead; I'd like to know."

From my close-approach contact with Calvin last night I already knew Amos hadn't contacted him before his death. Gordy was a long shot; I tried briefly to get him, but the distance was a shade too great. That left only one possibility. *Nelson? Are you there, Nelson?*

9

Yes, of course, Dale. What is it?

If Colleen's mental texture was one of warmth and love, and Calvin's one of calmness, Nelson's always struck me as predominantly nervous. *I was just in the neighborhood and thought I'd say hi.*

In the neighborhood?

Las Vegas. Light conversation was often lost on Nelson. *Listen, Nelson, I've been trying to track down some questions about Amos's death.*

What sort of questions?

Oh, just some loose ends. Nelson's nervousness was contagious, and I didn't want to prolong the contact. Besides, Lieutenant Bond was waiting. *I wondered if Amos had had a chance to contact you before the end.*

No, he said, almost too quickly. *But I might have been out of range.*

Where were you?

I flew down to Baja for a couple of days. His tone said it was none of my business where he and his Piper Comanche had gone. *I was flying back when the news came.*

Okay, just wanted to check. You doing okay?

Save your sympathy, Dale. I'm fine.

Right. I'll be talking to you later.

Bond nodded when I relayed the conversation. "That was Nelson Follstadt, right? Do you think you can believe him?"

I bristled. "Of course. Why would he lie?"

He shrugged. "I hear he has some psychological problems."

"Well . . . yes, he does, but he's improved a lot lately. And he's been away from the other telepath for nearly ten years, so there's no place to go but up."

"Come again? What other telepath?"

This wasn't really the time for a lecture, but Bond truly

didn't understand. And I've always tried to avoid littering my path with mysterious statements and obscure hints. "Oh, well, you've probably heard that telepaths can't get too close to each other. That's because the contact gets stronger with decreasing distance, and the two personalities begin to meld into one. At about twenty miles apart—theoretically—the strain becomes too great and both telepaths go permanently insane."

Neither Bond's face nor his thoughts were very pleasant. "Is that what happened to Nelson Follstadt?"

"Fortunately, no. The telepathic ability grows with age, and it's only as you get into the teens that it becomes strong enough for any risk of insanity to show up. Nelson just happened to grow up in the same city with another fledgling telepath, and before they were identified and split up the small effects had gradually built up into a mild paranoia. But, as I said, Nelson's improving."

"What about the other telepath?"

"He committed suicide six years ago." One of our group's worst failures, I reminded myself bitterly.

"Oh." Bond was silent for a moment, wondering if he should ask his next question. I let him take his time. "There's one other thing I've been wondering about," he finally said. "I've heard rumors that you people can . . . well, force normal humans to do what you want. Is that true? And if so, why didn't Mr. Potter stop the hijacking?"

"It's true, in about the same way the CIA and certain religious cults can impose their will on people. It would take almost continuous contact between telepath and subject for several days straight to accomplish it, though. Amos couldn't possibly have done anything in the time he had."

"Hmm. Okay, I'm surprised the CIA hasn't shanghaied you, though. You sound like you'd be handy to have around."

"Some of us have been tested by various agencies. There are drugs that are faster and easier to use. Look, we're getting off the subject. Is there anything else you can tell me about Amos's death or about the hijacking in general?"

"Sorry." He shook his head. "You've got all the obvious facts; the others will have to wait for the lab work. If you'll give me your number, I'll get in touch when I know something more."

"I'd appreciate that." I wrote my Des Moines number on a card and, for good measure, added Calvin's. "I may be moving around in the next few days, but Calvin Wolfe here will be able to relay any messages."

"Fine." He gave me a thoughtful look. "Nelson Follstadt's closer, you know. Don't you trust him?"

"Sure I do. I just—well, Calvin's a closer friend."

"Yeah. Well, thanks for stopping by, Mr. Ravenhall. I'll be in touch."

"Thanks." I shook his hand again and left.

His last question bothered me all the way back to the hotel. Why *hadn't* I given him Nelson's number?—Especially since Nelson was closer to Eureka, where I had already more or less decided to go next. Was there something about that last contact I'd had with him that had bothered me?

Certainly, Nelson had been nervous, but that was normal for him ... wasn't it? I was beginning to regret having broken off the contact so quickly. My chance was now gone for further questioning; if I called back with the same questions I was likely to stir up Nelson's quiescent paranoia, and I couldn't take that just now.

I glanced at my watch. It was nearly noon. Flopping onto my back on the bed, I closed my eyes. *Calvin? Yo, Calvin?*

Hello, Dale. Learned anything interesting?

Yes and no. I've found the cop in charge of the investigation has some of the same questions I do, but he doesn't have the answers either. Is Gordy still due in here at six, and when is he heading over to Eureka?

Yes, and tomorrow morning.

I need a favor. Would you ask him to delay either leg of his trip by twenty-four hours?

Well . . . I suppose I could ask him. Why?

I'd like to go up to Eureka myself and look around. No partic-ular reason, I added, anticipating his next question. *I'd heard Amos had suspended his psychotherapy practice and was working on something special. I'd like to check it out.*

I can save you some trouble, if that's all you want. According to Gordy, Amos was trying to build some kind of electronic gadget for locating new telepaths.

My jaw dropped. *You're kidding. I hadn't heard a whisper about that. I didn't even know it was theoretically possible.*

Me neither, to both comments, until Gordy told me last night. Apparently Amos didn't want it spread around, in case things fell through.

Now that I thought about it, I remembered Amos had earned a master's in electrical engineering before switching to psychology. *How far had he gotten?*

Gordy didn't know. He was planning to try to find out when he went up there.

I pondered. *Calvin, I'd still like to go to Eureka tonight.*

Okay, I'll try to work things out with Gordy. If not, you two'll be in contact range within a few hours and can hash it over between yourselves.

Thanks. One other thing. I hesitated. *Nelson told me he was in Baja when Amos died. Is that true?*

Calvin was silent for a moment, and I could sense his surprise. Accusing another telepath, even implicitly, of lying was serious business. *As a matter of fact, I don't know. Nelson is a bit of a maverick sometimes, and I'm pretty sure he occasionally takes his Comanche out for a short spin without telling anyone. I think he resents having his movements watched so closely, especially when he doesn't think it necessary.*

I grunted. That was just great. *Maybe I should give him personal notice that I'm heading to Eureka. I'll talk to you later, Calvin. Thanks for your help.*

Sure. Good hunting.

For a moment I just lay there, thinking. Then I rolled over, snared the phone, and placed a call to the airport.

I got into Eureka at eight that evening and rented a car for the drive out to Amos's home. I'd never been there before, but Gordy had given me detailed directions earlier in the day and I found the unpretentious little ranch house without difficulty. Mrs. Lederman, Amos's long-time housekeeper, was waiting there for me; with typical foresight, Calvin had phoned to tell her I was coming.

"I'm pleased to meet you, Mr. Ravenhall," she said when I had identified myself. "Please excuse the mess; I haven't felt much like cleaning today."

"It looks fine," I assured her. Her plump, middle-aged face had lost most of the signs of recent crying; the scars in her psyche would take much longer to heal. I didn't intend to pry, but the texture of her surface thoughts made it obvious that she had loved Amos deeply. I wondered how he had felt about her, and the thought inevitably turned my mind toward Colleen. . . .

Wrenching hard, I forced myself back to business. "Mrs. Lederman, did Amos say or do anything unusual before he left? Anything that might imply he was worried or suspicious about something?" She shook her head. "I've been thinking about it ever since Mr. Wolfe called from Colorado this afternoon and I can't come up with anything. Amos seemed a bit preoccupied when he returned from Los Angeles about two weeks ago, but that cleared up quickly and he went back to work on his telepath finder—I expect you've heard of that by now."

"Yes. Who besides you knew he was working on it?"

"Gordy Sears, of course," she said. "I think he was Amos's closest friend. And I believe Mr. Follstadt knew about it, too."

"Nelson?" That made sense, I suppose. One main use of the gadget would probably be to locate young telepaths before any accidental psychic damage occurred, and knowing such a thing was in the works might ease any fears Nelson had about being hurt like that again. "Would you let me see where Amos worked?"

"If you'd like," she shrugged, and I caught something about a mountain retreat from her mind. "But most of his electronics work was done at his cabin in the Sierra. It was more peaceful there, he used to tell me; nobody else *thinking* nearby."

She led me down the hall to Amos's workroom, and I poked around there for a few minutes without finding anything interesting. "Can you tell me how to get to his cabin?"

"Well . . . it was sort of private, but I guess it'd be okay now. But it'd take five or six hours to get there. You ever driven mountains at night?"

"Enough to know I don't want to try it in an unfamiliar area. I'll head out in the morning. If you'll give me those directions, I'll go now and get out of your way."

"No need for that," she shook her head. "I've made up the guest room for you."

"Oh. Thanks very much, but I don't think I ought to stay."

"It's no trouble. I'm leaving in a few minutes, anyway, and you'll have the place to yourself. Amos was always hospitable,

Mr. Ravenhall," she added, as I opened my mouth to refuse again. "I know he would have wanted you to stay here."

What could I say to that?

She gave me a quick guided tour of the premises to show me where everything was, and then left, locking the front door behind her. I watched her car disappear down the road and then, moved by an obscure impulse, returned to Amos's workroom.

Off in one corner of the room was a small writing desk almost buried under neat piles of paper and correspondence. I'd ignored it the last time I came through, but now I went over and gazed down at it. A proper investigation should include a search of Amos's papers . . . but I had no right to pry like that. Besides, if I found something significant, would I even know it? I still didn't really know what I was looking for. Resolutely, I started to turn away . . . and as I did, the return address on one of the envelopes caught my eye. It was that of a Las Vegas casino.

Frowning, I picked up the letter. It was unopened, post-marked the day before Amos's death. Feeling guilty, I opened it.

The message was very brief:

Dear Mr. Potter,

Thank you for your note of the 4th. We are quite interested in your proposal, and would very much like to discuss it in person with you. Please let us know when it would be convenient for us to fly you down for a meeting.

It was signed by one of the biggest names in Las Vegas.

I reread the letter twice without making any more sense of it. What was Amos doing getting mixed up with Vegas casino owners? What kind of offer was he making? And was it pure coincidence that Amos had subsequently died in that very city?

Some of those questions might be answered if I could find the carbon of Amos's original letter, but a two-hour search convinced me that it wasn't anywhere in the house. Unless Amos had destroyed it or Mrs. Lederman had taken it away, there was only one other place it was likely to be. More than ever, now, I wanted to get to Amos's mountain retreat.

I was rudely awakened from a restless dream by an insistent knocking at the base of my mind, and it took me a second to realize that I was being contacted. *Yes?*

It was Gordy. *Dale, are you all right?*

Sure. I sneaked a look at my watch. Four thirty, and I was lying fully clothed on Amos's guest room bed. *Why do you ask?*

When you hadn't checked in by midnight Calvin and I started getting worried. We thought something might have happened to you.

Just fatigue, I assured him. *I'm sorry, though; I had intended to contact you last night. I guess I was more bushed than I thought. Listen, I may have something interesting here. Did you know Amos had a cabin in the Sierra?*

Yes, but I don't know where it is.

I do. I repeated the location Mrs. Lederman had given me. *I understand he did most of the work on his telepath finder up there; I'm going to go see how far he got with the gadget. And to check on something unexpected that's just cropped up.* I described the contents of the letter I'd found.

What do you think it means? a new voice asked.

I jumped. *Calvin? Damn, but you startled me—I didn't know you were listening in. Come to think of it, how come you're within range?*

Because I'm in Salt Lake City, he explained. *I flew here last night to give Gordy a hand in raising you. Now, what about this letter?*

I haven't the foggiest. But I think it might be important.

Maybe, Gordy said cautiously. *I gather you'd like me to stay here in Vegas until you're finished with everything?*

If you would. I think it would make things simpler if I didn't have to keep track of where you were going to be. Another day or two at the most.

Okay. Nelson will calm down eventually, I suppose.

How's that?

You didn't know? No, I guess not. He was going to fly up to Eureka after I left to attend Amos's funeral. He was furious that we were delaying things so that you could go running around robbing Amos of his last shred of dignity.

That last was a direct quote, Calvin added.

I winced. *Yeah. I'm sorry. But I still think it's got to be done.*

We're not blaming you, Dale, Calvin said. *Just finish up as quickly as possible, okay?*

Will do, I promised. *Look, I'd better let you two go. I'll contact you when I get to the cabin. Honest.*

Gordy chuckled. *Okay. See you.*

I stared out the window at the predawn darkness for a full minute. Further sleep would be impossible; something in the back of my mind was urging speed. Swinging my legs over the edge of the bed, I located my shoes and headed to the kitchen for a fast breakfast.

Half an hour later I was driving towards the rising sun.

I'd half-expected Amos's cabin to be some rude shack on the side of a mountain, and was therefore vaguely surprised to find a quite modern-looking structure, complete with phone and power lines snaking their way down the mountain. With the key Mrs. Lederman had left me, I let myself in. The interior was as modern as the Eureka house, but not nearly as tidy; Mrs.

Lederman probably didn't get up here very often. It was basically a single room, efficiency style, almost a third of which was taken up by a long work table holding about a ton of electronic equipment. In the center of the work table was Amos's telepath finder.

There was no doubt as to what it was. Clearly homemade, it consisted of a metal box the size of a portable tape player with a pivoting direction pointer protected by a plastic dome mounted on top. There were only two switches: on/off and general/tare. *Calvin? Gordy? Anyone home?*

Right here, Calvin answered. *Where are you, Dale?*

At Amos's cabin. I've found the telepath finder.

You made good time, Gordy grunted, sleep-cobwebs still evident in his mind. I'd forgotten they'd been up much of the night trying to contact me. *What's it look like?*

I described it for them. *That's it?* Calvin asked. No *range meter or anything like that?*

Nope. Maybe Amos planned to work on one next. Of course, you could always get range by triangulation.

Right. Have you tried it yet?

No. I wanted you two here when I did. Any ideas what this general/tare thing is?

There was a pause. *A tare is a deduction of the container's weight when weighing something,* Gordy said. *Maybe that eliminates the operator's effect.*

That makes sense, I agreed. *Okay, brace yourselves. Here goes.*

With the second switch set at "general" I reached out and flipped the device on. Instantly, the needle on top swiveled around and came to a stop pointing at my belt buckle. I took a couple of steps to the right; the needle followed me.

Seems to work, I told the others. *Now I'll try it on "tare."* I flipped the second switch and waited.

Nothing. The needle moved a fraction toward the west, but

was still pointing at me when it stopped. I flipped the switch back and forth a couple of times, but the needle refused to move farther than a few degrees. *This part isn't working.*

You sure? Gordy asked.

Yeah. I'm standing on the finder's north side, so if it edits me out it should swing around to point south-east, where you two and Nelson are. It certainly shouldn't point north by west. I turned it off. *We can worry about this later. I'm going to see if I can find that carbon.'*

One corner of the work table was piled with papers. Leafing through the whole stack would take only minutes; as it happened, my search was considerably snorter. *I've found it.*

Read it to us, Calvin said.

I skipped Amos's identification of himself and his list of credentials. The interesting part was in the second paragraph:

> It has recently come to my attention that one of our group has been making periodic visits to your area for the purpose of "gambling"—I use quotation marks because, for him, certain games will not be governed by chance. No names need be mentioned; I do not intend to aid you in catching or prosecuting him, but merely wish this unfair practice to stop. My efforts to dissuade him have failed, so as a last resort I am offering you a deterrent in the form of a telepath finder. . . .

Gambling? Gordy seemed shocked. *Who of us would do something like that? That's just crazy.*

I think we all came up with the same name simultaneously. Calvin was the first to admit it. *If Amos was right, there's only one of us who has really convenient access to Vegas, who can sneak in and out without too much risk of close-approach problems.*

I sighed. *You mean Nelson?*

DAMN YOU ALL! WHY CAN'T ANY OF YOU MIND YOUR OWN BUSINESS?

All three of us jumped violently. It was Nelson's voice, but so convulsed with fury as to make it almost unrecognizable. *Hey, Nelson, take it easy,* I said. *We didn't know you were listening in.*

Of course not. You'd much rather plot my destruction in private, wouldn't you? You and that holier-than-thou Amos. Well, I warned him!

Something was wrong here. Even given Nelson's strong emotion, his contact shouldn't be this strong. *Nelson, where are you?* I asked carefully.

You! he all but spat. *It's your fault. You couldn't let Amos die in peace. You couldn't let well enough alone. Now you're going to get what he got.*

Damn you, Nelson! Gordy suddenly interjected. *You killed him, didn't you? Amos caught you sneaking into Vegas, so you conditioned those thugs to hijack the plane and kill him!*

It was his own fault, Nelson shot back. *It was none of his damn business how I make my money. I* had *to do it—can't you see that?*

He'd gone from angry to pleading in the space of a single sentence, and I didn't like it a bit. Was he starting to crack up?

You'd like that, wouldn't you? Well, if I go, you're going with me!

And that shook me clear down to my toes. It had come up so quickly and so unexpectedly that I hadn't noticed: Nelson and I were in close-approach contact.

Nelson was only a hundred miles away!

And getting closer, he mocked me. *I know where you are, too; I listened to you give the directions to your pals this morning. I'll be overhead before you know it.*

Nelson, are you nuts? Gordy cut in. *You'll kill both of you.*

And why not? You're all out to destroy me anyway. I might as well take one of you with me. I've got nothing to lose now.

Dale, get out of there, Calvin ordered. *You've got to try and get away from him.*

I took three steps toward the door and froze. *Get away where? I don't know what direction he's coming from!*

Nelson laughed. His thoughts were getting progressively louder, and it was becoming harder and harder to hear Gordy and Calvin over the noise. Calvin had to virtually shout his next message. *Use the telepath finder. Maybe it really is working.*

I sprang over to the table, snatched up the box, and flipped the switch. In "tare" mode it once again pointed north by west—and stayed there even when I moved out of the way. Instead of coming straight up from San Diego, Nelson had circled around and was bearing down on me from the north. Clutching the box like a talisman, I ran outside to the car.

And then the nightmare began.

There was no way I could outrun Nelson, and we both knew it. His Piper Comanche had a cruising speed of at least a hundred eighty miles an hour and could travel in a straight line, while I had to stay on winding mountain roads at a quarter of his speed. If I could have gone at right angles to his path, let him overshoot me, I might have had a chance. But it was already too late for that sort of trick. Nelson had complete access to my surface thoughts, and there was no way for me to make any plans without his knowledge.

You see? It's useless to struggle. Give up; it'll be easier on both of us.

I gritted my teeth and drove on, trying in vain to shut out the increasing pressure slowly crushing my mind. A curve came up, too fast. I tapped on the brake, managed to negotiate the turn without losing too much speed. Every fiber of my being was screaming for me to get away, but I had no intention of driving off a cliff for Nelson's convenience. Wiping my palms, one at a time, on my pants, I tried to think.

I was completely cut off from Calvin and Gordy now—the close approach had been blocking any other contact practically from the minute I left the cabin. They would know enough to call the police, of course, but there was little chance the cops could help me. It would be less than an hour before Nelson closed to the twenty-mile gap that would ensure mental disintegration for both of us. The Air Force? They could act swiftly, but they'd first have to be persuaded to get involved. And in a completely nonmilitary situation like this, the chances of that were essentially zero.

A reddish haze, more felt than seen, was growing at the edge of my mind. *Nelson, why are you doing this to us? It can't gain you anything.*

You've all worked against me: you, Amos, Calvin—everybody. You've robbed me of the money and power I could have had—that I deserved. *But at least I command my own death. And before that I'm going to make you fear me. You* are *afraid, aren't you, Dale?*

He knew I was. For himself, Nelson felt no fear: only pain, anger, and morbid satisfaction. His death wish wrapped around me, tinging the reddish haze with black. Blinking back tears of agony, I kept going.

I don't know how long I drove, or how many close calls I had with the many cliffs I passed. Indeed, I hardly even noticed the road any more; I drove by sheer reflex. As inexorably as the tide, Nelson's mind slowly washed over mine. Our thoughts, memories, and emotions intertwined, becoming bent and altered by the force of the collision. I saw his decision to kill Amos, and his conditioning of an airline attendant and three drifters to set up and execute the hijacking. I watched the agony of Amos's death, and knew that he'd realized, too late, what was happening. Nelson's current plan was laid bare; how he'd tried to beat me to the cabin and destroy both the telepath finder and the evidence of his gambling. I felt his lust for power, his anger and frustrations—at himself, me, the work!—his self-doubts . . . and all this was becoming part of me. I was slowly being lost in this thing, this Dale/Nelson creature which was being created; and the knowledge that Nelson was similarly being swallowed up only added to my terror.

And all too soon, I saw the end approaching.

I mean that literally, for in a very real sense whatever there was that was still Dale Ravenhall was now occupying two separate bodies. I could actually see both the road ahead of me and the more majestic view from Nelson's Comanche. I could feel the plane's vibration, touch two different steering wheels . . . and I knew the agony would soon be over.

Yes, *soon we'll be dead.* Was that my thought or Nelson's? Not that the distinction mattered much any more. I paused for a moment to look through Nelson's eyes, to gaze at the mountains I would never see again . . . and, suddenly, a sharp left-hand curve around a cliff loomed ahead.

I gasped, and Nelson's death wish within me fragmented as a surge of survival instinct snapped a portion of my mind out of the growing chaos. Stomping hard on the brake, I wrenched the wheel hard to the left; and as the squeal of tires filled my ears, I saw I had overcorrected. The side of the mountain rushed at me, and I leaned back, bracing for the crash.

The world exploded with a ghastly crash and everything went black.

I woke up slowly, painfully, and with a sense of complete disorientation; but what I noticed first was the silence. It was just me again, Dale Ravenhall, and the other presence was gone. Was I dead?

He's awake.

I cringed involuntarily as the thought touched my mind. The other knew it immediately and hastened to reassure me. *It's all right, Dale, it's all right. It's just me, Colleen. You remember me?*

I swallowed hard and, timidly, reached out. *Is that really you, Colleen?*

It's really me. And Gordon and Calvin are here, too, if you feel like talking to them.

How're you feeling? Gordy asked.

Better, I answered. I was starting to wake up now, and memories were coming back. *Where am I?*

Sacramento, Calvin told me. *They airlifted you there after you crashed your car. You were pretty lucky; minor injuries only.*

Yeah. I was dreading the next question, but I had to ask it. *What happened back there? How did I escape?*

Nelson crashed. Went into a dive somehow and ran smack into a mountain. The experts think he must have turned and come down too fast; there's no evidence of mechanical failure.

I nodded within myself. In those last seconds I'd been in the Comanche's cockpit as well as in my own car—and in the latter I'd turned left, hit the leftmost pedal, and pushed on the wheel. Apparently, I'd done the same in the plane. But I couldn't tell the others what had happened. Not yet.

Calvin was speaking again. *You've been under sedation for the last three days while a handful of top psychiatrists did some tests. They say you've got all the symptoms of dissociative hysteria, but that you have a good chance of recovering with proper care and some hard work.*

Unbidden, tears formed in my eyes, and I clenched my teeth

to keep them back. *Maybe. But who's going to come out of this recovery? Dale Ravenhall? Or a Dale/Nelson mixture?*

There was a pause. *We don't know, exactly,* Colleen said gently. *But whatever changes have been forced on you, you're still Dale Ravenhall. Hang onto that thought, that reality. You're still our friend, and we'll stick by you and give you all the help we can.*

Even if I turn out to be partly Nelson?

We would have done the same for Nelson, Calvin said. *He was one of us, too. Try not to hate him, Dale.*

I don't hate him for me. But I won't soon forgive him for killing Amos the same way he tried to kill me.

What do you mean, the same way?

I sighed. I wanted so badly to just forget all this. But they had a right to know. *Nelson wasn't in Baja when Amos was killed. He was in Las Vegas.*

But that's where his conditioned hijackers took the plane. Colleen sounded confused.

Which is exactly what he wanted. Don't you see? Picture Amos rushing helplessly toward a fatal contact with Nelson, who is pretending he is there just by chance. You all know how noble and selfless Amos was. What would he do in that situation?

There was a long pause, the texture of which changed from puzzled to horrified to very sad. *He would have committed suicide rather than let them both die,* Calvin said at last. *That's what happened, isn't it?*

I nodded wearily, and Colleen must have sensed my fatigue. *I think we'd better go now and let Dale get some rest,* she said. *Dale, we'll be here as long as you are, so just call whenever you want to talk. Okay?*

Sure. Thank you—all of you.

Take care, Dale. We'll talk to you later.

I turned my head to the side against my pillow. Sleep was

pulling at me, and I welcomed the temporary oblivion it would bring. *I am Dale Ravenhall,* I said to myself and to the universe around me. *You hear me? I am Dale Ravenhall. I am Dale Ravenhall. . . .*

I was saying it right up to the moment I fell asleep. Down deep, I knew it wasn't completely true.

DARK THOUGHTS AT NOON

Like a crazed hawk the Piper Comanche dives at me through the red mist. I am flying her; desperately, I grip the wheel, trying to keep the car's screeching tires on the road winding through the mountains. Agony clouds my vision, permeates every fiber of my being. In the distance I hear a bell ring. Ask not for whom the bell rings . . . no, that's not right, but I can't remember how it should be. Beneath me the road sweeps past/the toy-like mountains crawl past. I am Dale Ravenhall/I am Nelson Follstadt/I am Dale/I am Nelson—pain pain pain. The bell rings again—

And as quickly as it began, the daymare was over. I was back in my house on the outskirts of Des Moines, trembling slightly with reaction. Downstairs, the front doorbell rang.

I took a deep breath and got up from the desk chair where I'd been sitting, feeling my shirt stick to my back as I did so. I headed out of the room, and was halfway down the stairs when the call came.

Dale, are you all right?

It was Colleen, of course; she's usually the only one who can tell when I've hit one of my daymares. *Sure, Colleen,* I assured her. *It wasn't too bad this time.*

At a hundred thirty-odd miles away in Chillicothe, Missouri, she was still far enough away from me to edit the thoughts I sent her, but even so the fib was a waste of time. *Oh, Dale,* she sighed, and I instantly felt like a heel as warmth and strength flowed from her, chasing away the final bits of the vision's darkness. *It'll get better, darling—it* has *to. Do you want to tell me about it?*

Not really. I'd found out months ago that talking about the daymares didn't do anything to eliminate them. *Look, honey, there's someone at the door. I'll call you back when I'm free.*

All right, if you're sure you're all right. I love you.

I love you, too.

We broke contact, and I felt the usual frustration well up inside me. Frustration at my daymares, at Colleen's quiet refusal to return to her beloved Saskatchewan as long as I still needed her close by; but most of all, frustration at the universe's uncaring decree that had kept us apart all our lives. And once more I swore I was going to find a way around that law, no matter what it cost me.

I continued down the stairs, and as I reached the front hall I caught the first wisps of thought from those waiting outside my door. There were two of them, one of whom I recognized almost immediately from the texture of his surface thoughts. The other was a stranger, but knowing Rob Peterson had brought him here made his business obvious. Reaching the door, I opened it wide. "Come in, Rob; Mr.—ah—Green," I said, pulling Ted Green's name from Rob's thoughts.

Green blinked, and I felt him reflexively shrink back as he realized what I'd just done. Rob just grinned and strolled on in; after four months of working for me he'd long since gotten used to telepathic shortcuts. With only a brief hesitation and a measuring look at me Green followed. Pretending I hadn't noticed, I closed the door behind them, then led the way to the living room. We sat down, and I got right down to business.

"First of all," I said, addressing Green, "what has Rob told you about my project?"

"Nothing, really." He shrugged. He'd taken the farthest chair from me that courtesy permitted, and while he wasn't quite out of range there, the thoughts I could get were barely surface ones. But Rob was closer, and his thoughts verified Green's words. "He told me you needed something electronic built, and that I'd be working with the most intriguing bit of gadgetry I'd ever see." He smiled shyly. "How could I pass up a come-on like that?"

It was right then that I decided I didn't like Ted Green. The shy smile was pure affectation, completely out of sync with the cool, calculating mind I'd already glimpsed there. That sort of gambit used by that sort of person, I've found, is usually an attempt at emotional manipulation, a practice I detest. "How indeed," I said shortly. "Before I tell you more, I want it clearly understood that this information is strictly confidential, and that whether you take the job or not you'll keep it to yourself."

"I understand."

"All right." I pursed my lips, mentally preparing myself. I didn't want another daymare now. "Have you ever heard of Amos Potter?"

"Sure," was the prompt reply. "He was a telepath from California—worked as a psychologist, I think. He died last April during a plane hijacking, stabbed by one of the hijackers. Seems to me that was just a few days before your own accident, wasn't it?"

I forced a nod. Amos hadn't been killed by the hijackers, but had been forced into suicide by a megalomaniac Nelson Follstadt; and my "accident," as he called it, was Nelson's attempt to do the same to me. But there was no point in telling Green how much of the story the official version had left out. "Amos also had a master's degree in electrical engineering, and he left us an interesting device: a black box that locates telepaths."

Green blinked with surprise, threw a glance at Rob. "I'll be da—sorry. How does it work?"

I gestured to Rob. "We don't know yet," he said. "Most of the electronics are perfectly straightforward, but there are two components that Amos apparently made himself. They're the heart of the finder—and we still don't know how they work."

"Interesting," Green murmured. He looked at me. "May I see them?"

"Sure. The workroom's in the basement; the stairs are around that way."

I let Rob lead the way downstairs, bringing up the rear myself. Green, I noticed with grim amusement, practically walked on Rob's heels in an effort to stay as far away from me as possible.

I'd only lived in the house for about five months, having moved in just after my return from California with the telepath finder, and the basement thus hadn't had nearly enough time to fill up with ordinary homeowners' junk. That was just as well, because with the workbench and electronic gear Rob had brought in the place was already pretty crowded. In the center of the table, wired to an oscilloscope, was a crab-apple-sized lump of metal.

"That's one of them," Rob said, pointing it out. "We've got seven—Amos left us eight but I ruined one getting it open."

Green stepped over to the table and carefully picked up the sphere. "Heavy," he grunted. "What'd you find inside?"

"A couple of commercial IC chips, an inductor coil he apparently wound himself, and some components that unfortunately were connected somehow to the inside of the shell and which I ruined when I cut it open. But we've got lots of data on its characteristics."

Rob pulled over a fat lab notebook and within ten seconds the two of them were embroiled in a technical discussion about six miles over my head. I didn't even bother to try and follow it; I was more interested in learning as much about Green as I reasonably could. Moving to within two or three feet would have given me complete access to both his surface thoughts and a lot of the stuff underneath, but he was keeping me in the corner of his eye, and I didn't want to push him too hard. So instead I kept my distance and worked on picking up the high points of his personality.

He wasn't going to be as easy to get along with as Rob had been; that much was obvious right from the start. Along with his manipulative tendencies, Green had more than his fair share of egotism, ambition, and something I took to be contempt for people he considered inferior to himself. But he seemed smart enough, if the speed at which he assimilated Rob's pages of numbers and graphs was any indication, and Rob at least seemed to think he could be trusted to keep my secret. If he was willing to work for the pittance I could afford to pay, I decided at last, the job was his. His personality I could live with or stay clear of.

After a while Rob ran out of words, and Green turned back to me. "I think I understand," he said. "These kernel things apparently act as antennas for whatever it is you guys broadcast, covering a broad enough spectrum to pick up all of you and plot a resultant. I gather that it works; so what do you need me for?"

"I want you to use those—kernels," I said, adopting his term for Amos's gadgets, "to design and build something entirely different. You'd be working mainly for the challenge of it, though; I can't afford to pay you much."

"Which is why you wanted another grad student instead of hiring a real EE," Green nodded. His tone was noncommittal, but I could tell he was already hooked.

"More or less. Having known Rob for the past four years helped, too. All right. What I want is a device that'll block my telepathic ability."

Green frowned. "You mean like something to make the broadcast directional?"

"No—something to kill it altogether, the way a copper shell around a radio transmitter will absorb the signal."

"But why would you want—" He broke off, having answered his own question with impressive speed and accuracy, even given that my long-distance romance with Colleen was reasonably well known. "Temporary blocking, I assume?"

"Right." Though there were times I'd wished to be rid of the damn talent permanently. "When do you want to start?"

"I haven't said yet I'd take the job," he said, a bit testily. I hadn't been wrong earlier; he didn't much like having his mind read.

Rob, as usual, saw the humorous side of his friend's reaction and chuckled. Green flashed him an annoyed look, then managed a wry smile. "Right—I don't *have* to say things like that here, do I?

Okay. How about if I come in Saturday morning—say around eight-thirty?"

"Sounds fine. I'll see you then."

I leaned against the front door for a minute after I let them out, feeling the contacts fade as they walked to the street and Green's car. I knew I should be happy I'd found a replacement for Rob so quickly; it was only a week ago that he'd realized how much preparation his upcoming prelims were going to take. And yet, despite Green's apparent qualifications, there was something about him that made me uneasy. There'd been something going on beneath the level I could read, something . . . *sinister* was far too harsh a word; maybe *opportunistic* fitted the sense of the feeling better. I probably should insist on a deeper probe into

Green's mind before I let him examine Amos's devices further, a part of me realized. But my pragmatic side quickly scotched that idea. As long as he made me a telepathy shield it was a matter of supreme indifference to me what kind of schemes his ambitious little mind might be hatching.

Sighing, I pushed away from the door and headed back to the living room. Patience is a virtue, I told myself firmly. Flopping down on the couch, I put it carefully out of my mind and reached out. *Colleen?*

I'm here, Dale, her answer came immediately.

We talked for a long time, and the afternoon shadows were cutting sharply across my minuscule lawn by the time we broke contact. Spending time with Colleen invariably improved my mood, and I was sorely tempted to ignore my psychologist's standing order and pretend the latest daymare simply hadn't happened. But reason eventually prevailed. Hauling the vision out of my memory, I went over it with a fine-tooth comb. By the time I finished I was depressed again, a mood I'd had to put up with a lot lately—Nelson had always been the melancholy sort.

If only I'd had a telepath shield five months ago. . . .

Whatever other qualities Green might or might not have possessed, I had to give him full credit for punctuality; he arrived on Saturday at eight-twenty-five sharp. I took him downstairs and spent nearly half an hour showing him where all the equipment and supplies were. He still tended to shy away from close contact with me, but since his personality hadn't changed markedly in the past two days such avoidance was mutually agreeable.

"So what are you going to do first?" I asked when I'd finished the grand tour.

"Double-check some of Rob's numbers," he said, pulling an

ancient wave generator over toward the center of the table. "I want to see if flipping polarity on any of the kernel's bias terminals will affect the output the way he said it does."

I pulled a chair over to the far end of the work bench and sat down, resisting the urge to suggest that would be a waste of time. He already thought I was too impatient. "What will that tell you?" I asked instead, trying to sound merely curious.

"It'll tell me if energy is disappearing into the thing—if so, it may be acting as a transmitter instead of a receiver. Your shield might consist of one or more of these things blasting out an interference signal."

"Wouldn't it be easier to absorb the telepathic signals instead?" I suggested. "Then you could use them as receivers, the way they're designed."

"It might be," he said. "But I want to know my possible options before I start."

He returned to his work, his mind filling up with technical thoughts . . . but even so he couldn't hide the fact that his last statement had been at best a half truth. He had another reason for wanting to do this experiment, a reason I couldn't quite pick up at the distance I was at.

I thought about it for several minutes in silence. Two days ago I'd been willing to let Green do anything he wanted as long as he got me a shield, but now I was having second thoughts. After all, the telepath finder was Amos's final legacy to all the rest of us, and I had a certain amount of responsibility to make sure it wasn't ruined.

I puzzled at the question for a minute, then came to a conclusion. Leaning back against the wall, I sent out a call. *Calvin? Are you there, Calvin?*

Who's that—Dale? Calvin answered, a bit groggily.

I grimaced; I'd forgotten Saturday was Calvin's only morning to sleep in and that it was only a little after eight Pueblo time. *Yeah. Sorry, I didn't mean to wake you. I'll call back later.*

No, that's all right, he assured me. *I got to bed at a reasonable hour last night. What's on your mind?*

I wondered if Gordy had finished going through all of Amos's things, both at Eureka and at his mountain cabin. Specifically, I wanted to know if he found anything else relating to the telepath finder—notes, schematics; that sort of thing.

Um . . . you got me. I can call and ask, if you'd like.

I would, but you can wait until later. Whether he was in Eureka or at home in Spokane, Gordy would be on Pacific Time, and I had no desire to be the one responsible for waking him up this early.

Okay. Calvin hesitated. *I talked to Colleen yesterday. She said you'd had another daymare.*

Yes. It wasn't too bad, though.

Calvin didn't buy that any more than Colleen had. *Uh-huh. Any changes in the vision? Content, texture, length—anything?*

I sighed. *Not really,* I admitted, *unless you want to count the fact that my doorbell got incorporated into it. Aside from that it was just a straight replaying of Nelson's attempt to kill both of us. And before you try to think up a euphemistic way to ask, yes, I still get some of it from Nelson's point of view.*

He was silent for a long moment, but it wasn't hard to guess what he was thinking. Among the candle flickers of ordinary humans, we telepaths stand out like carbon-arc searchlights, the strength of our mental broadcast and sensitivity enabling us to communicate over hundreds of miles. But the price for this unique companionship is a heavy one: at anything less than a hundred miles apart the contact is strong enough to be painful, and at a theoretical distance of twenty miles both personalities would disintegrate totally under the strain. Nelson and I had been close to that limit when he finally took a wrong turn and crashed the plane he was chasing me with into a mountain. I'd survived the encounter . . . but not unscathed. The Dale Ravenhall I'd once been had been bent and altered by the force of the mental collision, changed into something that was part Dale and part Nelson. Permanently? No one knew. But the fact that some of each daymare still came heavily flavored with Nelson's memories was ominously suggestive.

Well, Calvin said at last, *it's only been five months, after all. A lot of simpler psychological problems take longer than that to heal.*

I snorted. *Thanks a whole bunch.*

Sorry, he said quickly, and I grimaced. In earlier days he would have recognized that kind of statement as the banter it was. Now, he was bending over backwards to avoid stepping on any toes, real or otherwise. Nelson had been the touchy sort.

It's okay, I reassured him. *I know you were trying to be encouraging. Uh . . . you don't have any plans to travel east in the near future, do you?*

I could come over any time. Why?—do you need some close-approach contact?

Not really. I wasn't ready yet to have all my surface thoughts open to another person, good friend or not. *I just thought maybe you'd be willing to stay in Minneapolis or Dubuque or somewhere for a week or two and let Colleen get back to Regina for a while.*

That could probably be arranged. Are her friends in Chillicothe getting tired of her company, or is she just homesick?

No to the former; probably to the latter. Not that she'll admit it, of course—she takes her baby-sitting duties seriously.

Uh-huh. Well, look—I'll talk to her and check the location log to make sure I wouldn't be flying in on top of anyone else and then get back to you. Okay?

Sure. Thanks; I really appreciate it. And don't forget to check with Gordy about any other telepath locater stuff.

Right. Talk to you later.

I came out of the contact and glanced around the room, reorienting myself. Everything was as I remembered it . . . except that Green was gazing sideways at me from the work bench, his expression wary. "It's okay," I assured him. "I'm not going to faint or anything."

"I know," he said. "Who were you talking to?"

"Uh—Calvin Wolfe."

"Pueblo, Colorado; right?"

"Yes." Frowning slightly, I touched his thoughts. What I found surprised me. "You've been reading up on us lately, haven't you?"

Again, there was that little flicker of resentment that seemed to come whenever I demonstrated my telepathic ability on him. "For a couple of days, yeah. I wanted to know what I was getting myself into. It must be nice to be able to talk to someone that far away so easily."

"You can do almost as well by telephone," I told him shortly, "and without the disadvantages we've got."

He shrugged. "Not much of a disadvantage. All you have to do is stay out of each other's way. Big deal."

If I'd been a violent man I probably would've hit him. Instead, I suddenly felt a need to get far away from such stupidity. "I'll be upstairs if you need me," I told him with as much civility as I could manage. Without waiting for a response, I left.

The call I was expecting came about eight hours later, after Green had gone home for the day; and to my mild surprise it was Gordy himself who made it. *Gordy, where are you?* was my first question.

On a plane somewhere near Billings, Montana, I believe, he said. *I'm on my way to Minneapolis; going to be doing some work there for the next couple of weeks.*

Such fortuitous timing, I told him. *Calvin couldn't get away?*

Even eight hundred miles away I could sense his embarrassment. *You make it sound like we're all conspiring to put one over on you,* he protested. *We're your* friends, *Dale.*

Yeah, I know. Feeling like a heel was becoming a full-time job here lately. *What's the word on Amos's things?*

I've gone through everything from top to bottom and back again. No notes, no plans, no schematics, no extra equipment other than what you've already got. Either he deliberately destroyed all the documentation or the design of the finder was so obvious to him that he could just sit down and cobble one together. Sorry.

Me too. I thought about the implications of that. From Rob's struggles with the kernels I found it hard to believe they'd been *that* easy to make. Had Amos foreseen other applications for his invention, applications he perhaps hadn't cared for?

My telepath shield, for example?

Gordy broke into my musings. *Look, Dale, don't you think it's about time, you let the rest of us in on what you're doing with all that stuff?*

My first impulse was to tell him that they'd find out when I was good and ready and not a solitary second sooner. But that was clearly Nelson talking. *I don't know,* I said instead. *I'm trying to make something new out of the things Amos developed for his finder. If it works—well, it'll benefit all of us. Let's leave it at that for now.*

Gordy was silent for a long moment. *You know, Dale, it's possible to play these things too close to the chest. If we'd known that Amos had caught Nelson making quiet trips to Las Vegas we might have implicated him in Amos's death before he had the chance to try to kill you. You could be running the same kind of risk here.*

I'm being careful, I told him stubbornly. My doubts about Green rose unbidden before my eyes; ruthlessly, I crushed them down. *I just don't want to raise any false hopes, that's all.*

All right, he said after another pause. *But be careful, okay?*

Sure. Enjoy your flight, and I'll talk to you later.

Yeah. Take care.

I sat where I was for a long time afterwards, my book lying ignored on my lap. Once again I felt torn between my natural desire for caution and my almost suffocating urgency to possess a telepath shield. Colleen was practically within my grasp—how could I permit anything to get in the way of that? Besides, what earthly use would a telepath shield—or anything else Green could make in my basement—be to a normal person? A defense against the highly unlikely possibility of one of us eavesdropping on a private conversation? Ridiculous, when thirty feet of distance would achieve the same end. No—I *had* to be reading Green wrong . . . and I didn't need to be reminded that Nelson had had a strong touch of paranoia.

Nevertheless, that evening I went out and bought a burglar alarm, and by the time I went to bed I had it rigged so that anyone entering or leaving my basement would trigger a light and quiet buzzer in my second-floor study. Now, whenever Green tried to leave I would know in time to get within telepathy range of him before he got out of the house. A rather simple precaution, to be sure—but then, I wasn't really expecting any trouble.

The days lengthened into weeks, as days have a way of doing, and progress on the shield remained depressingly slow. Green's idea about reversing the biases hadn't panned out, and he'd been forced to seek out new approaches. Fortunately, he didn't get discouraged as easily as I might have, his failures merely spur-ring him to stronger efforts. He began to spend more and more time at my house, sometimes arriving while I was still eating dinner and not leaving until after midnight. What made his single-mindedness all the more astonishing was the fact that he still felt acutely uncomfortable around me, avoiding close contact and sometimes even going so far as to fill his mind with technical thoughts to try to forget I was within range. Apparently he was simply the type who enjoyed a challenge for its own sake.

I had a couple more daymares during that period, too, one of them while Colleen was back in Regina. Fortunately, Gordy was still in Minneapolis at the time and helped me get through those first few shaky minutes afterward. I'd wanted him to keep quiet about it, but he insisted that Colleen had a right to know, and the upshot was that she was back down at her Chillicothe listening post within twelve hours. I was pretty upset with her for inter-rupting her R and R, and I think it was probably that mood that triggered the milder daymare a day later. It was really little more than an aftershock, but it was enough for Colleen; after that, she wouldn't have left me again if the whole midwestern United States had caught on fire. Gordy, too, found reason after reason to stretch out his Minneapolis visit, and when he finally left, Calvin found a plausible excuse to spend some time in Dubuque.

What with all this companionship therapy taking up a lot of my attention, it was early October before I finally noticed some-thing was off-kilter.

It began with an afternoon call from Rob Peterson, who was trying to get hold of Green and thought he might be with me. During the course of the conversation I discovered Green hadn't shown up at any of his classes for nearly a month, a figure that coincided uncomfortably well with the first of his six-to-midnight sessions in my basement. When I asked him about it later, Green admitted he'd been neglecting his schoolwork, but claimed he'd be able to catch up once he finished my shield. As usual, he stayed right at the edge of my range, so I wasn't able to confirm that he was telling the truth; and not wanting a scene I let him go back to work without further cross-examination. I soothed my conscience by reminding myself that he was a grown man, perfectly capable of deciding how to use his time.

But the whole thing seemed funny somehow—I couldn't reconcile this sudden neglect of his studies with the ambitious and calculating personality I'd already glimpsed in him. It bothered me; and gradually I began staying on the first floor whenever Green was in the house, where I could pick up his surface thoughts as he worked in the basement. He knew, of course—my footsteps would have been audible above him—and I could sense an almost frantic note in his attempts to cram his thoughts with technical details of his work. But enough got through. More than enough . . .

I waited until I was sure, and then I confronted him with it.

"You've had it for two weeks now, haven't you?" I said, anger struggling for supremacy with other emotions I was afraid to accept. "You know how to make a telepath shield."

"I don't *know* if I do," he protested. Hunched over the workbench, a soldering iron still gripped in his hand, he watched me with slightly narrowed eyes, as a rabbit might a fox. "I've never tested it."

Hairsplitting; but it *was* a genuine lack of certainty, and that had been enough to fool me for nearly a week. Belatedly, I wondered if perhaps I'd gotten the rabbit and fox roles reversed. "Well, let's not waste any more time. Turn it on."

"All right." Standing up, he went to the far end of the bench. A bulky, three-level breadboard assembly rested there, built into a framework that looked like it'd been made out of leftover angle iron. Three of Amos's kernels glittered among the tangle of electronic components. Plugging the device's cord into an outlet, Green flipped a switch and vanished.

It took a fraction of a second for my eyes to register the fact that Green was, in fact, still standing there in front of me, that it was only his mind that had disappeared from my perception. I must have looked as flabbergasted as I felt, because Green's lip twitched in a smile of sorts. "Like it?" he asked.

"I—yes," I managed. "How does it work?"

"Best guess is that it creates a sort of dead zone where telepathic signals get absorbed. I don't know for sure, though."

"I told you that was the approach to take," I said, feeling a little light-headed. "Will it block other telepaths, too? We project a lot more strongly than you do."

He shrugged. "Try calling someone."

I did; and because I was afraid of false hopes I tried for a solid three minutes. But at the end of that time I was convinced. *Colleen* . . . With an effort I dragged my mind back to Earth. One more important question still needed an answer. "All right. Now tell me what you've been doing these past two weeks, while you were supposedly working on the shield."

He radiated innocence. "I *have* been working on it—I've been trying to make a more practical model." He indicated the breadboards. "You see, this one is big and heavy, with an effective range of probably no more than a hundred feet, and it requires one-twenty line current. I think I can make one that would run off a battery and have almost half a mile of range— and the whole thing fitting inside a briefcase. Another—oh, month or so—and I should have it."

It was a good idea, intellectually, I had to admit that. But all of my hopes and dreams had suddenly become reality and I knew I didn't have the patience to wait another day, let alone an entire month. "Thanks, but no. This one will do fine."

He blinked, and I got the impression that my answer had surprised him. "But . . . I'm not finished here, Mr. Ravenhall. I mean, I promised to build you a practical telepath shield. *This* thing's hardly practical."

"It's practical enough for me," I said, frowning. Goosebumps were beginning to form on my suspicions—he had no business fighting that hard for a two-dollar-an-hour job. "Before we continue, what say we make things more interesting and turn off the shield?"

He made no effort to reach for the switch. "That's not necessary," he sighed. "I *was* bending the truth a little. I've already been trying to design an entirely different gadget using those kernels, and I was afraid you'd send me away permanently once I'd finished the shield."

"What sort of gadget?"

"A mechanical mind reader."

"A *what?*"

"Well, why not? The kernels clearly pick up telepathic signals. Why shouldn't the signals be interpretable, by a small computer, say?"

I opened my mouth, closed it again as the potential repercussions of such a gadget echoed like heavy thunder through my mind. By necessity, each of us who'd had this gift/burden dropped on us had long ago thought out the consequences of misusing our power. The potential for blackmail, espionage of all kinds, or just simple invasion of privacy—I was personally convinced it was only our extremely limited number and the fact that we were thus easy to keep track of that had kept us from being locked up or killed outright. A mechanical device, presumably infinitely reproducible, would open up that entire can of worms, permanently. "Forget it," I said, finding my voice at last. "Thanks for the shield; I'll give you your final pay before you leave." I turned to go back upstairs.

"Wait a minute," Green snapped. "I *can't* forget it, just like that. This thing'll be a gold mine if I can get it to work. I've put a hell of a lot of work into it—I can't quit now."

"A gold mine for whom? You and a select clientele of professional spies?"

"It doesn't have to be that way," he protested. "Psychologists, for instance—mind readers would be a tremendous help in their work. Rescue teams could locate survivors in earthquakes or collapsed buildings. Doctors—"

"What about bank robbers? Or terrorists? Or even nosy neighbors?" I shook my head. "What am I arguing for? The subject is closed."

Green expelled his breath in a long, hissing sigh, and his expression seemed to harden in some undefinable way. "I'll have to collect my tools," he said stiffly.

I hesitated, then nodded. "All right. I'll be upstairs writing your check."

I didn't head up right away, though, but crossed instead to the dim corner where the fusebox was. The telepath shield I'd coveted for so long had abruptly become something that could be used against me, and I had no intention of letting Green leave here under its protection—I wanted to know whether he'd really given up or had something else up his sleeve. One of the peculiarities of this house was that the basement lights were all on one circuit and the outlets on another. Finding the proper fuse I pulled it . . . and across the basement, just barely within range, I felt Green's thoughts reappear. Simultaneously, drowning out that faint voice, came a frantic duet.

Dale! Are you there, Dale; can you answer?

Here I am, I said hastily. *What's all the fuss?*

Oh, thank heaven. Colleen's thoughts were shaking with emotion. *We thought something terrible had happened. Calvin and I have been trying to contact you for nearly five minutes.*

Another daymare? Calvin asked, trying to sound calmer than he really was. I didn't blame him; a daymare that had lasted that long would have been a real doozy.

No; this was something good *for a change.* I told them about the telepath shield, trying to recapture my earlier enthusiasm for the device. But that glimpse into Green's ambitions had dampened things considerably, and I was barely able to keep my report on the positive side of neutral.

Calvin, at least, saw the potential hazards immediately. *Do you think it's wise to let this Green character run around loose?* he asked when I'd finished. *If he can make a telepath shield who knows what else he can do?*

There shouldn't be any problem, I assured him. *Amos's special gadgets are the key, and he doesn't know how to make them. I'm sure of that, but I'll double-check before I let him leave.*

I don't know, Colleen mused. *I don't trust him. He sounded—oh, too ambitious, I suppose.*

My own thoughts skidded to a halt. *Wait a second. When did you* talk *to him?*

Last week. She sounded surprised. *He got my number here from my Regina answering service. Said he was calibrating Amos's finder and needed to know where I was. I assumed you knew.*

I frowned . . . and at that exact instant both Colleen and Calvin vanished from my mind.

It was so unexpected that I wasted a good ten seconds trying to reestablish contact before I noticed that the faint touch of Green's thoughts was also gone and finally realized what was happening. I spun around, but too late: Green's legs were just disappearing up the stairwell. Clutched in one hand was something that looked like a small briefcase.

With a shout, I went after him. But his lead was too big, and by the time I ran out my front door he was already diving into the front seat of his car. With a squeal of tires he took off into the night. Seconds later I was tearing down the street behind him, gunning my old Chevy for all it was worth.

And the chase was on.

At first I thought it would be over quickly. I caught up to him with almost ridiculous ease, as if his car was in even worse shape than mine. But as we cleared the edge of town his lead began to open up slowly, and by the time he turned south on I-35 he was staying a comfortable quarter-mile ahead of me.

For me the drive was like an inside-out version of that horrible race through the California mountains. The road here was flat, and I was the pursuer instead of the pursued; but the same sense of terrified urgency was wrapped suffocatingly around me. Clearly, Green had lied about the portable shield—and I, the great telepath Dale Ravenhall, so caught up in my own selfish desires, had let him get by with it. Bitterly, I wondered what else he'd lied about . . . and whether I'd ever get a chance to warn the others. His strategy seemed clear: by forcing me into a chase like the one in California he was trying to trigger a daymare, one that would undoubtedly be fatal even given the sparse traffic and relatively straight road. And with the shield going full blast in Green's car it would be a very lonely death. More than once I tried to drift back out of range, hoping to at least let Colleen or Calvin know what had happened; but each time Green spotted the maneuver and matched it. I wondered what he would do if I stopped completely, to either call Colleen or phone the police. But I didn't dare try it. If I let him out of my sight I knew I'd never see the shield or the rest of Amos's kernels again. Grimly, concentrating on Green's taillights, I fought down the panic bubbling in my throat and kept going.

I don't know how long the chase lasted; my mind was too busy damning my shortsighted stupidity and fighting off potential daymares to think about time. Green got off the interstate at Osceola, heading east on 34. He didn't stay on the road long, though, turning south again on 65. Twenty-odd miles later he picked up a county road heading west, and from that point on I was thoroughly lost. I dimly remember that we were on some road labeled B when we crossed over into Missouri, but all the rest were just anonymous two-and four-lane roads, passing through or near sleeping towns with names like Wooodland, Davis City, Saline, and Modena.

And finally, sometime in the small hours of the morning, Green pulled over to the side of the road and stopped.

I pulled up behind him, feeling a cold sense of satisfaction. He hadn't given me a daymare and hadn't lost me among the country roads of two states, and had now bowed to the inevitable. He was outside the car now, the briefcase he'd taken from my house held across his chest like a shield. I got out, too, and walked toward him, watching for concealed weapons. "All right, Green, it's all over," I told him. "Let's have the shield and whatever else you stole."

In the headlights I saw him shake his head minutely. "Before you do anything hasty," he said, his voice strangely tense, "I suggest you look at the sign up there."

Frowning, I glanced over his shoulder. Highway 65 was cutting across the landscape directly ahead; a dimly lit sign along its side announced eleven miles to Chillicothe.

Chillicothe?

I felt the blood draining from my face as I refocused on

Green. "Yes," he nodded. "She's within the twenty-mile limit. If I flip this switch you'll both be dead instantly."

The big toggle switch sticking out of the briefcase looked the size of a baseball bat under his hand. There was no way for him to miss it if I jumped him . . . and looking at his eyes I knew he was half expecting me to try just that. "All right, let's both relax," I suggested through stiff lips. "What do you want?"

"For starters, I want you and Colleen Isaac together. There's no point taking both cars; we'll go in mine. I hope you know where she's staying—all I've got is her phone number. You'll drive, of course."

"Of course," I said mechanically. *Colleen,* I thought. *What have I done?*

There was no answer.

She was waiting outside her motel room door when we pulled up, her expression drawn but controlled. I got out of the car and walked up to her. For a moment we gazed into each other's eyes. Then, almost of their own volition, our hands sought each other and gripped tightly . . . and a moment later she was in my arms. "It's all right," I whispered to her, trying to project confidence I didn't feel, and to hide the disappointment that— despite the danger we were in—I *did* feel. I'd had such romantic dreams about this moment, dreams that would now be forever poisoned in my memory.

Behind us, Green cleared his throat. "We'd better get moving," he said, sounding almost apologetic. "Both of you in the front seat, please."

"Just a second," I objected, turning halfway around but keeping one arm around Colleen. "Doesn't she at least get to bring a change of clothes?"

"She didn't seem surprised to see us," he countered. "That means she was expecting us. The police may be on their way right now."

"I wasn't expecting you." Colleen's voice was slightly higher-pitched then I'd expected it to be and had a slight accent. But it was steady enough. "We assumed you were using your telepath shield to stop Dale from talking with us, But I didn't suspect you were here until I was also cut off a minute before you arrived. I didn't call the police."

"But one of your friends might have," Green growled, showing signs of agitation. "Grab your purse and let's *go!*"

He didn't relax again until we were five miles out of Chillicothe, heading east on 36. I held Colleen's hand as I drove, though whether for her comfort or my own I wasn't entirely sure. Strangely enough, she seemed the calmest of all of us, and was the one who finally broke the brittle silence.

"You know, Ted, this really can't gain you anything," she said, turning her head to the side so that Green could hear her. "By now every telepath on the continent knows about you and your machine."

"That's fine with me," Green grunted. "I'm going to need cooperation from all of you, anyway, so there's no reason to keep it secret. Except from the police, maybe. I hope no one's been stupid enough to call them."

"What is it you want?"

"An electronic telepath," I told her. "And he apparently wants us to sit around and watch him make one."

"I wish it were that easy," Green said. "But it's not. I figure I'll need at least ten kernels to make it, and even then it'll only be a one-way mind reading device—I can't get the damn kernels to transmit anything to speak of."

In spite of the danger, I felt a wolfish smile crease my face. "Ten kernels, huh? And you've only got four left—you left three in the shield in my basement. So you're licked even before you start."

"No!" His exclamation was so unexpected I jumped, nearly

swerving out of my lane. "I can figure it out—could have figured it out. But you weren't going to let me." He paused, and in the mirror I could see him fighting for self-control . . . and it was then that I suddenly realized he was as scared as I was. He'd clearly been spinning some high-flying hopes for this particular rainbow, and my adamant opposition had apparently goaded him into an act of desperation that he wasn't really ready for. Now, he was beginning to see just how deep the hole was he was digging himself into.

Colleen must have sensed that, too. "Ted, you don't have to do this," she said. "Let Dale take me back to my motel and then leave him with the shield, and it'll be over. There won't be any charges or other repercussions, I promise."

"What about my mind reader?"

Colleen hesitated. "I'm sorry, but I'm afraid we can't permit Amos's invention to be used in that way."

"Then forget it."

"Green—" I began.

"Shut up," he said. "I have to think."

His ruminations took the better part of an hour, during which time he had me change roads twice. I kept my eye on him in the mirror, hoping he would fall asleep. But he remained almost preternarurally alert the whole time.

Finally, he seemed to come to a conclusion. "Ravenhall, 63 ought to be coming up pretty soon," he said. "Take it north."

"Where are you taking us?" Colleen asked.

"Back to Iowa. I know a little resort near Rathbun Lake where you can rent cabins. We can stay there for a while."

"Taking us across a state line is a federal offense," I pointed out to him.

"How do you figure? I'm not kidnapping you. If you want, you can both get out right here.

I didn't bother to reply.

What with the circuitous route Green made me drive we didn't arrive at the resort until after eight in the morning. My secret hope, that the place might be closed until spring, was quickly dashed; either the warmest October in thirty years had induced them to stay open past their usual closing date or else they catered to the kind of hikers and fishermen who ignore the weather anyway. Green left us alone in the car while he went in the office to register. I tried to think of a plan—any plan—while he was gone. But it was no use. I'd been driving all night, much of it at the edge of nervous prostration, and my mind was simply too fatigued to function. Even as I drove up the gravel road to our cabin I felt my consciousness beginning to waver, and I just barely remember staggering through the front door with Colleen holding tightly onto my arm. Somehow, I assume, she got me to the bed.

I came up out of the darkness slowly and unwillingly, glad to escape the nightmares that had harassed my sleep but dimly aware that something worse was waiting for me in the real world. I opened my eyes to an unfamiliar ceiling, and even before Colleen spoke it had all come back.

"How are you feeling?"

I turned my head. She was sitting in a chair next to the bed, light from the window behind her filtering through her hair in a half halo effect.

"Groggy," I told her. "How long did I sleep?"

"Almost ten hours. I didn't see any point in waking you."

I looked at my watch. Six-oh-five. My stomach growled a reminder that I'd missed a couple of meals. "Did you sleep at all? And where's Green?"

"Yes, I took a couple of short naps. Your friend's out in the living room."

"He's no friend of mine." I turned my head the other way and realized for the first time that the cabin wasn't the simple one-room design I'd expected. Colleen and I were in a small bedroom that took up maybe a third of the cabin's total floor space. The door that sat between us and Green looked solid enough, but it opened inward and had no lock that I could see. I wondered how Green thought he could keep us in here.

"Don't try the door," Colleen said, as if she'd somehow penetrated the shield and had heard my unspoken question. "He has the switch on his telepath shield fastened to it with a piece of string. He sealed the window, too."

I hesitated halfway through the act of rolling out of bed, then continued the motion and got to my feet. Walking around the end of the bed, I went to the window behind Colleen. He'd sealed it, all right; a dozen nails and screws had been driven through the wooden sash and into the frame.

Behind me Colleen's chair creaked, and a moment later her hand tentatively touched my arm. "Dale . . . what does he want with us?"

There was no point studying the window any further; it was clear that without a screwdriver and claw hammer I would never get the thing open. Turning around, I faced Colleen, taking her hands in mine. "You heard him—he wants a mechanical mind reader. I gather he thinks we can help him make one."

"How? Does one of us have something he needs?"

I shook my head. "I don't know." It was odd, a disconnected part of my brain thought, how small a part of its target a camera could really capture. I had hundreds of photos and videotapes of Colleen, but not a single one of them had done her justice. Even tired, hungry, and with a horrible death crouching like a leopard over her shoulder, there was a vivaciousness about her that the films had never really showed. I'd known her energetic joy of life through her thoughts, of course; but to see it reflected in her face was an entirely new and delightful experience. If we died now, I would have had at least that much.

If we died now. The thought short-circuited my rising romantic mood and brought me back to Earth. There were a dozen questions that urgently needed answering. Giving Colleen's hands a squeeze, I let go and walked back around to the door. "Green?" I called through the panel. "You awake out there?"

"Come on out," was the immediate response. "The door's safe to use."

I opened it and stepped into the main part of the cabin, noting in passing that Green's booby-trap string was not tied to the doorknob but to another nail driven into the door at knee level. Green was sitting on a small couch across the room, a glowing lamp at his shoulder. On his lap, the switch close to hand, was the telepath shield.

"I thought you weren't ever going to wake up," Green commented. "There're some hamburgers in the sack on the table—you can heat them up in that one-quart oven over there. Cokes are in the fridge."

I was too hungry to bother with the oven. Colleen, with a lower tolerance for American fast food, took her burgers and headed for the cabin's tiny kitchen. Green waited until we were settled at the table before speaking again. "I've been making a list of the equipment I figure I'm going to need," he told us, holding up a piece of paper clearly torn from a second hamburger bag. "I figure that with a small x-ray machine I can figure out how everything is put together inside one of these kernels. If not, there are a couple of other things I can try. A good computer would be helpful in designing the mind reader's circuitry, and since I'll probably need one anyway to interpret the telepathic signals we might as well get that, too."

"Just where do you expect to get the money for all of this?" I asked around a mouthful of food. "If you're expecting the rest of the telepathic community to fork it over, you can forget it. None of us has the resources you're talking about."

"You fly all over the country whenever you want to, don't you?" he scoffed. "That isn't exactly cheap."

"Most of us have small stipends from universities that are studying us," Colleen explained to him. "The amounts aren't nearly enough to supply you with x-ray machines and computers, though."

Green's mouth twitched. "Well . . . then I guess you'll have to earn the money some other way."

"Such as?" I asked. Most businesses, I've found, aren't all that enthusiastic about having telepaths on the payroll."

"I suppose industrial espionage would be the most profitable," he said, watching me closely.

If he was looking for a reaction, he wasn't disappointed. Some breadcrumbs, tried to go down the wrong way, and it took me half a minute to cough them out. "Forget it," I snarled when I could talk again. "If you think we're going to do *that*—"

Colleen cut me off with a hand on my arm. "Ted, we can't do that," she said, her voice calm and reasonable. "We're all rather well known; certainly the security departments of any major corporation would recognize us instantly."

"Then you'll have to hit key employees at off hours," Green said stubbornly. "Or else wear disguises. I *need* that equipment—don't you understand?"

"And what about us?" Colleen asked. "Don't you see what involving us in crime would do to the trust we've built up between ourselves and the general populace? We can't survive without that good will, Ted."

"I'm sorry. I really am. But it's not my fault." He shifted his gaze to me, where it became more of a glare. "If *he* hadn't been all noble and virtuous and had let me keep going, none of this would have happened."

"Oh, sure—blame it on me," I growled. "Why not blame your parents, society, and the planet Jupiter while you're at it?"

He ignored me. "I want to know how to contact Calvin Wolfe—I know he's a friend of yours and his Pueblo phone's unlisted. I also want something I can say to him that'll prove you two are with me."

My mind raced. Was there some way I could slip in a clue as to where we were? Rathbun, reservoir, lake—I couldn't think of any way to code any of those words so that Green would miss it. I'd never been here before, so referring to a past visit was out. Distance from Des Moines? I hadn't the foggiest idea. I was still trying to come up with something when Colleen gave him Calvin's number and unconsciously undercut my effort. "Just give him your name," she told Green. "He knows who you are."

"Okay." He stood up and gestured toward the door. "We'll have to find a phone booth to make the call from; I don't want anyone tracing us here."

It was an hour before we got back to the cabin, Green having taken us halfway to Ottumwa to get the distance he wanted. We were left in the car while he made the call, and he wouldn't tell us anything about it afterward except that Calvin had agreed to take up the matter with the rest of our group.

"Do you think that's the truth?" Colleen asked me when we were locked again in the relative privacy of our room.

"Probably," I told her. Outside the window the evening had faded into night, and the lights from two or three other cabins could be dimly seen through the trees. Too far away to see a signal, even if I could think of some way to send one without tipping off Green. "Calvin would agree to anything at this stage to gain time." Pulling the shade, I turned on the light and sat down on the bed next to Colleen. The light switch had gone on with a loud click; no quiet SOS possible with that. "I just hope we don't get some gung-ho SWAT team bursting in with M-16s blazing."

"I doubt if there's any danger of that," she sighed. "We'd already decided to keep the authorities out of this when the shield cut me off."

I nodded; I'd rather hoped they'd seen things that way. At the moment no one but us knew it was even possible to build an electronic mind reader. If the word ever got out, chances were *someone* would eventually figure out how to do it. "Good. I guess. Anything else happen while I was out of touch?"

"Yes, but nothing that'll help us here." She shifted position to stretch out on the bed, closing her eyes against the overhead light. "I called your friend Robert Peterson on the phone and asked him to go over to your house and see what was wrong. He called me back on your phone with the news that your car was gone and your house lit and unlocked. Calvin wanted to know whether there was anything there that could be a telepath shield. Robert said there was a heavy monstrosity in the basement that had three of Amos's devices wired into it, but that he couldn't tell what it was without more study."

"Yeah. How *do* you test a telepath shield?"

"Obviously, with a telepath. Gordon was going to catch the next plane to Des Moines, and Scott will most likely come up from New Orleans now that I've also disappeared. He was anxious to get involved and has always rather liked me." She opened her eyes briefly. "Something I just thought of: could Robert modify Amos's telepath finder to locate a *lack* of telepathic signals?"

"Like this shield?" I shrugged. "I don't know, but I doubt it.

We had to take apart the finder to get parts for the shields; Rob would have to rebuild as well as redesign it. And, anyway, he hadn't gotten much into design work when Green took over." A fresh wave of shame and anger washed over me. "I should've waited until Rob was available again," I muttered.

Colleen was silent for so long I began to think she'd fallen asleep. Turning off the light I lay down beside her, hating both Green and myself and wondering if I was tired enough to escape into sleep myself for a few hours. Then Colleen stirred. "Dale . . . why did you do it?"

It took me a moment to understand what she was asking. "For us," I told her. "I wanted to be able to see and hold you, to share more than just my thoughts with you. I—when I say it like that it sounds pretty selfish, doesn't it?"

"A little," she admitted. "More like Nelson Follstadt than Dale Ravenhall."

I sighed, closing my eyes in an effort to block the sudden tears forming there. Nelson again—always it was Nelson. Was I never going to be free of him? Or were my motivations and judgment going to be forever skewed by what he'd done to me in the California mountains? It was like carrying my own personal ghost along with me, someone to fowl up everything I did, someone—

Someone to blame.

The thought leaped out at me with almost physical force. Was I using my psychological injury as a scapegoat, a convenient excuse whenever anything went wrong? I didn't really believe it—certainly didn't *want* to believe it.

But the possibility was there . . . and blaming other people *had* been one of Nelson's most annoying traits.

And I'd just argued myself in a circle. I never argued in circles. Or, rather, Dale Ravenhall never had. . . .

Colleen's arm slid over my chest, breaking through the spiral of fear and self-pity. "It's all right, Dale," she said soothingly. "We'll get out of this somehow."

For a long time she held me tightly, as if comforting a child. Gradually, my black depression began to lighten; and as it did so my need for her changed, both in nature and urgency. Her response, whether from love, fear, or a combination of both, was so strong it surprised me . . . but within seconds surprise and all other emotions were crowded out by the passion exploding within me.

For the three years since I'd fallen in love with Colleen this moment had formed the basis of virtually all my fantasies . . . and yet, now that it was here, the act was tinged with an unexpected sense of frustration. It wasn't just the circumstances, or the presence of Green on the other side of the door, but rather the missing dimension that even the casual sex of my younger years had had. For the first time in my life I was cut off from the thoughts and emotions of my partner, forced to rely on the subtle physical cues I'd never really bothered to learn. I botched it—botched it badly—and though she didn't say anything I knew she was disappointed. I tried to apologize, but I couldn't find the words, and had to settle for holding her close until she fell asleep.

I stared at the shadows of tree branches swaying across the window shade for at least an hour after that, tired but not really sleepy. With time, I knew, I could learn to be a better lover to her—but time was the least certain commodity in our world just now. I wondered how long it would take Green to get the money and equipment he wanted . . . and I wondered how long the batteries powering the shield would last.

Eventually, I fell asleep.

We both woke fairly early the next morning. That turned out to be a mistake, because the day quickly became one long study in boredom. Green had slipped out before we woke and had brought back donuts and coffee and the necessary ingredients for sandwiches. That last was a disappointment; I'd hoped for the chance to break the window and escape when he left to buy lunch. But as usual, he was one move ahead of me.

To his credit, he also brought back a couple of decks of cards and three paperbacks of the sort found on grocery store book racks. But neither Colleen nor I were great shakes as card players; and I, at least, was too wrapped up in my own real troubles to have any patience with someone else's fictional ones. Besides, the covers of the books strongly suggested they contained a fair amount of sex and/or romance, and after the fiasco of the previous night I knew I wouldn't be able to handle that.

So instead of reading I spent some time going over our room, searching for something I could use as a tool or weapon. It was a small room, though, and it wasn't even eleven o'clock before I gave up.

Mostly, Colleen and I talked.

There wasn't much about each other we didn't already know, of course; but good friends can always find something interesting to talk about. We discussed world topics, history—one of Colleen's pet interests—and our fellow telepaths, and reminisced a good deal about the five years we'd known each other. By a kind of unspoken agreement we avoided talking about our current situation, but the very fact we were using spoken words at all was a continual reminder of what was happening. I could feel a tenseness in Colleen's body as we lay side by side on the bed, and my own attempts at conversation were blunted by my preoccupation with the problem of finding a way out of this mess I'd created.

The damnable thing about it was that, barring some slip on

Green's part, I couldn't think of a single way either to escape or to get the telepath shield away from him. And the more I thought about it the more I realized that we didn't even have the threat of official retribution to hold over his head if he flipped that switch—he could probably claim that I'd been so delighted with my new shield that I'd set up this little informal honeymoon trip with Colleen and that I'd dragged him along to take care of the electronics, which had unfortunately failed. With us gone it would basically be his word against Calvin's, and if Green had been smart he wouldn't have said anything to Calvin that actually involved the words *ransom* or *blackmail*. The bad thing about such a scenario was that, once he had what he wanted, Green might feel he had to kill us to maintain the charade.

Nelson had tried once to kill me. Now, it seemed, his ghost had given itself a second chance. I only wished Colleen hadn't been the means it had chosen—but, then again, her inclusion might have been deliberate. Nelson had hated all of us.

Sometime in the middle of the afternoon Colleen and I made love again, at her request, and for a while I was able to forget the danger we were in. Perhaps if I'd been paying closer attention to her I would have noticed the tension had left her muscles by then, leaving behind an almost unnatural calmness, and perhaps I would have wondered what that meant. Perhaps; but probably not. I'm not very good at reading physical cues.

Evening came, and Green again was too smart to leave us alone while he went for food. Apparently he'd become convinced that the police really hadn't been called in, and so he piled us into the car and we went out to a restaurant together. His new-found confidence went only so far, of course; the place he chose was a dark, intimate one with high-backed booths, where our chances of being recognized by anyone were minimal.

I'd expected dinner to be a strained affair; but while it was so for me the others seemed surprisingly relaxed. Colleen kept Green talking, both about himself and his ambitions. If I'd paid closer attention to the conversation I might have learned why succeeding with his mind reader project was so important to him. But my full attention was on the briefcase sitting upright on the seat next to him, and on the arm resting casually on top of it. Even when cutting his steak his left hand never moved far enough away from the switch for me to risk any action. I hardly tasted my own food, and felt almost resentful that Colleen so obviously enjoyed the expensive filet mignon she'd ordered.

The ride back to the cabin was quiet. Colleen huddled close to me the whole time, her hand stroking my thigh in a way more suggestive of fear and loneliness than of passion. Her friendly chatter in the restaurant, I guessed, must have been an act to put Green at ease, and now that I'd been unable to take advantage of the trick an emotional letdown was setting in. I wished that I hadn't been so quick to shoot down her suggestion that Rob might be able to gimmick together a telepath shield locater; at least that would have left her some small hope to cling to.

I parked out front as usual and we went into the cabin, Green with his damn briefcase keeping well back. Colleen turned on the light and we headed toward the bedroom; but as Green closed the cabin door behind us she touched my arm and stopped, turning to face him.

"Well, go on in," Green said, as I followed Colleen's lead and turned around. Green had stopped just inside the door, his expression more puzzled than wary. Not that he needed to worry; we were a good fifteen feet away from him, and even with the shield hanging loosely in his hand we both knew I couldn't possibly get to the switch before he did.

But Colleen didn't move. "No," she said calmly. "We can't let you continue with your plans, Ted. An electronic mind reader would bring chaos upon a world that already is sorely lacking in privacy—surely you recognize that. Do you care so little about other people that you would do something like this to them?"

"Oh, come on," he growled, clearly not in the mood for an argument. "You're blowing this way out of proportion. Only the wealthy and powerful are going to be able to afford mind readers—and they're only going to use them on each other. Besides, once I've sold enough mind readers I'll be marketing these telepath shields anyway. You'll have the status quo back before you know it."

I stared at him—the man was even more cold-bloodedly mercenary than I'd realized.

Colleen shook her head slowly, and for the first time I noticed her face was unnaturally pale. "No. We can't allow it."

"You can't stop me," Green said flatly.

"Yes, I can." Colleen paused, and I heard the faint sound of tires on gravel outside as one of the other campers returned for the evening . . . and without warning Colleen screamed.

It was a piercing, mind-curdling scream, so loud and so unexpected that for a second it literally locked my muscles in place. Across the room Green jerked violently, nearly dropping the briefcase; but before either of us could do anything more the scream cut off as abruptly as it had begun—

And Colleen was holding a knife hara-kiri fashion to her stomach.

For just an instant there was a deathly stillness in the room. I don't know how Green looked in that first second; my full disbelieving attention was riveted on Colleen. The knife, still greasy from the steak she'd been cutting with it half an hour previously, glinted with a horrible light from between her hands. Her eyes seemed black in contrast as they stared unblinkingly at Green.

"The game's over, one way or another," she said, her words sort and rapid, but with an iron cast to them. "You will set down that case and step away from it, or I will kill myself. I expect you understand."

With an effort I shifted my gaze to Green. He understood, all right; his face had gone a pasty white. If Colleen died before he could hit the switch his power over me would be gone . . . and I would kill him. "It won't work," he half croaked, half whispered. "You can't die fast enough. Your brain will live too long."

"Perhaps." Colleen's voice was still glacially calm. "But many people will have heard my scream, and some of them could be coming in the door at any time. You won't be able to pass our deaths off as strokes or heart attacks, not with a knife in me. And even if you manage to get away, you've left fingerprints all over this room." Outside, a car door slammed. "Here they come," Colleen said. "Decide, Ted. Now."

Green growled something deep in his throat, but I hardly heard him. Nausea was trying to turn my stomach inside out, and I fought desperately against the white spots forming before my eyes. But it was no use. The parallel was too close: Amos, too, had died of a self-inflicted knife wound in defense of someone else. The scene in front of me shimmered and faded . . . and the daymare began.

Amos, you're coming too close; it's beginning to hurt.

I can't stop, Nelson. My plane's been hijacked.

You have *to stop. You* have *to! It hurts, it hurts.*

You're going to let her die, aren't you, Dale? She's going to die, just like Amos did.

No! I shouted, and even as I stood in the middle of it I felt the vision quiver. This wasn't the usual pattern . . . and with sudden clarity I saw that Nelson's death-wish within me had overreached itself. These were *Nelson's* memories, not mine, given to me in distorted form during our close approach five months ago. They had no basis of reality in my own mind to draw strength from. Illusions only . . . and with all the force I could gather I hit them with the strongest reality I had.

I AM DALE RAVENHALL! I screamed to Nelson's ghost.

And with a shudder the vision shattered.

I'd apparently been gone only a second or two, because the tableau was just as I'd left it. Running footsteps were audible outside, and Green half turned toward the door, his face contorted with indecision. His hand twitched—and I moved.

With my left hand I slapped Colleen's right elbow forward, knocking the knife point away from her body, and with my right I plucked the weapon from her loosened grip. Green looked back at the motion—and with a yelp ducked as I hurled the knife toward him with all my strength.

It bounced butt-end first off his shoulder, throwing him off-balance for a second. But it wasn't enough, and I wasn't more than a third of the way to him when his scrambling hand got to the switch. He froze for a single heartbeat, panic etched across his white face . . . and then he flipped it.

And nothing happened.

My charge ground to a halt as confusion slowed my muscles. The agony I'd expected—the red haze of pain as two minds crashed together—it simply wasn't there. I looked around, half afraid I was the only one unaffected, that I would see Colleen stretched on the floor in death; but she, too, merely looked bewildered. I turned back to Green, and as I did so the footsteps outside ceased and the door was unceremoniously slammed open.

Two men charged in: Rob Peterson and a big blond man I'd never seen before . . . or rather, never seen except in photos.

"Are you two all right?" Gordy asked anxiously, looking back and forth between Colleen and me.

And finally I understood.

"It was plain dumb luck that we spotted you leaving that restaurant back in Moravia, or whatever that town was named," Gordy said, shaking his head. "We'd figured you to be a good five miles farther west, and when we cut through the edge of your shield I thought you'd passed us, heading for points unknown, and that we were going to have to start all over again. It's a good thing Rob recognized Green's car."

I nodded, feeling the tension drain slowly out through my arms as I held Colleen tightly to my side, and let my gaze wander. Green was sitting on the ground by Gordy's rented van; in the dim light streaming from the cabin's windows he looked like someone who'd just been condemned to purgatory. Rob, sitting cross-legged inside the van to take maximum advantage of the dome light, was doing a quick check of the wiring in Green's stolen telepath shield and fitting it with fresh batteries. And behind him, tied down securely in the van's cargo area, was the bulky shield Green had first demonstrated for me down in my basement. Chugging quietly beside it was the gasoline generator that supplied its power.

"Only two days," Colleen murmured. "It seemed much longer, somehow."

"To us, too," Gordy agreed. "If I never see another field of corn stubble I'll be perfectly happy."

I sighed. "Okay, I give up. You didn't just quarter the whole state until you found us, and I don't see anything that could possibly be a telepath shield locater in here. So how'd you do it?"

"With the best locaters you could possibly use for the job: two telepaths." Gordy glanced down at Green with what looked like rather cold satisfaction. "Green here made the mistake of telling Calvin that his gadget had a half-mile range, and once I got to Des Moines a little experimentation with the model he'd left behind showed us that the shield absorbs *all* telepathic signals trying to pass through it, whether or not the sender is actually within the field. By then Scott was in Chillicothe, so we had him stay put while Rob and I drove a hundred-mile-radius circle around him. We were just lucky that you'd gone to ground inside that range—we would have had to start all over again with a new circle otherwise."

"All set," Rob reported, hopping down from his perch and handing me the briefcase. "I've rewired around the switch, too, so don't worry about bumping it."

Gingerly, I took it. "What now?"

Gordy answered immediately; clearly, he'd already thought this through. "Rob and I will take Green away in his car while you drive Colleen back to Chillicothe in the van—you'll have both shields that way. I'll call Scott as soon as I'm clear here, so he'll be out of the way by the time you get there. After you drop her off, you can bring the van and shields back to Des Moines. I guess Rob or somebody will have to go retrieve your car later."

"Where will you be?" I asked him.

He hesitated, glancing at Green. "I'll be in the Dubuque area for a couple of days, I think," he said softly. "Even without access to Amos's devices Green knows too much about telepath shields. I don't think we should take the chance."

Beside me, I felt Colleen shiver. It had been done before, I knew; Nelson had used cult-style brainwashing techniques to condition the men who'd hijacked Amos's plane. With the insights and feedback telepathic contact permitted, the process wouldn't take Gordy more than three or four days. Looking at Green's grim expression, I realized that he'd already figured out what we would have to do. I almost felt sorry for him, but decided to save my sympathy for Gordy instead. "I suppose you're right," I said. "Do whatever you have to."

The three of them left a few minutes later. Standing together by the van, Colleen and I watched their tail-lights disappear among the trees. The sound of crunching gravel had been swallowed up by the rustling of leaves before she spoke. "We really don't have to leave here right away, you know," she pointed out. "Now that Green's gone, perhaps we could stay here for a few days."

"And try to repair the damage that's been done to my dreams?" I shook my head. "No. It's too late for that."

"I'm sorry." Her murmur was barely audible.

"Don't be," I said quickly. "It wasn't your fault. It's just that . . . we were like two cardboard cutouts in there. All of what makes you *you* was missing."

The words were hopelessly inadequate, and I knew it; but even as I groped for better ones I felt her nod. "I know," she said, and there was no mistaking the note of relief in her voice. "Your telepath shield made us normal people for two days . . . but we can't *be* normal people; not really. Maybe with enough time and effort we could learn some of the techniques, but it wouldn't be the same. I think perhaps we've been spoiled by our ability, even while taking it for granted. Even if the machines could somehow be made foolproof . . ." She shook her head.

"I understand." I sighed. "I'm sorry, Colleen—sorry for everything. It seems sometimes like everything I've done the past five months has gone wrong."

"Oh, I don't know," she said, attempting a light-hearted tone. "You saved my life a few minutes ago, when you took my knife away."

I snorted. "Even there I didn't have any choice. I couldn't let you die like that. It was how Amos died . . . how Nelson killed him."

She shuddered. "I guess we'd better go," she said, her voice dark again.

I nodded silently and we climbed into the van. It was strange, I thought, how dreams so seldom live up to their expectations. I'd wanted to be able to hold Colleen, to talk to her, and—*yes, admit it*—to make love to her. Now, all I could think about was getting a hundred miles away from her as fast as I could . . . so that we could be together again.

I was tired of being alone.

Starting the engine, I put the van in gear and we headed off into the night.

BLACK THOUGHTS AT MIDNIGHT

One by one, the last few cars and trucks vanished from the interstate, disappearing down exits to their homes, or—in the case of the trucks—pulled off into rest stop parking lots or entrance ramp shoulders by their drivers for a few hours of sleep. By midnight, new headlights were showing up only once every ten or fifteen minutes, in either direction. By one o'clock, even those stragglers were gone.

And I was alone. Alone, with a lopsided island of rolling pavement in my van's misaligned headlights the only barrier between me and the darkness outside.

I had forgotten, or perhaps never fully known, just how dark the night was.

An absence of light, my educated mind told me; nothing more or less than that. But that was a civilized definition, created by civilized city dwellers for whom darkness was merely not enough light to read by. Out here, driving through North Dakota under a starless November sky, things were far different. The night had a life and a reality of its own; a malevolent life, stirring ancient fears deep within me. Beyond the range of my headlights the world ceased to exist; to my left, I could all but visualize ethereal hands pressing blackly against the side window.

Half an hour yet to the Canadian border. Border crossing formalities, time unknown, particularly if they decided to give me grief over the bulky apparatus strapped down behind my seat. Six more hours after that to Regina.

Seven hours, plus or minus. Seven hours before I could get to Colleen.

I shouldn't have thought her name. *Dale?* her thought brushed sleepily across my mind.

I clenched my teeth. Damn it all—I'd woken her up. *It's all right, Colleen,* I told her, burying my own tension as best I could and working hard at being soothing. If she came fully awake again— *It's all right. Go back to sleep.*

I held my breath; but even as the first flickers of pain began to show through her fogged mind the codeine-laced medicine she'd taken three hours ago glazed it over again. *Okay,* she said, already slipping back down. The word faded into vague, non-verbal sensations, then disappeared entirely.

I took a careful breath, hearing my teeth rattle together with the strain as I did so. Seven more hours to go. Seven more hours of utter helplessness, piled on top of two weeks' worth of steadily growing fears and frustrations. Fears, frustrations, and questions . . . and the horrifying revelation that had driven me onto this road eleven hours ago.

She'll make it, Dale.

I gritted my teeth. *Damn it all, Calvin—no one invited you to listen in.*

He didn't reply, but just stayed there, quietly radiating calm and patience and strength . . . and my anger evaporated, leaving me feeling like a rat. As he no doubt knew I would. *I'm sorry,* I apologized grudgingly. *I know you're just trying to help.*

I didn't notice until after I'd said them how easily my words could be construed as a backhanded insult. I hadn't meant them to come out that way, or at least I didn't think I had. It hardly mattered, though, not with Calvin Wolfe. Even when he noticed insults, he had the kind of overdeveloped patience and secure self-image that let him shrug such things off without even thinking about it.

As he did now. *That's okay,* he assured me, the patience and calm and strength undiminished. *I know you've been under a lot of pressure lately. Where are you?*

I tried to remember the towns that had been on the last exit sign, but it was a futile effort. I'd passed far too many exit signs since leaving Des Moines. *Thirty-odd miles south of Canada.*

You're making good time, he said, and I caught just a hint of uneasy disapproval as he made a quick estimate of the speed I'd been doing. *About due for another break, aren't you?*

I snorted gently to myself. *Who are you, my mother?*

Some of the patience cracked, just a little. *Come on, Dale— you're not going to do Colleen and her migraines any good at all if you conk out at the wheel doing seventy.*

I gritted my teeth, fighting against the swirling emotions within me. He was right, of course; I wouldn't do them any good that way. Not Colleen, not her headaches, not— *I won't fall asleep*, I growled, pushing the thought aside and reaching down for the two-liter bottle of cola wedged beside my seat. Working the cap off one-handed, I took a good swig. *If you're worried about it, you always can tell me stories to keep me awake.*

The patience cracked a little further. *Instead of that,* he countered, *why don't you tell me one? Like, for instance, just what exactly is wrong with Colleen?*

You know what's wrong, I said, the words coming out with the easy glibness of two weeks' practice. *She's suddenly started developing migraine headaches. The doctors don't know yet what's causing them.*

But she *knows.* It was a statement, not a question, without a whisper of doubt behind the words. *And so do you.*

I could have denied it—*had* denied it, in fact, several times in the past twelve hours, vehemently and with a fair imitation of wounded dignity. But it was the Nelson part of me that was the consummate liar . . . and after eleven hours on the road, that part was as weary as the rest of me. *You're right,* I conceded. *She figured it out yesterday evening, and I—well, sort of bullied her into telling me this this morning.*

And you responded by loading the telepath shields into a rented van and charging hell for leather to her rescue.

A decision that had been less than popular among my fellow telepaths. Every one of the five with whom I shared normal communication had told me in so many words that going to Regina to hold Colleen's hand was a noble but essentially useless gesture. My stock reply had been perhaps unnecessarily blunt. *Colleen and I discussed it between ourselves,* I told Calvin shortly. *What's going on is our own personal business. Period.*

Is it? he countered. *Is it really?*

There was something in his tone. Something that told me he had figured it out. *Calvin. Please—just let it alone.*

I can't do that, Dale, he said, almost gently. *This is going to impact on all of us.* He hesitated. *Colleen's pregnant, isn't she?*

I sighed. *Yes.*

There was a short silence, and even through my fatigue and worry I found it blackly amusing to watch the three different directions Calvin's thoughts went skittering off in. On one hand were the mainly scientific questions of dominant versus recessive genes, and what the odds were that the child Colleen was carrying might not have been a telepath at all. Beneath that line of thought was another, more worried set as he considered what would happen to both of them as the fetus continued to develop, putting dangerous close-approach pressure on both minds.

And buried almost invisibly behind both of those was the *really* worrisome question: whether I had known the woman I loved had been sleeping with another man. How I was feeling about the whole thing, whether what I was really doing was charging to Regina to confront her with it . . .

You misunderstand, Calvin, I told him. *It's my child Colleen's pregnant with.*

Close-approach distance—the distance at which two telepaths had surface-thought communication with each other whether they wanted it or not—was supposed to be around a hundred miles. Off-hand, I couldn't remember if any of us had ever close-approached a sleeping person before, but with my own fatigue already tugging at my eyes—and with Colleen's mental patterns being heavily damped by the codeine—it didn't seem like a good time to experiment. As Calvin had pointed out, wrapping my van around a tree wouldn't do anyone any good.

So, just outside Brandon—maybe two hundred crow-wise miles from Regina—I pulled off the road, revved up the portable generator in the rear of the van, and switched on both of the telepath shields.

And a portion of my world went black.

It was an eerie and decidedly scary feeling, made all the worse by the lonely darkness around me. Ever since my early teens, when my telepathy had first begun to develop, there'd been a sort of permanent haze of thought-clutter that added an unobtrusive background to every waking minute. Most of it came from normals out beyond my twenty-foot sensitivity range, and

I'd long since gotten so used to it that I had to stop and concentrate before I could even hear it. But with the shields on, all that was gone.

Three of us—Colleen, Gordy Sears, and I—had spent varying amounts of time in the shield a little over a month ago, and we had yet to come up with an adequate verbal description of the experience. *The gap where a tooth used to be* had been Colleen's best attempt; *growing up next to a waterfall and then going deaf* had been Gordy's.

What I remembered most was being with Colleen . . . and at the same time, not being with her. Everything that I loved about her—her kindness, her patience, her sense of humor—everything that made her the woman she was had been hidden from me, hidden behind expressions and gestures and vocal tones that I'd never learned how to read. It had been the most acutely lonely experience of my entire life.

And now here I was heading back into that loneliness again. The loneliness, and the risk of horrible death if both shields should somehow fail at the same time.

Perhaps Calvin was right to be worried. Perhaps the ghost of Nelson Follstadt I carried within me was still trying to kill Colleen and me.

Maybe this time it would succeed.

I reached Colleen's house a little after eight in the morning; and had just about decided to break down the door when she finally answered the bell.

My first look at her as she fumbled with the storm door latch was a shock. Her face was pale and drawn, with lines etched into the skin that hadn't been there five weeks ago, and her shoulders seemed rounded with fatigue.

And then the storm door came open, and she was in my

arms. "Dale," she said into my shoulder. Her body trembled against me; and yet, even as I winced at the tiredness and memory of pain in her voice, I could tell that the pain itself was gone. The telepath shields, blocking the deadly searchlight-strength blazes of our two minds, had also wiped out Colleen's headaches.

We got in out of the doorway—it was just above freezing outside and all Colleen was wearing was a thin robe—and she led me to the living room. "You made good time," she said, sinking onto a well-worn couch and rubbing at her eyes.

"I was inspired," I told her, carefully setting down the briefcase containing the portable telepath shield before collapsing next to her. At the outskirts of Regina, with the end of the long road in sight, I'd experienced a small adrenaline rush, but most of that had already faded away. "How are you feeling?" I asked, slipping my arm around her shoulders and holding her against me.

"Better than I have in weeks," she sighed. "My head hurts a little, but I think it's just left-over muscle tension. Nothing like the migraines." She paused, as if listening. "It's so quiet."

I looked down at her, a shiver running up my back. "You don't mean . . . you weren't getting any actual *thoughts* from the baby, were you?"

She shook her head, her hair swishing across my nose and cheek with the movement. "Oh, no. I just meant . . . you know. Outside."

The background thought-clutter. "Yeah," I nodded understanding. And it wasn't just the clutter that was gone; so too was the effortless communication with the rest of our group. A communication and friendship that all of us had grown accustomed to—for most of us, the only real friendships we had. Slowly, it was starting to percolate through my numbed brain just how much Colleen was going to have to give up here. "I'll be right here with you," I assured her. "The whole eight months, if you need me."

"I know," she said, and yawned.

I yawned, too. "We'd better get you back to bed before we both collapse right here," I said. Gathering my strength, I stood up and took her hands. "Come on; let's go."

She was practically sleepwalking by the time I got her to her bedroom. My original plan had been to go back outside and unload the other, bulkier telepath shield from the van before sacking out myself; but seeing Colleen stretched across the bed was too much for me. There would be plenty of time for such details, I told myself as I took off my shoes, after I'd caught up a little on my sleep.

It was four-thirty in the afternoon when I finally awoke, reasonably rested but with that stiff feeling I always get when I sleep in my clothes. Colleen didn't stir as I eased carefully out of bed and tiptoed out of the room. In the living room I put on my shoes and coat and headed out to check the van.

The gasoline generator had run out of fuel while we slept, shutting down current to the floor-model telepath shield that had been running off of it. The shield itself was probably still operating—Rob Peterson had installed a battery backup system just two weeks ago—but the silent generator still gave me an uncomfortable feeling in the pit of my stomach. Our limited experiments with the backup had showed that even fully charged batteries faded in a matter of hours, as opposed to the seven to ten days of power a similar pack provided to the more efficient portable model sitting inside by the couch.

Not that we could afford to trust either shield by itself, which was why I'd brought both of them with me. Later this evening I would manhandle the larger model into Colleen's house and plug it into regular line current. But with sundown only another half hour away I decided I might as well hold off until full darkness, when any nosy neighbors who happened to be watching would have less to see.

It took only a minute to drive outside the house shield's half-mile range and pull over to the curb. Switching off the ignition, I stretched back against the cold van seat, and for a moment just listened to the background thought-clutter that once again filled the corners of my mind. Gordy's old inadequate image of living by a waterfall flicked to mind . . .

Dale?

With an effort, I forced my mind from the quiet exhilaration of just being normal again. *I'm here, Gordy,* I acknowledged.

You all right? Calvin's thought joined in. *We've been trying to reach you all day.*

I'm fine, I told him. *Sorry, about that—I lay down for a short nap that stretched out a bit.*

Yeah, we thought that might be it, Gordy said.

Not that it stopped us from worrying, Calvin added dryly. *Do remind Colleen to turn her phone back on when you get back to the house, too.* He paused, and I could sense him brace himself. *So . . . how is she doing?*

The pain's gone, I told them. *When I left a few minutes ago she was still sleeping like a baby.*

Ah. Gordy's reaction to the simile was brief and low-key, but it was enough to confirm that Calvin had filled him in. As I'd rather expected he would. *It was a close-approach problem, then,* he added.

You expected otherwise? I countered mildly.

Not really. Gordy hesitated. *We didn't tell anyone else, by the way. We thought that timing should be up to you and Colleen.*

Though such considerations hadn't stopped Calvin from

spilling the beans to Gordy . . . Shaking my head sharply, I cut the thought off. Calvin, Gordy, and I were the only ones of our group Colleen could regularly reach from Regina. It was only fair that her best friends be let in on what had happened, and to hell with Nelson's paranoic tendencies. *Thanks, I appreciate that*, I said. *I take it, then, that you think we should tell everyone?*

I don't see how you can avoid it, Calvin said. *Colleen's going to have to stay in the telepath shield for the next eight months, minimum, and someone's bound to notice in all that time that she's disappeared from sight.*

Besides, why would you want *to keep something like this secret?* Gordy added. *The first child born to anyone in our group, let alone to two of us? It ought to be something to cheer about.*

I grimaced. *And what about the telepath shield? Should we cheer about that, too?*

There was a slight pause, and I felt Gordy's enthusiasm deflate a bit. *Ouch*, he said.

At the very least, I agreed with perhaps an unnecessary touch of sarcasm. *Word leaks out about that and we're going to be right back where we were with Ted Green last month.*

They thought about that for a long moment. *Maybe we can still keep it private knowledge within the group*, Calvin offered doubtfully. *Colleen doesn't have any real commitments she can't bow out of for the next few months, does she?*

Her doctor knows she's having headaches, I pointed out. *If she's at all competent she isn't going to drop it just because Colleen says everything's all better now.*

There was another moment of silence. *We'll think of something*, Gordy said at last. *For the moment the main job is to keep Colleen and the baby healthy. Is there anything we can do to help?*

Not that I can think of, I told them. *If I come up with anything, I'll let you know.*

Okay, Calvin said. *You think we ought to set up some regularly scheduled contact time when you'll be outside the shield?*

Maybe later we'll need to do something like that, I said. *For now, I don't think it's necessary. I'll have to leave in a couple of days, anyway, if I'm going to get the van back to Des Moines before the rental period runs out.*

You want me to fly in to stay with her while you're gone? Gordy offered.

A brief surge of jealousy flashed through me before I could suppress it. Absurd, of course—Gordy was nothing more to Colleen than a good friend. *Let me see how she's doing when she wakes up,* I suggested. *If she feels like she'd like company, I'll let you know.*

Unless you'd rather I not even offer. . . ?

So he'd caught the flicker of emotion. *No, of course not,* I said, feeling my face flushing with embarrassment. *Sorry—Nelson must have taken over for a minute.*

There was a short, awkward silence, and I realized my apology had made things worse instead of better. Neither Gordy nor Calvin had made any secret lately of the fact that they thought my close-approach with Nelson had become altogether too convenient a catch-all excuse for me. *Sure, Dale,* Gordy said at last. *Anyway, let me know what she says.*

Right. Well, I suppose I'd better get back. See if she's woken up yet and find an out-of-the-way corner to hook the big shield up in.

Okay, we'll leave you to it, Calvin said. *Take care of her, Dale, and keep in touch. Maybe on your drive back to Iowa we can hold a round table on just how we're going to keep all of this quiet.*

And who all we're going to keep it quiet from, Gordy added. *Say hi to Colleen for us, okay?*

Sure, I said, turning the van's ignition key again. *And don't worry about it. We've got plenty of time to come up with a workable plan.*

And I really believed that as I broke contact and turned around to head back to Colleen's. Really believed that we had weeks—even months—to come up with a good story.

If I'd only known that I had, instead, exactly four minutes . . .

I saw the flashing red lights two blocks away; but it wasn't until I got past a camper parked on the wrong side of the street that I realized the ambulance was pulled up directly in front of Colleen's house.

I bounced the van half up on the curb right behind it and scrambled out, banging my shin on the door in the process. I hardly noticed, my full attention on trying to see into the slightly ajar ambulance doors. There was no one inside, which meant she was still in the house. Racing across the lawn, I threw open the front door and dashed into the living room. "Colleen?" I called.

"Over here," her voice said from my right. Skidding to a halt, I turned to find her sitting calmly on the couch, a stethoscope-armed woman seated beside her and a group of three men standing in a loose circle around her.

All of them, at the moment, looking at me. And doing nothing else.

"What's going on?" I asked when I got my voice back.

"This is Dr. DuBois," Colleen told me, indicating the woman beside her. "She tells me—" she swallowed— "that I may have lost my baby."

I stared at Colleen, then at the doctor, then back at Colleen. "I don't understand," I said. "What—I mean how—?"

I was interrupted by a loud beep and a flurry of unintelligible speech from one of the paramedics' belts. "Doctor. . . ?" he asked, pulling the radio from its holder.

DuBois nodded, a strangely hard set to her mouth. "Yes, you might as well go ahead," she told him. "There's no emergency here now."

He nodded, acknowledging the call with some kind of number code as he and the other two men brushed past me and left. I closed the door behind them and watched as they hurried across the lawn, my thoughts a swirling mass of utter confusion. Only hours earlier I would have sworn the baby was perfectly fine; and now *this* . . . "How? I asked the doctor again."

DuBois opened her mouth; but it was Colleen who answered. "Because the headaches have stopped," Colleen answered for her.

I frowned at her, saw the tight look in her eyes. As if she was pleading silently with me to understand . . .

And abruptly, I did. Somehow, probably through all the tests Colleen had been taking, DuBois had discovered she was pregnant and realized where the migraines were coming from. But with the headaches now stopped—and with no way to know about the telepath shield—she had come to the only conclusion possible, that one of the two conflicting minds had ceased to exist.

Relief washed over me. Relief that the baby was not, in fact dead; relief that now we didn't have to think up some story about the migraines to get the doctor off Colleen's back.

All of that assuming, of course, that DuBois was indeed thinking the same way I was. "You mean that the headaches were because—?" I asked, trying to draw her out.

DuBois nodded, the eerie hint of flashing red fading from her face as the ambulance outside drove off. "Because Colleen and her baby were far closer together than two telepaths can safely be," she explained. She looked at Colleen. "Is this—?"

"He's a good friend," Colleen told her. "He understands about telepaths."

DuBois nodded and turned back to me. "Then you must understand that both of them were in great danger," she said gently. "In fact, that's why I brought an ambulance here this evening, to get Colleen to the hospital for an emergency abortion. As it happened—" she shrugged slightly—"in this case Nature provided her own solution."

I shivered, memories of my own close-approach with Nelson flashing to mind. DuBois saw, misunderstood. "Don't worry—I'm sure Colleen will be all right," she assured me. "We'll make sure tomorrow. Unless—?" She looked back at Colleen, eyebrows raised.

Colleen shook her head. "Tomorrow will be early enough. I'd rather not start a full examination right now."

"Okay." DuBois reached over to squeeze Colleen's hand, then stood up. "I'll see you tomorrow morning, then—ten sharp. But don't hesitate to call before then if you have any problems."

She pulled her stethoscope off her neck and dropped it into her bag. Picking up her coat, she got into it as she walked to the door. I opened it for her, she nodded her thanks—

And suddenly her eyes widened, and her mouth fell open, and the whole thing went straight to hell. "You're Dale Ravenhall," she breathed, staring at my face as if seeing a ghost. "You're one of—" She spun to look at Colleen, twisted back to stare at me. "You can't *be* here."

On the couch behind her, Colleen had gone white. Her mouth worked soundlessly, her eyes wide with helpless horror . . . and beside her, nestled coyly against the couch where I'd first put it down, the briefcase containing the telepath shield seemed as large and obvious as if I'd parked an elephant there.

DuBois mustn't find out about it. At all costs, she mustn't find out.

She was still staring at me. Swallowing hard, I closed the door and took a careful breath. "What I'm about to say," I told her, "is something you must promise to keep to yourself. I mean *absolutely* to yourself. Is that clear, Doctor?"

She hesitated a fraction of a second, then nodded. "I promise," she said gravely.

I nodded back, wishing to heaven I wasn't in the middle of the telepath shield. If she was lying through her teeth, I'd never know it. "All right. You can test for this tomorrow, but my guess is that the baby is still fine. What seems to have happened is that both he and Colleen have totally lost their telepathic abilities."

Behind DuBois, Colleen nearly fell off the couch. "It seems to be a side-effect of the pregnancy," I rushed on before she could blurt something that would pop the bubble. "A safety mechanism, I guess; otherwise, like you said, a telepath couldn't possibly live through a pregnancy."

DuBois nodded slowly. "I see," she said thoughtfully. "Strange, indeed."

"Not all *that* strange," I argued, digging desperately for half-remembered facts as I fought to create something reasonable-sounding on the run. "I mean, a woman's digestive system shuts down during labor, doesn't it?"

"Yes, but that's hardly comparable," DuBois shook her head, turning to look at Colleen. "This is more like a controlled stroke, or possibly something like hysterical amnesia. Either way, it implies that some part of her brain has completely shut down." She looked back at me, her eyes shining with sudden excitement. "Yes. And if so, it means we should finally be able to discover where exactly in the brain the telepathic talent originates."

Even with the cool air leaking in from the front door beside me, I felt sweat beginning to collect on my forehead. "I really don't think this is the time to put Colleen through a whole battery of tests," I suggested cautiously.

"Why not?" DuBois countered, turning back to Colleen. "Don't you see what this might mean, Colleen?—after years of warm-air speculation, we could be on the edge of finally learning what makes you tick. Learning how and where the telepathy comes from—maybe figuring out how to turn it on and off at will—"

"And what will all this testing do to my baby?" Colleen asked quietly.

A lot of doctors would probably have popped off with a brusque or even patronizing dismissal of the question. To DuBois's credit, she didn't. "It should be safe enough," she said instead. "There's no way to guarantee that, unfortunately, not with a fetus with the abilities this one clearly has. But medical science has had a lot of experience with non-intrusive testing over the past couple of decades, and I think the chances of danger will be extremely small."

Colleen looked past her at me, her eyes pleading. "But if there's even a *small* chance she'll be hurt . . ."

We discussed and argued and bargained with DuBois for over an hour. In the end, we gave in.

You told her what?

I clenched my teeth. *Will you for God's sake settle down, Gordy?* I said. *It's no big deal.*

I'm so glad you're more relaxed about life these days, he came back acidly. *I don't suppose you've by any chance considered the possible consequences of this stupid lie of yours?*

So what was I supposed to do, tell her about the shield?

Why not? She could probably have been trusted with the secret.

"Probably" isn't good enough, I insisted. *And I'm sorry if the lie wasn't up to your usual standards. Next time I have to come up with one on the spur of the moment I'll ask for sealed bids.*

Gordy's comeback would probably have been a juicy one, but Calvin cut in before he could speak. *All right, everyone relax,* he said in that calmly authoritative tone of his. *What's done is done. Let's concentrate on figuring out how this is going to affect Colleen.*

How it's going to affect her is that she's going to get hauled off to the hospital tomorrow, Gordy said blackly. *What are you planning to do, Dale, walk her back and forth between testing rooms lugging the shield?*

I turned to peer out the van's side window at the brightly lit building beside me, my breath making a patch of frost on the glass as I did so. *As it happens, I'm sitting outside the hospital right now,* I told them. *As long as I park reasonably close in tomorrow the shield should have no trouble covering the whole building.*

That's fine for tomorrow, Calvin pointed out. *What happens when they find out that none of her brain cells have in fact closed up shop? Is DuBois the type who'll push for more tests?*

Like at the Mayo Clinic or somewhere equally far out of town? Gordy added before I could answer. *Blast it all, Dale—you should have just told DuBois that you weren't you.*

It wouldn't have helped any, I insisted. Actually, that approach hadn't occurred to me until it was too late—our faces had been splashed on the world's TV screens enough times over the years that I never even considered trying to bluff my way out. But I'd had plenty of time since then to realize why it wouldn't have worked anyway. *She was already busy scheduling Colleen in for tests when the shoe dropped. Or were you thinking that during all that she might miss the fact that Colleen was still carrying a live fetus?*

She might have concluded that the baby's telepathic abilities had been burned out, Calvin pointed out. *But I suppose that would simply have called for a different set of tests. I'm afraid Dale's probably right, Gordy; the minute the doctor commandeered that ambulance, anything he or Colleen could say or do would only have bought us a temporary reprieve.*

Thank you, I said, passing over the point that the only "us" really involved here were Colleen and me and the baby. *And as for season tickets to the Mayo Clinic, we've already been through that with DuBois. This is going to be a one-day, single-shot study marathon; guaranteed, end of argument. They get all the data they need tomorrow or they're out of luck.*

And if DuBois starts pushing anyway? Gordy persisted. *I know the type, Dale—you let her get her nose inside the tent and she's going to want all the way in.*

Her nose was in the tent the minute Colleen went to her for help with the migraines, Calvin said heavily. *No way to keep this from getting out, I don't suppose?*

I shrugged, the movement making my coat squeak against the van's seatback. *We can try, but I'm not optimistic. DuBois will want to publish anything she finds, of course, but we've probably got a few weeks or months before that hits the journals. More likely the simple fact of Colleen's pregnancy will leak through one of the people who help do the testing tomorrow.*

Any way you can identify the ones most likely to talk and maybe—I don't know—persuade them not to or something?

With my head inside the telepath shield?

I sensed Calvin's quick flash of annoyed embarrassment. *Oh. Right.*

For a moment there was silence. *I guess there's really nothing else we can do at the moment,* Calvin said at last. Reluctantly.

Not really, I agreed. *Before I forget, Colleen said that you might as well start passing the word to the rest of the group. Probably ought to wait until morning—there's no reason to wake people up for this.*

We'll do that, Calvin promised. *How is Colleen holding up?*

I hissed between my teeth. I would have given almost anything to have said she was doing well; or doing badly, or doing medium. But the simple truth was— *I don't know,* I had to tell them, hearing the undertone of frustration behind the words. *I'm . . . not very good at reading her.*

Another brief moment of silence, an awkward one this time. *You'll get better at it,* Gordy assured me. *Just give yourself time.*

I grimaced. Time. It was, indeed, one thing we were likely to have plenty of. *Right. Well . . . I'll talk to you both tomorrow.*

Colleen had a roaring fire going in the fireplace, and was sitting at the far end of the couch staring at it, when I returned from my reconnoiter and long-range discussion group. "Well?" she asked, not turning as I closed the door behind me.

"They're not exactly turning cartwheels," I admitted, shrugging off my coat and draping it over the nearest chair. "But they don't see what else we could have done."

"Except maybe telling Dr. DuBois the truth in the first place."

I winced. I'd defended my decision to lie about the shield— defended it successfully, too—in front of Calvin and Gordy. But defending it in front of Colleen was another matter entirely. "I'm sorry," I said. "I really think things would have been worse if we'd told her about the shield, but—well, I know it stepped on your sensibilities, and I'm sorry for that."

She nodded, still gazing into the fire . . . and belatedly the warning bells began tinkling in the back of my mind. "Colleen?" I asked, moving up beside her. "You all right?"

She still didn't look up . . . but from my new perspective I could now see the tear stains on her cheeks. "Colleen?"

"It's so lonely," she whispered. "So lonely, Dale. When you left to talk with the others . . . I've never been alone before. Not like this."

I sat down beside her and slid my arm around her shoulders. Her body trembled against mine. "It'll be okay," I said soothingly. Even I could hear how fatuous the words sounded. "It'll be okay. I'll stay with you as long as you want me to."

She sighed; a deep, shuddering breath. "I'm not going to make it, Dale. Not eight whole months—not like this."

"You'll make it, Colleen." More fatuous words. "You'll make it because you're not the type to give up. And because it has to be done."

"Does it? Does it really?"

I felt an icy shiver run up my back. "What alternative is there?"

She didn't answer . . . but then, she didn't have to. DuBois had already talked about the alternative. "Do you want to have an abortion?" I asked her in a low voice.

"What, kill the only child ever conceived by two telepaths?" A sound that was half laugh, half sob, escaped her lips. "What would the group say?"

"They'd understand," I told her. "Besides, now that we've got the telepath shield this can be done again. If anyone wants it done."

For a long minute the only sound in the room was the crackling of the fire. "What happens after the baby is born?" Colleen asked at last. "I can't stay in the shield for eighteen years."

"I know." That much, at least, was obvious. "We'd have to put him up for adoption. Scott's got a lot of connections with lawyers in the New Orleans area, and Lisa knows everyone important from Philadelphia to the Canadian border. We'll have them quietly get the wheels grinding."

She didn't say anything, just shifted beside me and brought her hand up to rest on her abdomen. "I don't know. None of the options . . . I just don't know."

"Me, too," I told her. "Look, we don't have to make any major decisions tonight. Let's just get you through DuBois's marathon of tests tomorrow and see how you feel then. All right?"

"Sure." She stared at the fire for a minute, then sighed. "It's funny, you know. When I was a little girl I dreamed about being a mother—played house with my dolls for hours at a time. Then I hit puberty, and all the strange sounds I'd been hearing all my life sharpened into words, and I found out what I was . . . and I knew I'd never be able to have children. The dream died slowly, kicking and screaming all the way. But finally I had to accept it."

I thought about my own hopeless love for Colleen all these years, and the way the telepath shield had suddenly made it possible. And what had happened afterward. "Sometimes dreams like that find a way to come back to life," I told her. "Though not always quite the way you envisioned them."

She sniffed, twice, and abruptly I realized she was crying again. "I'm scared, Dale," she said between silent sobs. "I'm scared that I'll hate the baby for what I'll have to go through for her. Or else that I . . . won't be able to give her up."

There were things I could have said. Soothing things, words of comfort and assurance and trust, none of which would have done the slightest good whatsoever. And so I did the only other thing I could think of to do.

I wrapped my arms around her and held her tightly against me, and listened helplessly as she cried.

* * *

Along with Nelson's paranoia and general lack of honesty, I had also picked up some of his boundless confidence; but by morning my own natural caution had reasserted itself, and we wound up fudging a bit on my original plans. Instead of both of us driving together to the hospital, we took separate vehicles: Colleen in her own car with the portable telepath shield in the trunk, me in the van with the larger line-current model and gasoline generator chugging away in back. It meant I had to stay with the van most of the day, lest the generator's puffing exhaust line poking out the back doors attract unwelcome attention, but even that was probably a blessing in disguise. Much as I hated abandoning Colleen to DuBois's gauntlet of tests without being there to hold her hand, I'd begun to wonder if it would perhaps be more than a little foolhardy to parade together all day among dozens of hospital staff and patients. As long as DuBois was the only one who knew about Colleen's "lost" telepathic powers—and as long as she didn't break her promise to keep that knowledge confidential—there was a chance of stuffing the lie back into its bottle with a minimum of embarrassment. The minute someone else recognized me, that chance would be gone.

Early December in Regina is hardly the time or the place to be sitting outside in a van for hours on end, but it turned out not to be as bad as I'd feared. The weather, I gathered, had been somewhat warmer than usual for that time of year, and with the generator churning out a modicum of heat behind me and the blazing sunlight turning the van's dark-blue interior into a wrap-around radiator, the temperature stayed reasonably tolerable.

Reasonably tolerable is still considerably short of warm, though, and my teeth were beginning to chatter when, six hours after our arrival, Colleen finally drove her car up beside me and gave me a tired nod. I nodded back and started the van, and twenty minutes later we were home.

"How'd it go?" I asked her, taking off my heavy boots and standing on one of the floor heating grates. My toes tingled unpleasantly with returning sensation.

"Nothing I haven't had before," she sighed, dropping into a chair at the kitchen table and closing her eyes. "Sort of a repeat performance of all the tests we went through when we were first identified as telepaths. Plus a couple of encores they've dreamed up since then."

Those tests were nearly a decade in the past, but I still remembered them. Vividly. "The full spin cycle, in other words."

"Something like that." She opened her eyes. "I don't know about you, but they didn't let me have any lunch and I'm starved. How's your cooking?"

"Tolerable," I told her, "but all my best meals take at least an hour from scratch to fork. You up to waiting that long?"

She made a face. "Not really."

I nodded and reached for my boots. "Me, neither. What's your preference in fast food?"

She gave me directions to a chicken place and I headed back out to the van . . . and it was as I was preparing to pull out of the driveway that I first noticed the man sitting in the parked car down the street.

Waiting for someone to join him from one of the houses, I decided; but even so, I watched in the mirror as I headed down the street, half expecting him to pull out behind me. He didn't, and after the first wave of foolishness passed I forgot about him.

Until, that is, fifteen minutes later when I returned with the chicken and saw him still sitting there.

Perhaps if I hadn't just spent six hours sitting in a van in the middle of a Saskatchewan winter that wouldn't have struck me as quite so odd. But I had; and it did. Enough so that I made sure to lock up the van before I went inside, and immediately after eating went back out to bring the line-current telepath shield into the house. The sun was starting to go down by then, its heating effects long gone, but the man was still sitting in the car, a black silhouette against the pink clouds to the west.

By the time I had the shield inside and started searching for a good place to plug it in, Colleen had retired to her bedroom with a book. By the time it was ensconced in a corner of her back bedroom study and plugged in, the book was on the floor and she was sound asleep. Those two weeks of migraines were still taking their toll, I reflected, and a full day of medical tests certainly hadn't helped. Turning off her bedside reading lamp, I covered her with a quilt and bedspread and tiptoed out, closing the door behind me.

Two minutes later, wrapped up again in coat and scarf, I slipped quietly out the back door and padded through the half-frozen mud in the back yard around to the side of the house. Flitting between the house and detached garage, I came up to the side of my van and peered cautiously around it.

The watcher in the car was still there. Crouching against the van, partially obscured from his view by a section of hedge, I watched my breath make clouds of pale white and tried to figure out what to do. Under other circumstances, it wouldn't have been a problem—with a sensing range for normals that was just under twenty-five feet, I would have had no trouble sneaking up close enough to find out who he was and what he was doing here. But with two telepath shields blasting away behind me, that was out of the question.

I was still trying to come up with a plan when he came up with one for me. From his direction I heard the faint sound of an engine being started, and a moment later his headlights came on and he pulled away from the curb to head leisurely down the street. Fifteen seconds later, I was on his trail.

He drove sedately, heading in toward the center of the city, without any sign of nervousness or awareness of my presence that I could detect. Which was just as well, given that everything I knew about tailing a car had come from watching TV cop shows. I tried to hang back in the waning rush-hour traffic, more worried about being noticed than I was of losing him, and waited impatiently for us to reach the edge of the telepath shield's half-mile range.

It came, as usual, suddenly. One moment, nothing; the next, the background of mental sound filled the back corners of my mind. *Calvin? Gordy?* I called.

Right here, Calvin came back immediately.

Me, too, Gordy added. *So; how'd Colleen's tests—?*

Later, I cut him off. *I've got a problem.*

I gave them a thumbnail sketch of my situation, and for a minute they were both silent. *Could be he's just a reporter,* Calvin suggested slowly.

That would be bad enough, I reminded him. Ahead, my quarry turned right at a small cross street. *It would mean that someone at the hospital leaked the news about Colleen's pregnancy.*

In which case you'd better just turn east and keep going, Gordy said tartly. *You let a reporter get a clear look at you and that cock-and-bull story about Colleen losing her telepathy will start its long slide down the tubes.*

Unless he already has *seen me,* I pointed out grimly, reaching the corner and turning to follow. Hard to tell, not knowing the town, but it seemed to me we were heading back out of the main entertainment sections. *In which case running does nothing but leave Colleen here to face the wolves alone.*

Gordy considered that. *So you follow him outside the shield's range and find out?* he said doubtfully. *Seems risky, especially if he* hasn't *recognized you yet.*

If I set things up right he won't have a chance in hell of spotting me, I reminded him. *All I need is a crowded restaurant or bar or something—*

And what if he's not a reporter? Calvin put in.

My thought broke off in mid-sentence. There was an ominous darkness in Calvin's tone. *What do you mean? Who else could he be?*

Calvin seemed to hesitate. *What if it's Ted Green?*

I felt my mouth go dry. *But that's impossible,* I managed. *Isn't it?*

It most certainly is, Gordy said, his voice allowing for no argument. *Everything Green knew about the shield was blocked. Permanently.*

But maybe—

I said permanently, *Calvin,* Gordy all but snarled. There was anger in his tone. Anger at the implication he hadn't done the job right—

Anger with a clear haze of pain beneath it. When it was all over and we'd questioned him about it he'd shrugged off Green's brainwashing as merely distasteful and tiring. Now, for the first time, I was getting a glimpse of just how thoroughly he'd played down the horror and sheer dirtiness of the experience. Briefly, shamefully, I wondered if I'd ever thanked him properly for his sacrifice.

But now wasn't the time for such things. *Could it be a friend of Green's, then?* I suggested. *Someone who knew he'd been working for me and put two and two together afterward?*

It would have to be damn good addition, Gordy grunted. But he said it thoughtfully, not defensively, and there was a growing uneasiness behind it. *But I don't suppose there's any point in taking chances. I'll give Colleen a call and have her call the police.*

They're going to need a reason to pick him up, Gordy, Calvin cautioned him.

I'm not worried about him, Gordy said shortly, and I sensed him scooping his phone off the hook. *This particular guy can't do anything with Dale sitting there on his tail. But he might not be working alone.*

My heart seemed to seize up inside my chest. I hadn't even thought about that . . . and I'd left Colleen alone, asleep and helpless. *Gordy—*

Shut up—it's ringing.

I shut up, and for a moment I drove in silence, listening to the sort of faraway echo effect that always comes of listening in while another telepath speaks aloud. Gordy gave Colleen a quick summary of what we thought or suspected and told her to call the police and tell them she'd spotted someone skulking around the neighborhood. I could hear the worry in her echo-effect voice, and for a long minute wondered if I should just turn around and get back to her. But even as I heard Gordy hang up—*Uh-oh . . .* I said.

What is it? Calvin asked sharply.

My cue, I think. A block ahead, my quarry had turned into a pocket-sized parking lot. Pulling smoothly to the curb, I killed my lights and watched as he got out and headed across the street. He disappeared into a building with a garish neon sign in the window—somebody's night club, it was called, I couldn't quite read the name from the angle I was at. *This is it,* I announced, opening the van's door and stepping down. It was quiet—strangely quiet—with only a few cars moving anywhere within my sight and no pedestrians at all. The skin on the back of my neck tingled; swallowing, I headed for the building. *I get the distinct feeling I'm not in the better part of town,* I told Calvin and Gordy, trying not to let my sudden nervousness show through.

It was a wasted effort. *Dale, maybe we'd better call this off,* Calvin said. *Who knows what you might be walking into there?*

He's probably not a reporter if he's in a place like that, Gordy added. *And if he's something shady, you sure as anything don't want to confront him.*

It was a sentiment I could wholeheartedly agree with. But even as I weighed the pros and cons in my own mind, my feet kept on walking . . .

Dale?

Quiet a minute—I'm listening. I took another few steps toward the night club, the action putting me within listening range of another handful of the bar's patrons; and it was immediately clear that my darkest fears had been for nothing. *It's all right,* I told them, letting out a quiet sigh of relief. *There's nothing particularly sinister here. A little off-beat, but it seems safe enough. I'm going in.*

I opened the door and pushed my way in through the blast of warm, smoky air that swept out past me, and gave the place a quick once-over. It was more or less what I'd expected from my telepathic assessment of the clientele: dim lighting, unimaginative decor, and a fairly loud music soundtrack playing in the background. I was, however, a bit surprised by the young women dancing on the raised stage in the center of the room.

I think it's euphemistically referred to as exotic dancing, Gordy told me, and through the heavy tension in his tone I caught just a glimpse of amusement at my surprise.

Right. Anyway, it explained the curious sense I'd had coming in, an aloof sort of lust. It was, I decided, probably difficult to get really worked up, even by a semi-nude dancer, in a large room with a bunch of other men.

And there were a fair number of men there, considering the early hour. Most were sitting on stools pulled up against the stage area, but a handful of tables and booths further out were occupied, as well. All eyes were on the dancers, which was fine with me: my quarry would never even see me coming. Piece of cake.

Unless he spotted you following him, Calvin warned. *Be careful.*

Sure. As casually as possible, I sauntered away from the door, eyes darting for likely prospects as I sorted through the cacophony of thoughts surrounding me. It wasn't quite as bad as trying to follow a conversation at a crowded party, fortunately, since looking directly at a person usually sharpened that particular mental voice. I walked slowly past the near side of the stage, shifted direction slightly toward the tables and the booths—

I'd been wrong. There was one pair of eyes most emphatically not on the gyrating women. A pair of eyes locked solidly on my own . . .

Oh, my God.

What? Calvin and Gordy demanded together.

My mouth had gone dry. *There's a murderer here,* I told them. *John Talbot Myers, wanted in Toronto for three killings during a bank robbery.* For a brief second I thought about trying to escape; but it was instantly clear that even trying it would be suicidal. From his back booth, Myers had seen me walking slowly around as if looking for someone, and was already half convinced that I was either a cop or an informer. His thoughts were edging toward lethal, and I caught a reference to a gun—

Get out of there, Calvin snapped. *Now.*

Too late, I gritted. Too late to run, too late to pretend I hadn't noticed him; too late for anything.

Except . . .

I'm going to talk to him, I told the others. *One of you better call the Regina police and tell them he's here. I hope they believe you.*

Dale—

Quiet. Moving as casually as possible, I walked over toward Myers's booth. Nelson, I thought dimly, don't fail me now.

Myers watched me approach, and it seemed to me that I could see in his face the trapped-animal sense that I was hearing from his mind. A dozen wild plans fought for supremacy amid his swirling emotion, all of them involving the gun in his pocket; and as I slid silently into the booth across from him I realized with a start that the weapon was no longer in his pocket but was pointed at me under the table.

But I had a weapon, too, one he couldn't possibly know about. Less than three feet away from him now, I was finally close enough to dig beneath the surface thoughts for things he wasn't thinking about directly. Heart pounding in my ears, my hands folded lightly together on top of the table, I probed furiously for something I could use.

And found it. "Well," I said at last, trying to keep my voice brusque and quiet at the same time. "About time you showed yourself. You have any idea how many places I've been in and out of looking for you?"

It was not what Myers had expected me to say, and for a moment surprise flashed across his mind. But only for a moment. "I think," he said, softly, "that you have me confused with someone else."

"Give it a rest, John," I said coldly. "Unless you've decided you don't want us to help you, that is."

His face didn't change. "And just who is this 'us'?"

I sighed theatrically, probing hard. I needed to tailor my story to the basics of Myers's situation, and while I had a handle on the framework, I still lacked several crucial details. But with a properly phrased question—and a little luck—Myers would supply me with what I needed. "What do you mean, who are we?" I demanded, letting a little scorn creep into my voice. "Who the hell knows you're here in Regina?"

"Why don't you tell me," he challenged. He was smart, all right, or at least smart enough to know that you didn't volunteer information like that to a stranger . . . and totally unaware that in thinking the answer to my question he'd done exactly that.

"Alan Thomas, of course," I said with an air of forced patience, suppressing a shiver as I picked up a short profile of the man from Myers's mind. Thomas was an old colleague from Myers's youth, heavily into Regina's criminal underside and as twisted as Myers himself. "He asked me to help get you out of here."

"Did he, now." Myers still wasn't ready to take me at face value, but the uncertainties were starting to creep in. "Describe him for me."

I could have done so easily, of course; awaiting my answer, Myers had what amounted to a full-color portrait of Thomas hovering in the front of his mind. But along with the portrait came the seeds of an easier way. "Why don't I just give you the name 'John Alexander' instead."

If a mind could heave a sigh of relief, Myers's would have done so. "John Alexander" was the name that Thomas was going to have false identity cards made up in to facilitate Myers's escape from Canada. "So why didn't Alan come himself?" he grunted, and I heard a faint click as he put the safety back on his pistol. "For that matter, what the hell was he doing, letting you in on this?"

"Because the plan's gone to hell," I told him. *Calvin?*

Right here. I'm on the phone with the Regina police now.

I'm going to try and set Myers up for them. Listen in and cue them in on the story.

Got it.

"You've picked up a tail," I continued aloud to Myers. "RCMP. He's in here right now, watching you."

Myers swore gently. "Where?"

"Over there, watching the show by the stage." It was a safe

enough fingering; there were over fifteen men there. "We figure he's either waiting for confirmation of who you are, or else already has reinforcements on the way."

Myers's eyes and thoughts had gone icy. "Let's get going, then," he said, his voice gently vicious. "I'll go first; you deal with him when he follows."

I shook my head minutely. "No need. Alan's come up with a better way to lose him." I smiled sardonically. "We'll simply, right here in front of him, have you arrested."

For a moment his acceptance of me vanished, and I held my breath. And then he got it. "Oh, that's cute," he said, and I sensed a genuine if hard-edged humor at the whole idea. "Real cute. Uniformed cops, squad car, the whole works?"

"Depends on what Alan can get hold of," I told him, letting myself breathe again. "May have to go with plainclothes types and an unmarked car." Dimly, I sensed Calvin relaying the plan to the police, and I sent up a quick prayer that they'd go along with it. If they didn't, there would be a gunfight for sure. "But either way, very convincing."

Myers's eyes swept the stage, too casually. "What if he follows us or wants to ride along?"

"No problem," I assured him, probing again. Thomas had a lot of quiet contacts, one of whom— "One of Alan's people at Mountie HQ ran a profile on the guy, and he's apparently been slapped down more than once for trying to hog credit he didn't deserve and stepping on local toes in the process. The boys who're coming have been briefed, and they'll just tell him to go take a hike if he tries to muscle his way in."

They're on their way, Dale, Calvin interjected into my thoughts. *They say you're a damn fool for getting involved instead of calling them directly, but they're willing to go along with it.*

Good. Tell them to just go ahead and come straight in—Myers isn't altogether crazy about the plan, but he buys it and he won't offer any resistance.

I'll tell them. They'll be there in maybe three minutes.

Which meant I had to move now if I wanted to avoid being picked up in the net and losing whatever chance I had left of keeping my presence in Regina a secret. "Okay," I said, glancing at my watch. "They'll be here any minute. I'm going over there—" I nodded across the room— "where I can keep an eye on our Mountie friend."

Myers frowned. "Why? He's already seen you with me."

"That's the point," I agreed. "It means that after they take you out, he's got to choose which of us to follow. If it's me—no problem, I know how to lose him. If it's you—" I gave him a tight smile— "then I'll be behind him. Making sure he doesn't follow you very far."

Again Myers's eyes flicked over the men at the stage, and I caught him wondering why we were going to all this effort if I was going to take the Mountie out anyway. "I hope I don't have to do that, of course," I added. "Better all around if he just thinks the cops have beaten him to the punch and doesn't figure out what really happened for a couple of days. Nothing heats up a chase like taking out a Mountie."

Myers nodded agreement, and I knew beyond a doubt that I had him. I'd told him things only he and his ally Thomas should have known, had presented him with a plan that he found reasonable and even amusing, and had short-circuited all of his worries, almost before they were fully formed, by echoing his own thoughts back at him.

I nodded to him and left; and I was seated casually across the room when the four plainclothesmen came in.

I held my breath . . . but it went as smoothly and beautifully as could be. They came over to Myers, underplaying it exactly as fake cops following my script might be expected to do; nothing to disturb the men watching the show, but more than enough for an undercover Mountie to notice. Myers submitted to them without argument or fuss, acting to probably the best of his ability like a man pretending he actually was being arrested. One of the cops went so far as to give him a reassuring wink as the cuffs went on, and after that Myers would have gone all the way to the police station with them.

Which, of course, he was going to. I wondered briefly what his reaction was going to be, decided my imagination wasn't up to it. *They got him?* Gordy asked, his tone tight.

Just taking him out the door, I told him. *Like I said, a piece of cake.*

Glad to hear it. The hairs on the back of my neck pricked up; there was none of the limp relief I was feeling in his voice. *Then you'd better get back to Colleen. Right away.*

For the second time in fifteen minutes my heart seized up. *What's happened?* I demanded, on my feet and heading for the door. *Is she all right?*

She's fine, he said. *And it may not mean anything at all . . . but she just called to say that the police did indeed spot a prowler when they came by a few minutes ago.*

It was just as well that most of Regina's police were busy with Myers at the moment, because I broke most of the city's traffic laws getting back to Colleen's house. Every window was ablaze with light when I skidded roughly into the driveway—she must have turned on every switch in the whole house.

I'd taken her spare key along with me, but it proved unnecessary; I was still fumbling it out of my pocket when I heard the deadbolt being unlocked from the inside. A moment later I was inside, and Colleen was trembling in my arms.

Trembling hard. "What happened?" I asked, my eyes sweeping the room for signs of trouble. Nothing seemed to be out of place. "Did you see somebody?"

She shook her head. "No," she said, voice muffled in my chest. "I just—when Gordon called—and then the police came by and said someone was out there—" She took a shuddering breath. "I'm sorry, Dale. I'm acting like a child afraid of the dark."

"It's all right," I soothed her, feeling like a jerk. I knew she was still getting used to being isolated in the telepath shield, after all. If I hadn't left her all alone while I played private eye . . .

The shield.

She must have felt me stiffen. "What is it?" she asked, pulling away to look up at me.

"Come on," I said, taking her hand and heading toward the back bedroom. Calvin's speculations that Ted Green was involved with all this rose up before my eyes, and I found myself gritting my teeth as I pushed open the bedroom door.

Anticlimax. The telepath shield was right where I'd left it, humming sedately to itself. The portable shield—? I had another flash of dread, then remembered that it had spent the day in Colleen's car trunk and that it was still out there. For a moment I considered going out and bringing it in, but decided it was safe enough where it was. I reached for the light switch—

And paused. On the carpet halfway to the shield, some trick of lighting angle making it visible, was a small glob of mud.

Mud from my shoes, was my first hopeful thought, from earlier this evening when I brought it in. But between the driveway and the walk and the steps I'd been on concrete the whole distance.

But there was plenty of mud just outside the back door.

It took only a few minutes of searching with angled flashlight beams to find the rest of the trail, a trail that did indeed lead straight to the back door.

"He could have killed us," Colleen whispered, trembling against me again. I didn't blame her; I was trembling some myself. "If he'd taken it—"

"I doubt he meant to," I hastened to reassure her. I didn't doubt it at all; the chances were at least even that he'd intended doing exactly that, but had been scared off by the noise of Gordy's phone call. "Did the police get a good look at him?"

"I don't know, but I doubt it." She pointed toward the back of the house. "They said he disappeared back toward the Abbotts' house—that's the white one two houses down—and that they tried to cut him off but couldn't find him. They said they'd put an extra car in the neighborhood, but that there wasn't much else they could do."

Ten years ago, I reflected sourly, when we were still big news, the Regina police department would probably have fallen all over itself trying to protect her, and like as not we'd have wound up with a ring of armed guards around the house. But all the many and varied expectations of how telepaths would make the world a better place had gradually faded away, and with the rosy glow had gone our celebrity status.

Though of course it was only our relative obscurity these days which had allowed me to sneak unheralded into Regina in the first place. The universe, I reflected, contained no unmixed blessings.

"Well, I guess that'll have to do for tonight," I told Colleen as I double-locked the door and steered her back toward the bedroom. Despite obvious efforts to the contrary, she was already starting to sag with her earlier fatigue. "But tomorrow we'll do something more useful."

She nodded, either too tired to think about asking what I had in mind or else too tired to care. I helped her into bed, turned off the light, and tiptoed out. For the next few minutes I made a circuit of the house, making sure all the windows were locked and setting various jars and other breakable glassware onto the sills, the best impromptu burglar alarm I could think of. And wondered exactly what we were going to do when morning came.

Or more precisely, wondered exactly where we were going to go.

Colleen wouldn't like it, and I wasn't looking forward to telling her she would have to leave the city she loved, possibly for eight months, possibly longer. But I no longer saw any choice in the matter. Clearly, someone had recognized me and subsequently deduced the existence of the telepath shield, and now that somebody had seen the thing up close. If he decided to steal it, then the child Colleen was carrying was dead . . . because as long as she was pregnant, Colleen's life depended on having two functioning shields, one acting as backup to the other; and with one of them gone an abortion would be the only safe course of action. The migraines of the past month were abundant proof that as the fetus developed its close-approach pressures would continue to increase, almost certainly reaching lethal levels long before Colleen was ready to deliver.

And I was not going to risk losing Colleen. Period.

I finished my rounds, turning off lights as I went, and trudged back through the dark to the bedroom. By noon tomorrow we'd be gone, I decided as I lay in bed listening to the unfamiliar creaks and groans of a strange house in an unfamiliar neighborhood. We'd take the morning to throw some essentials into suitcases, and by noon we'd be on the road.

Eventually, despite the noises, my own fatigue caught up with me, and as I drifted to sleep I wondered distantly if perhaps I might be getting a little *too* paranoid.

I was not, in fact, paranoid enough. By noon tomorrow it was far too late.

It was nine-thirty the next morning, and I was still trying to persuade Colleen of the necessity of running, when the knock came on the front door.

For a frozen moment we just stared at each other. The knock came again; rising from the kitchen table, I moved quietly to the door. "Who is it?" I called.

The voice that answered was urbane and calm and educated. And very sure of itself. "The fact that you have to ask that question, Mr. Ravenhall," he said, "tells me all I need to know. Please open the door."

I heard a footstep as Colleen came up behind me. "Dale?— what is it?"

"Trouble," I hissed back. For a moment I hesitated; but there really wasn't anything to be gained by keeping him out. Mind scrabbling hard to come up with a new story to spin, I undid the locks and opened the door.

There were two men standing there. One, obviously the man who'd spoken, was balding and late-middle-aged, heavily wrapped up in an expensive coat and an almost visible air of authority. The second, standing a pace behind him, was much younger, with a coolness to his eyes that made me shiver. "I think you have me confused with someone else—" I began; but practically before I'd started into my spiel the middle-aged man pulled open the storm door and walked calmly in past me, the other right behind him. So much for that approach.

"Miss Isaac," the spokesman nodded to Colleen. "Please— both of you—sit down."

"Perhaps you'd like to state your business first," I said in my best imitation of hauteur.

Almost lazily, the older man turned and studied me. "Please sit down," he repeated, emphasizing each word just noticeably.

Silently, I stepped to Colleen's side and sat us down on the couch. My first hope, that we were dealing with overeager reporters, was gone now without a trace. Our visitor chose a chair facing us and eased himself smoothly into it, his younger companion remaining standing behind him. "Now, then," he said briskly, looking back and forth between Colleen and me. "I expect it'll save time and histrionics all around if I begin by telling you what I know. First: I know that you, Miss Isaac, are pregnant; possibly by Mr. Ravenhall here, though I'm not absolutely certain of that. Second: the child is itself telepathic—or perhaps potentially telepathic would be a better term; it certainly isn't doing any real mind-reading at this stage of its development. Third: the only way you and the fetus can stand being this close together is because you have a device plugged into the wall back there that somehow temporarily damps out your telepathic power, which is of course also the only reason Mr. Ravenhall can be here in this room with you. Now, does that pretty well cover it?"

I felt cold all over, the lie I was struggling to create dying stillborn. Or most of it, anyway. "Pretty well," I said calmly. "Except that the machine's effects aren't temporary. They're permanent."

He smiled indulgently. "Really. And you'd like me to also believe that your powers of persuasion are such that you could simply talk a killer like John Talbot Myers into giving himself up."

I glanced at the man standing silently over him, the taste of defeat in my mouth. "So it was you I was following?" He nodded once, still silent, and I shifted my eyes back to the other. "How did you arrange for Myers to be there?"

He smiled again. "I'd like to claim credit for that, but in fact it was pure happenstance. Alex here—" he gestured minutely toward the man standing over him—"was really only trying to get you out of the way for a while so that another of my people could examine the device he saw you bring inside after your long day at the hospital."

"I hope he got a good look before the phone call scared him away," I said coldly.

He cocked an eyebrow at me. "Your anger is understandable, Mr. Ravenhall, but totally unnecessary. He had explicit instructions not to tamper with the device. After all—" he shrugged— "I'd hardly go to all this trouble only to lose my child."

Beside me, Colleen stiffened. "What do you mean, *your* child?" I demanded.

"I mean," he said softly, "that when the baby is born I'll be taking charge of it."

"Like hell you will," I said, a flash of anger hazing my vision with red. "It's Colleen's baby, and whatever arrangements are made will be up to her."

"And her sponsors?" he asked pointedly.

I frowned. "What do her sponsors have to do with it?"

He looked at Colleen. "Your monthly stipend, Miss Isaac; the money without which you would have little or no way of surviving. It comes from the University of Regina, Regina General Hospital, and the Canadian Psychiatric Institute, correct?"

She hesitated, then nodded. "Yes."

His eyes came back to me. "And your funding, Mr. Ravenhall, comes from the Draper Fund for Basic Medical Research and the Iowa State University of Science and Technology. Correct?"

"You're well informed," I told him. "What's the point?"

His face hardened, just a little. "The point is that all of that money—*all* of it—comes from me. Not from some kindly bureaucracy or generous charity or the U.S. and Canadian taxpayers: from *me*. And not just yours, but all of your fellow telepaths', as well."

"What are you saying, then?" Colleen asked quietly. "That you own us?"

For a long moment he gazed thoughtfully at her. "I wanted to own you," he said at last. "And if I'd succeeded it wouldn't have been because I had to fight off the competition. Even before all the initial hype and media attention had died down, all of the hard-headed realists of this world had already come to the conclusion that your talent was far too limited to be useful. You could really only transmit words, which cut out any possibility of sending technical data or drawings cross-country; you had to get within thirty feet of your target before you could do any direct spying; and with the liberals in the legal system screaming about the Fifth Amendment you were reasonably useless for solving crimes." He smiled at me. "At least officially. I dare say John Talbot Myers is still trying to figure out what exactly happened to him." He sobered again. "But the most telling point of all against you was that, at least at the beginning, you were literally internationally known figures. Even now, while that recognition has slipped enough for you, Mr. Ravenhall, to walk anonymously into a night club in Regina, all the truly important people in the world would recognize you in an instant."

And at last it hit me. "And that's why you want Colleen's baby, isn't it?" I said. "Because if you can keep his existence a secret . . ."

"He'll be the Unknown Telepath," he finished for me. "And brought up to be totally loyal to me."

Dimly, I was aware that Colleen was pressing close to me; but at that moment all I wanted to do was wrap my hands around that neck and squeeze the satisfied look off his face. Without even thinking about it I surged to my feet—

"Sit down, Mr. Ravenhall," the man told me, his voice calm but abruptly icy cold. "I don't especially need *you*, you know."

I broke off in mid-stride, enough of my brain functioning again through my rage to see that his stooge Alex had his right hand inside his opened jacket. Just about where the business end of a shoulder holster would be . . .

And then Colleen's hand darted up to grip mine in an iron vise, and my last thought of resistance evaporated. For now, at least. Taking a deep breath, I sat down again. "You'll never get away with it, you know," I told him. "Colleen and I can't just disappear without someone noticing."

He shrugged, all affability again. "There's no reason why either of you should have to disappear. Miss Isaac can stay here, certainly until her condition begins to show, after which she can take a vacation for a few months and then return. You, of course, will have to eventually head back to Des Moines."

"Oh, certainly," I snorted. "And if I happen to meet with an accident on the way back—well, that's just the way it goes?"

His eyes hardened. "I don't like being called a murderer, Mr. Ravenhall," he said softly. "I like even less being called a fool. Do you think I've spent over four million dollars in the past ten years just to throw it away by killing you?"

Behind the haze of anger and helplessness, a small corner of my mind recognized that that was exactly the attitude I wanted to foster in him; but at the moment I wasn't interested in listening to reason. "If you expect some kind of future cooperation, you can forget it," I told him instead. "Not from me, not from any of the others."

"Perhaps, perhaps not," he said placidly. "You may be surprised—some of them may be more grateful for my assistance over the years than you are. Your late colleague Nelson Follstadt, for instance, was quite willing to assist me with some small experiments before his untimely death."

"Nelson was ill," Colleen said, her tone laced with contempt. "Only a bastard would take advantage of a man like that."

"I never claimed sainthood," the other said with an unconcerned shrug. "And, of course, there may be things you can do that don't require a surplus of cooperation. Sperm donor, for example—as soon as Miss Isaac delivers we can take that telepath suppressor apart and learn how to build others, and at that point the number of potential telepaths is limited only by our imagination."

"It'll be years before you get a return on your investment," Colleen reminded him. She was working hard at keeping her voice calm and reasonable, but the hand I held was stiff with emotion. "None of us developed our telepathy until adolescence; there's no reason why my baby should be otherwise."

He smiled. "I have nothing against long-term investments, Miss Isaac. You and Mr. Ravenhall are living proof of that."

"You won't get away with it," I told him, dimly aware that I'd already said that once this morning. "What's to stop us from calling the police down on you?"

He gave me an innocent look. "Down on whom? You don't even know who I am."

"You said you were funding all of us," I reminded him. "Those connections can be traced."

"Not in a hundred years of trying," he said. "Face it, Mr. Ravenhall, you can't stop me. Not even if you were so foolish as to try."

There was something in his voice that sent a chill up my back. "And what's that supposed to mean? That you're willing to lose some of your investment after all?"

"I'm always willing to do that if necessary," he said coolly. "But I'm actually not referring to myself at all here. All right; assume that you call the Mounties and relate this conversation to them. What do you suppose they'd do?"

"Throw your butt out of the country," I growled.

"Possibly, though I don't know what exactly they'd charge me with. And then?"

"Suppose you tell me," I challenged.

"You know as well as I do," he said. "The first child born to a telepath?—*and* the first known method to dampen telepathic abilities? You and your machine would be in secret custody somewhere in the northern Yukon within six hours. Or in Langley, if the CIA got to you first." He looked speculatively at Colleen. "Your child would disappear as soon as he was born, Miss Isaac; disappear into a Military Intelligence family, probably, so that he'd be properly prepared for the life they'd eventually put him to."

"Which is no different than the life you have planned for him now," she countered, her voice stiff.

He shrugged. "Working for me he would be in the United States, transmitting private messages or testing employees' loyalty or doing a little industrial espionage." He cocked an eyebrow. "Working for the CIA he would be in Eastern Europe or Iran or the Soviet Union, spying on people who would most certainly torture him to death if they caught him."

Colleen didn't say anything. Neither did I. There didn't seem to be anything left to say.

Apparently, our visitor could tell that, too. "Think about it," he said, getting up from his chair and buttoning his coat. "You either accept what I'm offering, Miss Isaac, or else you suffer through what the government will do to you and your child when they find out—and they *will* find out; don't think for a moment you can hide it from them forever." Stepping to the door, he paused and nodded courteously. "I or one of my people will be in touch. Good day to you." He pulled open the door and stepped outside. Alex locked eyes briefly with each of us, and then he too was gone.

And we were alone.

With an effort I unclenched my jaw. Colleen was still pressed tightly against me; bracing myself, I turned my head to look at her. "I'm sorry, Colleen," I said quietly.

She lifted her eyes to mine . . . and even as I watched, I could see the fear and hopelessness and near-panic in her face began to fade. Into a simmering anger. "He won't get my child, Dale," she said, her voice a flat monotone that I found more unnerving than a scream of rage would have been. "I'll die before I'll let him have my child."

My mind flashed to that horrible scene at Rathbun Lake, the frozen tableau of Colleen facing down Ted Green with a knife pressed against her stomach. "It won't come to that," I told her through suddenly dry lips. "We'll find another way. I promise."

She blinked away tears. "I know," she whispered.

She didn't say it like she believed it, but that was hardly surprising: I didn't really believe it myself. If even half of what our visitor had said was true, we were up against frightening amounts of money and power, and I couldn't even begin to imagine how we could hide Colleen from such power for the next eight months.

But I'd find a way. I had to. More than anyone else I'd ever known, Colleen had a solid sense of what things in this world were worth dying for; and at Rathbun Lake she'd proved she had the courage and will to carry out such convictions.

One way or another, she wouldn't be giving up her child into slavery.

* * *

Gordy and Calvin listened silently to my story, but even without words I could feel the anger growing steadily in both of them—in Gordy's case, an anger that was already halfway to full-blown fury. *He can't get away with it,* Calvin said when I'd finished. *If he's really the one funding us, we'll be able to track him down.*

We can try, I agreed. *He didn't seem to think it likely we'd succeed.*

Yeah, well, let's not take his word for it, okay? Gordy said bitterly. *You seem to be taking all this pretty calmly.*

Only because I've had two days to get used to it, I told him shortly. *And because Colleen and I have had time to think and plan. You see—*

I hope you didn't do your planning in the house, Gordy interrupted me. *Your lousy child-snatching-Fagin pal probably had the place bugged.*

Don't worry, we figured that, too, I assured him. *We did all our discussions in writing, most of it at night in bed with a small flashlight. And we burned the papers afterwards and flushed the pieces down the toilet.*

All in the best traditions of TV cop shows, Gordy growled.

You want to listen to this or not? The thing is, we've come to the conclusion that our Fagin pal, as you call him, isn't nearly as all-powerful here as he'd like us to believe. Whatever the size and scope of his business or organization or whatever, he's throwing only a tiny fraction of it our way.

Maybe that's what he wants you to believe, Calvin suggested. *Maybe he's just trying to lull you into a false sense of security.*

Why? Underplaying it makes no sense—he wants us to knuckle under, remember? To give up and let him have his way.

Then you're reading it wrong, Gordy concluded sourly. *He'd have to be an idiot not to throw in everything he's got.*

Which is exactly my point, I said. *He is throwing in everything he can; but that isn't very much.*

From Calvin came a sudden flash of understanding. *Ah-ha,* he said. *Of course. He can only use the people he can trust completely, because everything turns on his keeping the baby's existence a secret.*

At least until it's born, I agreed. *After that he can spirit the child away, and then even if the world finds out there's an unknown telepath on the loose they still won't know what he looks like and he'll be difficult or impossible to track down. But until then, every-thing's got to be kept secret, or the media will descend on Colleen and he'll have lost his chance.*

Then that solves our problem, Gordy said. *We call a news conference—*

And have Colleen vanish into some secret government strong-hold after all the hysteria fades a little?

Gordy's surge of satisfaction faded. *Maybe we can bluff him with it anyway,* he suggested, more doubtfully. *Tell him that he either backs off, or we blow the whistle and the hell with the consequences.*

It wouldn't work, Calvin said. *Dale and Colleen have had two days to do that, and the fact that they didn't will imply to him that they'd rather take their chances with him than with the government.*

That's what we hoped he'd think, I agreed. *Which is why we waited this long for me to leave. To make sure Fagin's watch-dogs didn't think I was heading out somewhere to whistle up the Marines.*

For you to—wait a minute, Dale, where are you?

On Trans-Canada One, heading east.

There was a moment of stunned silence. *You're leaving her?* Gordy asked, something darkly unpleasant bubbling beneath the surface of the words. *Just like that? Leaving her stuck all alone, with maybe one of Fagin's Neanderthals watching the house—?*

Oh, I'm sure someone's watching the house, I told him grimly. *Otherwise, Colleen could just pack up the shield and make a run for it. As it is, with the thing as bulky as it is—and with the garage unattached from the house—anyone watching the house would see her in plenty of time to go take her by the hand and lead her back inside.*

Like I said—trapped in the house, Gordy all but snarled. *Damn it all, Dale—*

And that's where they've finally made a mistake, I cut him off. *Colleen can leave Regina any time she wants to. Fagin doesn't know about the second shield.*

Gordy's growing tirade cut off in mid-accusation. *He doesn't know about it?* he asked, sounding incredulous. *How on God's earth did he miss something like that?*

I don't know, exactly, I admitted. *Best guess is that he simply never thought to look. Presumably his local people picked up on Colleen's pregnancy while she was undergoing all those tests at the hospital and tailed us home. They would have seen me haul the line-current model into the house, but I never got around to taking the portable one out of Colleen's trunk that night. By morning Fagin was in town and giving us his big pitch, so of course we just left it where it was.*

And it's still there? Calvin asked.

If it weren't, I wouldn't be having this conversation, I said, and despite myself felt a shiver run up my back. *Before I left this morning I took Amos's magic kernels out of the line-current shield.*

You what? *Dale—*

Gordy broke off, the texture of his thoughts more confused than anything else. Too many shocks in too short a time, I decided, and for a few minutes I drove on in silence, listening to the background clutter and giving them time to assimilate all of it. *We seem to be running about two steps behind you, Dale,* Calvin said at last. *Why don't we shut up and let you give us the rest of it.*

I sighed. *There's not much more to tell. The day after tomorrow—in the late afternoon, around sundown—Colleen will drive off as if going to the little mall around the corner from her house, and will just keep going. By then Rob Peterson will hopefully have had time to put together a new shield with the kernels I scavenged from the old one, and I'll head west to rendezvous with her. We'll hide her someplace where she'll be safe for the next eight months, get Scott and Lisa working on finding an adoption family when the time comes . . . and that will hopefully be that.*

Calvin seemed to mull that over; but Gordy's response was far more immediate. *It won't work. Not for long enough. God's sake, Dale, you really think Fagin won't be able to trace her? I mean, her license plates alone—*

If you've got a better idea, let's hear it, I snapped. *We've got between six and nine days now until the new batteries we put in the portable shield run out, and it'll take at least half a day for us to reach our rendezvous point. We simply don't have the time to set up anything more elaborate.*

So we've got until tomorrow night, Gordy said, his tone oddly dark. *Fine. Give me until then to come up with something, okay?*

I suppose I should have expected something like that, but the offer took me by surprise anyway. Calvin, who knew Gordy better than I did, was somewhat faster on the uptake. *We can't risk it, Gordy,* he told the other. *Suppose Fagin is having you watched? Or has access to airline reservation computers?*

I have a friend who's a private pilot, he said stubbornly. *She can fly me up there without anyone knowing where I've gone.*

Fagin could check on the flight plan, I pointed out, feelings of resentment stirring within me. This was *our* war, not his—

She can file a false flight plan, Gordy insisted. *She'll know how to pull something like that off.*

And then she's in the hot seat, too, huh? I growled . . . but I could see now that it was a losing battle. Gordy was determined to put his oar in here; with our blessing if possible, without it if necessary.

Calvin saw it, too. *I don't suppose there's really any way we can stop you,* he conceded. *Just remember that if you tip Colleen's hand there won't be any second chances.*

Even seven hundred miles away in Spokane I could feel Gordy's shudder. *I'll remember,* he said softly.

There was little enough time to spare, and I drove straight through the day, arriving in Des Moines just after one in the morning. On the way into town I stopped at a phone booth—I wasn't about to trust my home phone—and gave Rob Peterson a call. He was great; didn't ask any questions, just promised to be at my house at ten with all the equipment he'd need to put together a new telepath shield.

He was there on time, and I left him working while I returned the van to the rental agency. One of the employees drove me home, and on the way I had him do a leisurely drive around the block. If Fagin had anyone watching my house, I didn't pick him up. More evidence that he was running this on a shoestring . . . if, of course, I was reading the signs right. Given my recent record, I wouldn't have bet a lot on it.

It took me only a couple of hours to pack the stuff Colleen and I would need for our getaway, and after that I had little to do except worry. A little before noon Gordy arrived in Regina—apparently unnoticed by Fagin's friends—and spent the afternoon poking around town on errands he wouldn't discuss with either Calvin or me. I tried pressing him for information once or twice, but it was obvious he wasn't going to give me any, and by early afternoon I gave up the effort. Leaving Calvin to keep an eye on him, I settled down to wait, dividing my attention between worrying and watching Rob work. The worrying was what I did best.

I'd assumed that it would take at least a day to build the new shield when I'd set things up with Colleen; but on that, at least, I'd been overly pessimistic. By five-thirty that afternoon Rob had the device finished—a briefcase-sized one, this, instead of the bulkier model I'd scavenged the kernels from. I told Calvin to stand by and flicked the switch.

The background clutter—as well as Calvin's and Rob's thoughts—vanished. Getting in my car, I headed slowly down the street, and within a few minutes had confirmed that it did indeed have the same half-mile range as the model I'd left with Colleen. I reported to Calvin and drove back home, watching for parked cars with Fagin's watchdogs sitting in them. Again, if they were there, I couldn't spot them.

Rob was waiting just inside the door when I pulled up. "Well?" he asked eagerly. "Does it work?"

"Like a champ," I told him, clapping him on the shoulder and stepping over to where the mass of wires and chips and Amos's enigmatic kernels was sitting on the kitchen table. "You did great, Rob. Especially given that you'd never actually done this before."

He shrugged modestly. "Yeah, but remember I examined the stuffing out of the thing last month. Now if I could just figure out how Amos made those kernels we'd be in real business."

I nodded and flipped the off switch—

And an instant later my head filled with a din of shouting. *Dale! Are you there? Dale—!*

I'm here, Calvin, I said, the skin on my neck crawling. There was a note of near-panic in that tone— *What's wrong?*

Gordy's gone in, he said, and behind the words I could visualize clenched teeth. *The minute you confirmed the range and headed back home, he disappeared.*

God in heaven— *He can't do that,* I said, reflexively looking at my watch. It would be just about sundown in Regina, exactly the time we'd planned for her to make her break . . . except that Gordy was twenty-four hours early. *What in hell's name does he think he's doing? Colleen won't be ready yet.*

I don't know. Calvin hesitated. *But I think he may be up to something desperate. He's been . . . really brooding about this.*

Which I'd been too absorbed in my own thoughts to notice? But it was too late to worry about that now. *Did he tell you the name of his pilot friend?*

Yes—Jean Forster. Why?—you think she's involved in some way?

She's at least involved to the extent that she got him there, I reminded him grimly. *It might be a good idea to call the Regina airport and try to warn her about Fagin's goon squad—*

And with a suddenness I wasn't prepared for, Gordy was back. *Calvin, Dale—listen.*

I didn't get a chance to ask what it was he wanted us to listen to . . . but an instant later I got the answer anyway. As from deep in a well, I heard an angry voice. *Get out here, you son of a bitch. God damn it—look what you did to my car.*

I sensed Gordy being hauled all but bodily from a vehicle by two men, and I strained to try and see their faces through his eyes. It was no use; the images I could pull in were too weak, and in the dim light of dusk all I could see were silhouettes. But I didn't need to see them to guess who they were. Fagin's stamp was all over them. *Cute, friend—real cute,* the angry man snarled again, his silhouette raising as if on tiptoe to look past Gordy. *What, you figured you'd give her a head start and then catch up? You lousy son of a—*

Knock it off, Billy. The second man's voice was hard and calm and authoritative, and Billy shut up. *There's no real harm done. It was pretty stupid, you know,* he continued, talking to Gordy now. *We had orders to stop anyone we caught trying to take anything big out of the house—and that included garbage men. Take a look in back, Billy—make sure the thing's there.*

Billy's silhouette nodded and headed obediently off to the left, and as Gordy turned to watch him I saw that they were indeed standing beside a small garbage truck. Briefly, I wondered how Gordy had gotten hold of it. *Yeah, it's here,* I heard Billy call. *Uh . . . shouldn't we be getting on the phone and getting Harry on the trail?*

What for? the other asked calmly. *She'll be back. Any minute now, probably.*

Yeah, but if she didn't see him crash our car—?

The other man turned to face Billy's returning figure; and once again, Billy shut up. *She probably didn't,* he agreed quietly. *So what?*

Oh. Right. Billy nodded belated understanding. *The headaches'll start up again. That'll tell her he didn't get away.*

And I don't think she'll miss the implications, the other agreed. He turned, and I got the feeling he was peering down the street, looking for Colleen's returning car. *Though on second thought . . . come here; watch this guy for a minute.*

Billy's silhouette replaced his in front of Gordy, and he stepped over to a nearby car and leaned in the open door. He emerged with something in his hand, which he did something to and then held to the side of his head. A cellular phone, probably. *Harry? Warfield. Listen, I want you to cruise south down Albert Street to the highway—see if our pigeon has gone off the road some-where . . . No, I want you to* leave *her there—of course you bring her back home, damn it; we can go back and get her car later.*

Warfield reached in and hung up . . . and suddenly I sensed Gordy's mind tensing as he prepared for action. *She'll be back,* Warfield said, straightening up to face Gordy again. *Unconscious, maybe—probably with one hell of a headache—but she'll be back.*

No.

The word seemed to hang in the air, and for a moment I could sense Warfield and Billy staring at him. *What do you mean, no?* Warfield asked, his voice calm but with menace beneath it.

I felt my fingernails digging into my palms as I clenched my fists in agonized helplessness. God, he was going to ruin every-thing—it was far too soon to spill the fact that Colleen had her own telepath shield. I wanted to scream at him to shut up; but it was too late, he'd already said too much, and sooner or later now they'd have the rest of it. Impotent fury bubbled up inside me, turning my stomach inside out. All my worry and planning . . . and with a single word Gordy had betrayed it all. *I said, what did you mean, 'no,'* Warfield demanded again, taking a step toward Gordy. I braced myself—

And Gordy took a step toward Billy, slammed his fist into the goon's stomach, and ran.

It was probably the sheer unexpectedness of it that let him get away with it; with the telepath shield out of quick reach at the bottom of the garbage truck and with Colleen still well within the close-approach death zone, Gordy had literally nowhere to run, and both his captors surely knew that. But unexpected or not, Warfield clearly had good reflexes. Even before Gordy reached the back of the truck I could hear the sudden scraping of feet on pavement that showed the chase was on. Where the hell did Gordy think he was going—?

An instant later I found out. Gordy skidded to an abrupt stop at the rear of the garbage truck, threw a wild punch to keep Warfield back—

And slammed down the compression lever.

The sudden growl of the motor drowned out Warfield's startled exclamation; but Gordy's reply was only too clear. *I'm taking Colleen the one place your filthy boss can't reach us,* he shouted.

You stupid bastard, Warfield yelled over the grinding of the hydraulic crusher jaws. He leaped forward, grabbing Gordy by the shoulders and trying to force him away from the lever. But Gordy held his ground, wrapping his arms around the other.

And then the crusher hit metal, grinding away against the angle iron holding the telepath shield together . . . and, abruptly, as if by mutual consent, both men stopped their struggling. The grinding stopped, and I could see Warfield's silhouette draw back in confusion. *What the hell?*

Gordy looked slowly back at the garbage truck, as if not believing what he was seeing. *It . . . can't be,* he said, and even through the tunnel effect I could hear the bewilderment in his voice. *We agreed—if I didn't get away—*

He broke off, and I could just hear the electronic warbling of the car phone. Gordy glanced over that way, and I saw Billy reach in for the phone. *Get away from there,* Warfield ordered Gordy abruptly, shoving him away from the lever. *Must not have busted the thing all the way—*

Hey! Billy called, his voice odd. *It's Harry. C'mere—you gotta hear this.*

Warfield took Gordy's arm and marched him toward the car. *What is it?*

Harry found her car, Billy said, and now I could identify the emotion in his voice. Disbelief. *It's down by the lake. Next to a spot where it isn't all frozen.*

For a long moment Warfield just stared at him. Then, taking a long stride forward, he snatched the phone from Billy's hand.

Dale? Calvin? You both listening.

With a conscious effort, I unclenched my teeth. *We're both here, Gordy. What's—where's Colleen?*

On her way out of town in a car I rented and left at the lake, he said. *She'll meet you at the rendezvous you set up.*

Get out of there, Calvin put in, his voice urgent. *Now. Before they remember you're still there.*

Sorry, but I can't. Gordy's voice was calm . . . but beneath it I could feel a tightness. A tightness, and the winding up of courage; and over all of it, a strangely wistful sadness.

And suddenly I realized that Gordy was preparing himself to die.

Calvin's right, I snarled. *Colleen's in the clear—get out of there.*

I can't, he said again, and this time there was an edge to it. *I have to make sure they're convinced that she would rather die than give up her child to that kind of slavery, and that once the game was up that she would commit suicide rather than let me kill both of us. And they're not going to want me around to testify after that.*

I bit hard at my lip, searched frantically for a way to convince him . . . and then my brain seemed to catch, and I cursed my stupidity. *Calvin—get on the phone,* I ordered. *Call the Regina police, tell them there's a kidnapping in progress. Where are you, Gordy?*

A flicker of hope, the realization that maybe he wouldn't have to sacrifice himself after all— *The corner of Fourteenth Avenue and Rae Street—*

And suddenly Warfield spun around, his brain apparently catching, as well. *God damn it,* he snarled viciously, hand jabbing at Gordy. Now, *damn it.*

Here it comes, Gordy said, and there was no longer any tension in his tone. Just a quiet acceptance. *Good-bye. Tell Colleen that I love her—*

And then a shadow swung at his head, and the image was gone.

I don't know how long I stood there, staring at nothing and listening to the silence where Gordy had been. Gradually, I became aware that there was a hand on my arm. Blinking my eyes against a painful dryness, I found Rob gazing at me, his thoughts highly worried. "I'm all right," I told him. Even to myself my voice sounded dead.

He didn't believe it, of course. "Anything I can do to help?"

I shook my head. *Calvin?*

Here, Dale. I've got through to the Regina police, and they're sending a car. He hesitated. *I also told them about Colleen's car, and hinted that we suspected suicide.*

Yeah. It felt wrong, somehow, to maintain the lie; but if we didn't, then Gordy's sacrifice would have been for nothing. *You think they realized he was lying?*

I'm sure they didn't, Calvin assured me. *I think it just suddenly penetrated that with the shield supposedly destroyed he could get through to us again. They couldn't afford that.*

It made sense. The game was lost, as far as they knew, and their first priority now would be to cover their tracks. *What the hell's keeping those cops?*

Take it easy, Dale—it's only been a couple of minutes.

I sighed. *I'm sorry. I just . . .*

I let the sentence trail off. There really wasn't anything left to say. Dimly, through the moisture fogging my vision I felt Rob leading me to a chair, and allowed myself to be sat into it. Fagin would pay, I promised myself. If I had to track him down myself, and kill him with my own two hands—

Dale? The police have arrived on the scene, but there's no one there. Just the garbage truck.

Of course there's no one there, I said savagely. *They wouldn't just leave him there for the cops to—*

I don't know why it clicked just then. But it did . . . and suddenly my grief vanished into a surge of adrenaline. *He's not dead,* I told Calvin. *Of course he's not—what kind of an idiot am I?*

Dale, I know it's hard—

No, listen! I cut him off. *Listen! They wouldn't just kill him like that—Fagin would have their heads on poles. He'd want to question Gordy and make sure he was telling them the truth about Colleen.*

For a long moment Calvin thought about that, and despite his determination not to build up false hope I could sense a growing excitement. *You may be right,* he agreed. *In which case we should send the police to the airport, try and head them off.*

Yes—no. Wait a minute, let me think. Something Fagin had said . . . yes. *He knew Nelson,* I told Calvin. *Probably pretty well—he mentioned once that Nelson had done some experiments for him. Maybe the Las Vegas stuff that Amos caught onto.*

Maybe, Calvin allowed cautiously, wondering with a distinct undercurrent of uneasiness just where I was headed with this. *So what does that tell us?*

I grinned humorlessly, my lips tight enough to hurt. *It tells us,* I told him, *that for the first time since Nelson tried to kill me, he's going to do something useful.*

Calvin said something cautionary sounding, but I didn't wait to hear it. All my thoughts and senses were turned inward as I searched out that part of my personality which had come from my close-approach with Nelson. It was all still there, of course: the greed, the arrogance, the deception, the contempt for mankind in general and his fellow telepaths in particular.

Everything I'd fought so hard and for so long to bury was right there, just waiting against the barriers I'd painfully erected against it.

I thought about Gordy and Colleen . . . and let the barriers fall.

And nothing happened. Nothing at all. The Nelson part didn't surge out like poison gas under pressure; didn't flow out like an attacking army bent on destruction; didn't gloat, didn't cheer, didn't rage. It was just there, like nothing more or less than a memory. A dark memory, to be sure, full of pain and anger and terror; but a memory nonetheless.

It was perhaps the greatest surprise of a long day of surprises, that the very thing I'd feared so much for so many months would in fact turn out to be so utterly powerless. Perhaps it was just the healing effects of time; perhaps that deadly confrontation at Rathbun Lake had been the killing blow, only I hadn't realized it.

I was whole again.

There would be cause for quiet celebration later, perhaps, but not now. For now, Gordy's life was hanging by a thread . . . and that thread was somewhere in those memories of Nelson. Bracing myself, I plunged in.

And there it was. *Calvin? I got it. Fagin's name is Lawrence Barringer, and he's based somewhere in the Los Angeles area.*

Got it, Calvin said. His emotions were masked, but it wasn't hard to guess that he was wondering what that information had cost me. *You want to call the LA police, or should I?*

No one's calling any police. Not yet, anyway.

What? Dale, he's got Gordy, remember?

No he doesn't—and that's the whole point, I told him. *His goons have Gordy; and they're hardly likely to drag him to Barringer's house and dump him on the living room rug. They'll take him to some out-of-the way place and question him there.*

I felt Calvin's shiver. *You think they'll . . . torture him?*

My stomach turned, and for a long moment I dug again into Nelson's memories, searching for more details of Barringer's personality. They were there, all right; but even as I sifted through them it suddenly occurred to me that nothing I found here could be taken at face value. Colored as it all had been by Nelson's own warped mentality, there was no way for me to sort out objective fact from wishful or even malicious fantasy.

But I had to try. *Okay, here it is. From what Nelson knew about Barringer he was an absolute fanatic for secrecy in his activities. He'd rather take extra time and make sure he's not being watched or monitored than rush into something and find out later that the whole thing's been captured on tape. Given that—and given that they'll assume we'll call the cops in—my guess is that they'll sedate Gordy and drive him out of town, contacting Barringer from someplace reasonably distant. He'll send a private plane for them, again rendezvousing somewhere away from Regina, and fly them leisurely down to some quiet spot near Los Angeles where they hopefully won't be disturbed. That make any sense to you?*

Calvin pondered it. *I suppose so*, he agreed, almost reluctantly. *There really isn't any rush, after all—if Colleen's alive he's got eight months to track her down. You think Barringer will want to be in on the questioning?*

Yes. On that score I had no doubt at all. *Absolutely. He wouldn't trust it to anyone else, for one thing. And that's where we're going to nail him.*

Wonderful—except for one small problem, Calvin pointed out heavily. *Namely, we don't* know *where this quiet spot is that they're going to take him. Unless*, he interrupted himself with a sudden surge of excitement, *your friend Rob can put Amos's old telepath-detector back together. If he can—*

Sorry. I'd already had that idea, and found the flaw in it. *The kernels he would need for that are already being used.*

In the second shield; right, Calvin said, the excitement evaporating. *In that case, I don't see that we have any choices left, Dale. We have to call in the police and ask them to put a tail on Barringer.*

If we do that, I reminded him, *we lose Colleen's baby to the government.*

If we don't, he snarled with uncharacteristic harshness, *we lose him to Barringer. Or don't you think he'll be able to make Gordy talk?*

Yes, I'm sure he will. I took a deep breath. *As a matter of fact . . . I'm rather counting on it.*

It took Calvin nearly an hour of phoning to track down Jean Forster, Gordy's pilot friend, and ask for her help. Five hours later, just after midnight, she called me to announce that she and her twin-engine Beechcraft were at the Des Moines airport. An hour after that, we were airborne.

In many ways it was yet another echo of that desperate race to Regina only a few days earlier, and I found many of the same black thoughts swirling around and through my mind as we flew westward. Suspended between land and sky, the occasional concentration of town and city lights below clumping like distorted fun-house mirror images of the stars above, the sense of unreality was even stronger than it had been then.

As was the sense of desperate danger.

I died a thousand deaths that night. At least that many. I'd put on a good front when selling this whole scheme to Calvin, but I knew all too well that a hundred things could go wrong. If I'd read Barringer wrong—if he broke his pattern and decided that speed was more important than caution—then Gordy would be in Los Angeles and the interrogation over and done with long before we got anywhere near the scene.

And even if everything went exactly according to plan, it could still go bad. Horribly bad.

I was able to doze a couple of those long hours away, but mostly I spent the night wide awake, staring out the window at nothing in particular and wondering if I should just give up and abort this whole crazy plan. Colleen had a good head start; with luck, perhaps we could bury ourselves so deeply that even Barringer couldn't find us. And he surely wouldn't be stupid enough to hurt Gordy, no matter what happened.

It was a private battle I fought over and over again that night; and it was Jean Forster's presence beside me, more than anything else, that helped me push back the temptation each time it surfaced. From the beginning I'd had reservations about bringing her into this, and had given in mainly because there hadn't been any other choice; but ten minutes of sitting next to her in a cramped cockpit had laid every one of those reservations to rest. She was smart, competent, tough, and fiercely loyal to the small and select group of people she named as her friends. Just getting me this far had required her to litter our flight path with a half dozen broken FAA regulations, and she knew full well that her license was the least of what she was putting at risk tonight.

In many ways she reminded me of Colleen . . . and it wasn't hard to guess what both of them would say if I suggested abandoning Gordy now.

And so we headed west, swinging a bit northward to avoid getting too close to Calvin in Pueblo. We stopped once for refueling at a field Jean knew outside of Grand Junction . . . and finally, with local sunrise still half an hour away, we came in sight of the sea of lights that was Los Angeles.

For a few minutes—a few long, long minutes—there was nothing. I sat watching the city lights, sweating as I strained for a contact and fought back the fears and terrors swirling around me. We'd gambled, and we'd lost. Barringer had held the interrogation in Canada, or had flown Gordy here five hours ago, or had simply killed him to cover his tracks. Jean eased the plane a bit to the left, heading southwest toward the southern edge of the city—

And I felt it. Tenuous, weak, almost imagined; but definitely there. The touch of another telepathic mind.

Gordy.

Calvin? Calvin, wake up.

Here, Dale, Calvin replied with an alertness that showed he hadn't been asleep. *What is it?*

I've got him. And he's still unconscious.

I could feel Calvin's cautious relief. *Which means they haven't started on him yet. I hope.*

Yeah. Me, too. Muscles I hadn't even realized were tight were starting to relax. We'd gambled, and we'd won. Barringer had gone with the leisurely, secure approach after all, and we'd beaten him to the punch. *Have you heard from Rob yet, by the way?*

Five minutes ago, as a matter of fact, Calvin said. *He made it to Colleen's hideout and gave her the second shield, and she's on her way to wherever it is you two planned for her to go. I didn't want to wake you if you were trying to sleep.*

So Colleen, at least, was safe. One down, one to go. I took a deep breath—

And in a single instant the muscles tightened again. "Oh, my God," I whispered.

At least I thought I'd whispered it. Jean heard anyway. "What?" she snapped.

I forced my teeth to unclench. "He got stronger. Much too strong, much too fast. They're waking him up."

Take it easy, Calvin said, glacially calm. *It's bound to take them a few minutes to bring him up to where he can answer questions for them.*

"You want me to radio the police?" Jean called.

"Can't yet," I told her, willing some of Calvin's calm to flow into me. "We still don't know where he is." *Gordy?* I called. *Gordy, can you hear me?*

There was no response . . . but even as I strained I could tell our direction was correct. He was somewhere south of Los Angeles, and we were now heading straight toward him.

Straight toward him. As Nelson had flown straight toward me . . .

I shook my head to clear it. "We're going in," I called to Jean. "You remember the plan?"

She nodded. "You want belt or arm?"

"Belt," I said, reaching over to hook the fingers of my left hand into her belt. I'd rather have held her arm, but I couldn't trust myself not to tug it the wrong direction at a critical moment. Already I could feel the pressure building in my mind as we flew toward Gordy.

Toward Gordy . . . and toward the theoretical twenty-mile limit that would kill us both. In, at the Beechcraft's current speed, something like twenty minutes.

The pressure was growing steadily stronger, its edges becoming tinged with a red haze I remembered all too vividly. The fuzziness that was Gordy's unconscious mind was becoming ever clearer, and I could feel the first wisps of pain as the surfaces of our minds began to merge . . .

Dale? Calvin's thought was dim and faraway, a scream almost lost in a hurricane. *Can you hear me? Dale?*

I could hear him—just barely—but I couldn't answer. My mind was bending now, molding itself against Gordy's even as his bent against mine. Setting my teeth together, I fought against the pain, hunting amid the din of two minds clashing for the information I desperately needed. The darkness in Gordy's mind seemed to be lifting; with all my strength I tried to reach through it. To search beyond him—

And with a suddenness that made me gasp, I had it. Four men stood around him, one of them leaning close to his face. Reaching through Gordy's mind was a blaze of pain; fighting it back, I pressed harder. Through the man's eyes I saw Gordy, lying motionless on an ambulance-type stretcher; through his ears I heard the sounds of distant surf and even more distant traffic. And through his mind—

"Oc—Oceanside," I gasped. "They're in . . . Oceanside."

Dimly, I felt a hand shaking my shoulder, heard a voice shouting in my ear. "—address? Come on, Dale—give me the address."

I pulled the street and house number from the other's mind and choked them out; and then the pain was too much, and I fell back. Gordy's mind was growing clearer by the minute—

"Gordon Sears," a voice said into my mind—into Gordy's mind. "Can you hear me?"

A moment of silence. I wondered vaguely if Gordy, half asleep as he was, could feel the pain I was feeling. Wondered if it would keep him from answering, or would instead go the other way, sapping any strength he might have to resist them. "Yes," Gordy answered, the word coming first through his mind and then through his ears.

And then through my ears, as I repeated it aloud? Maybe. I couldn't tell for sure.

"Good," the voice came again through Gordy's mind. "Listen to me, Gordon—listen closely. I will ask you some questions and you will answer them. You will tell me the truth; because

I'm your friend, and I'm Colleen Isaac's friend, and her life depends on your telling me the truth. Do you understand that?"

"Yes," Gordy said again. His voice was dreamy, just like his mind. I wondered what kind of drug they'd used on him, but I was too afraid of the pain to touch the stranger through Gordy's mind again.

"Excellent, Gordy," the voice said. "Then tell me where Colleen Isaac is."

I could feel Gordy's mind fighting against the drug. "Gordon?" the voice asked again; and this time there was a hard edge to it. "Gordon, where is Colleen Isaac? *Where is she?*"

I could feel his mind weakening. Helpless in the drug's grip . . .

But Gordy's mind was not his alone anymore . . . and I had none of their poison in my body. "She's dead," I murmured, and heard the echo in my mind as Gordy's mouth obediently repeated the words. "She died . . . in Regina. In the lake. To . . . save me."

"She's not dead!" a new voice shouted. Barringer's voice. "She can't be dead, damn it—she *can't* be. *Where is she?*"

"She's dead," I said again, and an involuntary sob escaped our lips. The pain was a red haze over our mind, and I felt our fingers trembling in Jean's belt. We could let go, and she would pull up and take us away from the pain. But it was still too soon. Still too soon.

Barringer was screaming something else, but we could hardly hear him. All around us was the din of two minds wrenching against each other . . . "She's dead," we said once more. "She told me . . . she would rather die than lose her baby to . . . anyone."

And suddenly the screaming was gone. We tried to listen

through the noise, to hear what was going on; but the noise was too loud. The noise, and the pain . . .

"Dale? Dale!"

I blinked; blinked again as I realized there were tears in my eyes. That voice . . . and the pain was almost gone. And it was only me. "Wha—?" I croaked. There was no echo . . . "Jean?"

"It's okay, Dale," she said, and I could hear the almost limp relief in her voice. "God, for a while I thought we were going to lose you. To lose both of you."

Abruptly, I realized my fingers were still wedged in her belt. "Where are we? Wait a minute—we can't leave—"

"It's okay—it's okay," she soothed me. "The cops are there. Nailed Barringer and his goons red-handed. Soon as they radioed that they'd got him, I took off." She leaned forward to frown at me, and I heard the question in her mind. "Is—I mean, did it work?"

I took a deep breath. "He should be fine," I told her, answering the question she'd wanted to ask. We were heading east, now, heading back home. Ahead, the sky over the mountains was red with the approaching sunrise.

And the long night was over.

"It's not the Hilton," Colleen said, waving a hand around the two-room cabin, "but it's home."

"For the next few months at least," I agreed, looking out the window at the snow-covered mountains and trying hard not to think of how isolated she was going to be out here. "Certainly a great spot to get away from it all."

"There's room for two," she said.

I turned to see her gazing at me, her forehead wrinkled with concern. "Thanks, but I can't," I told her. "If I disappeared for too long someone would start to wonder if you really weren't dead after all. It would be a shame to blow a perfectly good lie like that."

"Certainly not after all the effort you and Gordon put into it." She smiled, but the smile didn't touch her eyes. "I don't think I'll ever be able to thank you for what you did for me. What you risked—"

"Colleen." I turned to face her and took her hands in mine. "It's over. Okay? Over and done with, and both Gordy and I are fine. Really."

"But the flashbacks—"

"Will go away," I reminded her. "Remember, I've been through this once before. Nelson's attack isn't much more than a bad memory now, and he and I got much closer together than Gordy and I did."

She nodded. Squeezing my hands, she let go and stepped over to stare out one of the windows. "I just . . . it's still going to weigh on my conscience, Dale. Neither of you is going to ever be quite the same again, and all because of me. I'm sorry if that sounds silly, but that's how I feel."

"Doesn't sound silly at all," I assured her. "Tell me, Colleen: who is that baby you're carrying?"

She turned to frown at me. "What do you mean?"

"Well, he's part you and part me, right? I mean, that's where he came from."

The frown was still there. "I don't understand what you're driving at."

I sighed. "We're all unique, Colleen, but at the same time most of who we are ultimately comes from other people. Not just our parents' genes—all of us, all our lives, are continually influenced by those around us. Our politics are molded by politicians and commentators, our tastes are influenced by our job or station in life . . . and we're forever exchanging styles and traits and interests and catch phrases with our friends." I shrugged. "It just happened that with Nelson and Gordy I got an accelerated version of the process."

She thought about that for a minute. "What about Barringer?" she asked.

Which meant the subject was closed, at least for now. Which was fine with me. I knew she'd think about it, and eventually realize I was right. "He's going to be far too busy treading legal water to bother us for a while," I told her. "There are half a dozen charges pending, up to and including kidnapping, and when the locals are done with him Canada's waiting to take their shot."

"But if they know Gordon was taken from Regina—?" She threw me a questioning look.

I shrugged. "If they figure that out, there really won't be any way to hide the existence of the shield any longer. But with Amos's kernels gone, I don't think the Regina police will be able to conclude anything from the mess they recovered from the garbage truck."

"But Barringer knows," she said in resignation. "So it was all for nothing."

I put my arm around her shoulders. "Not in the least. We saved you and our child from being snatched away into some form of slavery, didn't we? You call *that* nothing?"

"No, of course not. But—" She shook her head.

"It would have been nice if we could have kept the shield a secret," I conceded gently. "But to be perfectly honest, Gordy and I would have had to be fools to risk our lives for a machine. It's the people in this world that are important, Colleen—don't forget that. Not that a person as caring as you are is ever likely to. Must be why I love you so much.

"And speaking of love and people," I added briskly, squeezing her shoulders and stepping away, "grab your coat. I've got a surprise for you."

She blinked at me, sniffing back some tears. "What kind of surprise?"

"A nice one," I assured her, picking my own coat off the couch. "Something I stumbled on more or less by accident on the way in. Come on—and don't forget your hat and mittens."

We bundled up, and I led the way out into the frosty mountain air. In front of the cabin the snow-packed dirt road sloped gently upward, peaking at a cut in the mountains before sloping down toward the small mountain village a few miles away. I led us along the road for a few minutes; and suddenly Colleen, huffing along a step behind me, grabbed my arm. "Wait a minute, Dale, we can't go any farther. The edge of the shield—"

"Is right there," I pointed at a pair of branches sticking up out of the snow beside the road ten yards ahead. "Just don't pass the sticks there . . . and say hi to Calvin for me."

She stared at me. "What are you talking about? The shield's edge isn't sharp enough for me to do that."

"Agreed," I nodded. "*One* shield's edge isn't that sharp. But if you put two of them in line about a foot apart—we can mark the spots on your floor when we get back—and kind of lean forward, just a little, it turns out that you can stick your head far enough out for you to have limited communication without the baby knowing a thing about it. Go ahead—I tried it on the way in, and Calvin's waiting."

She didn't say anything; just threw her arms around me and hugged me close for a minute. Then, straightening, she walked tentatively toward my markers, head and shoulders hunched slightly forward.

And then, abruptly, she stopped . . . and I thought I'd never seen such a look of pure joy.

There was still a long road ahead of her, and much of it would be hard. But at least now she wouldn't have to travel it alone.

For a moment I watched her. Then, shivering with the cold, I turned away. There was, I'd noticed, a pile of boards stacked in the rear of the cabin, as well as a complete took kit, a spare sleeping pad, and an extra Coleman heater. With a little judicious hammering and some careful positioning, I ought to be able to put together quite a cozy little shelter for her up at the edge of the shield. I had the distinct feeling she'd be spending a lot of time out here over the next few months.

I walked back to the cabin, and got to work.

BRIGHT THOUGHTS AT DAWN

God's in His heaven/All's right with the world!

That had been one of my mother's favorite quotes when I was growing up. She'd trotted it out on good days and bad; sometimes in gratitude, sometimes in defiance. There'd been times when I disagreed with the declaration and the accompanying attitude, but I never once doubted she was sincere.

Now, fifteen years after her death, I still remembered the lines, wrapped as they were around my memories of her. Sometimes, I even repeated them silently to myself.

I couldn't speak for God right now. But things were definitely not right with the world.

You don't think I've tried to talk to him? Calvin Wolfe asked, his mental voice sounding weary. *I have. At least a dozen times. He just repeats that he's fine, and it's going to take time to heal.*

I nodded, feeling Calvin's own ache deep inside me. That was what Gordy Sears always said these days, to any of us who asked. And if you pushed him past that point, he would go into deflection mode and then simply stop talking.

You realize that's a contradiction in terms, Scott Lowell pointed out with more than a hint of lawyerly pedantry. *He technically can't be* fine *and* slowly healing *at the same time.*

You have to understand him, Scott, Colleen Isaac said. *Gordy is . . . complicated.*

We're telepaths, Calvin said heavily. *Complicated is part of the package.*

There was a moment of silence. I didn't know what the others were doing with the gap and the impromptu opportunity it brought for introspection. Calvin and Colleen were probably wondering what else we could do to help Gordy. Scott was probably mentally correcting whatever errors in grammar or logic he'd heard from us.

Me, I was wondering about Scott.

He was hardly an unknown, of course. The North American telepath community was made up of exactly eleven members: two in Canada, one in Mexico, the rest of us in the U.S. Hardly a group anyone could get lost in, so we all knew each other to one degree or another. Scott lived in New Orleans, just past the edge of my normal telepath communication range, which limited my contact with him. But he traveled around enough that he was sometimes able to drop in on conversations with my core group of Colleen, Gordy, and Calvin.

But lately, those contacts had been less and less frequent. I didn't know whether Scott was just too busy to touch base with us, whether he was taking a sabbatical from his fellow telepaths, or whether it was something else entirely.

Only now, suddenly, he'd come out of the woodwork?

Firmly, I pushed away the lurking suspicion. That was the Nelson part of my brain talking, the part of I'd absorbed when he forced me into the close approach that had killed him and nearly killed me as well.

Or possibly it was the Gordy part of me. He and I had also had a close approach, though neither of us had had any such intention of mutually assured destruction.

But Gordy was far more driven than I was, the type who saw a problem, worked out an answer, then went hell for leather until he made his solution work. Maybe his influence was why I was pushing myself so hard trying to analyze Scott.

Maybe it was also why I was trying to analyze myself. Because that was still one of the big unknowns about that incident and Gordy's current behavior.

What part of me had *he* absorbed?

In my humble opinion, there wasn't a lot of me that was worth absorbing. I didn't have Colleen's kindness or patience, I didn't have Calvin's nearly unshakable calm or his uncanny ability to share that calm with the people around him, and I didn't have Gordy's drive and problem-solving capabilities. I certainly didn't have Scott's precise and analytical mind.

What about you, Dale?

Scott's sudden question caught me flat-footed. *What* about *me?*

You're the one Gordy melded with, Scott reminded me, in case I'd needed reminding. *I assume you have some insights into his current mental state.*

It doesn't work like that, I told him stiffly. *I'm Dale with a touch of Gordy. He's Gordy with a touch of Dale. It's not like we're suddenly identical twins.*

And a touch of Nelson.

My throat went a little dry. *What?*

You're also Dale with a touch of Nelson, Scott repeated.

That didn't affect him, Colleen said before I could come up with a good response.

Anyway, he's long since worked that through, Calvin added.

So it didn't affect him *and he's* worked it through, Scott concluded dryly. *Again, a contradiction in terms. Curious.*

Or hilarious, depending on your point of view, I growled. *Don't you have some legal briefs to file or something?*

Dale, Calvin cautioned.

That's all right, Calvin, Scott said calmly. *I'm a lawyer. I'm used to being disliked.*

I felt my face warming. *No, Calvin's right,* I said. *Sorry, Scott. This Gordy thing has me on edge. Tension brings out the worst in me.*

Apology accepted, Scott said. *And I apologize in turn. I shouldn't have brought up Nelson in the first place.*

Apology accepted, I said, trying not to sound grudging about it. *As to Gordy, I don't think there's anything we can do except wait for him to get over this latest funk or whatever it is. When that happens, I'll try talking to him again.*

Good, Scott said. *Well, I should probably go. I'm heading to Boise this weekend for some skiing, which will put me in good range of all of you. I'll touch base when I get there; hopefully, we'll have time for a more leisurely conversation.*

Before you go, one more question, Colleen said, her voice studiously neutral. *I heard you're representing Lawrence Barringer now. Is that true?*

I felt my mouth drop open. Barringer, the ruthless bastard who'd tried to get hold of Colleen's baby and had drugged and interrogated Gordy—

My firm *is representing Lawrence Barringer,* Scott corrected calmly. *I personally am not.*

Is there a difference? Calvin asked, sounding as sandbagged as I was. Apparently, Colleen hadn't shared that tidbit with him, either.

Of course there's a difference, Scott said, his calmness starting to sound a little strained. *I won't meet him, have any direct dealings with him, or communicate with him or his attorneys.*

Unless that changes, I said.

It won't, Scott said. *May I remind you that the laws of the state of Louisiana still apply. I cannot interact with any clients, judges, clerks, or opposition attorneys except via audio or video media, and I must maintain a distance of at least fifty feet from any of them.*

I'm sure Barringer will make sure to scrupulously abide by all that, I said acidly. *Since when do kidnapping charges in California translate into hiring a Louisiana law firm?*

Since the charges allege that Gordy was transported across state lines, Scott said. *That automatically makes them Federal. We have extensive experience in Federal law, so his personal lawyers hired us. Any other questions? Good. As Dale said, I'm sure I have briefs to file or something. Good-bye.*

I felt small flicker of emptiness as he broke contact and his mind disappeared from our little group. *Huffy much?* I said.

Wouldn't you be if someone accused you of working with someone like Barringer? Calvin countered.

Colleen was asking, *not accusing,* I countered. *And you didn't—*

I broke off, my face warming for the second time in as many minutes. *Sorry,* I apologized, also for the second time. *I know you were in the middle of that mess right alongside the rest of us.*

No problem, Calvin said with his trademark calmness. *Like you said, Gordy's got us all on edge. Colleen, are you all right?*

I'm just a little tired, she said.

You sure? he pressed. *I know you were having morning sickness a while back.*

It's nothing, Colleen assured him again. *Just part of being pregnant.*

I frowned. Colleen had told me privately a week ago that the morning sickness seemed to have passed. Had it come back? *You feel like a little company?* I asked. *I could drive up for a few days.*

Thanks, but I don't want to put you to any trouble, she said. *I know how much you have on your plate right now.*

A small shiver ran up my back. The only things I had on my plate were trying to keep track of what was happening with Barringer and checking in occasionally on Rob Peterson and his continuing efforts to figure out what Amos Potter had put into the electronic kernels he'd created that were all that was keeping Colleen and her unborn baby alive. *It's not that bad,* I assured her. *Nobody's going to miss me for a couple of days.*

All right, she said, maybe a little too casually. *Let me know when you leave and we'll work out a schedule.*

Right. We'd figured out a way to layer our two telepath shields so that she could lie on a cot with her head just outside the field and her baby just inside. But it was awkward, the shelter I'd cobbled together outside her cabin was drafty and uncomfortable, and she couldn't stay out there for hours on end. Usually she just came out when she felt like talking to one of us, but we had a schedule ready to go if we needed more frequent communication. *I've got some loose ends to tie up, but I should be able to leave by noon tomorrow.*

That would be wonderful. Thank you, Dale. Good-bye.

Good-bye, Colleen, I said. *See you soon.*

Sooner than she might expect, actually.

Because that noon thing had been for Calvin's benefit, maybe Gordy's, definitely Scott's if the latter two were listening in. In point of fact, I had every intention of being on the road by dawn at the latest.

Deep inside me, I knew it wasn't polite to lie to my friends that way. But lying and paranoia had been part of Nelson.

And like Scott said, part of Nelson was now part of me.

Typical telepath-to-telepath conversational range was limited to around nine hundred miles. Close-approach started at about a hundred miles, the distance where we started feeling mental pressure and increasing pain.

The good part, if you could handle the discomfort, was that close-approach became a sort of private chat room, the two participants able to speak at a lower broadcast power that prevented anyone else from listening in. It also led to the kind of mind-to-mind and soul-to-soul connection normal humans could never truly experience.

The bad part was that if you pushed that closeness too far, the mutual pressure would eventually stress both minds to the point where they started to merge. I'd experienced that twice, and it wasn't pleasant.

At twenty miles, or so the calculations suggested, both participants would die in a blaze of brain-frying insanity.

I was half an hour past the U.S./Canadian border when I hit the hundred-mile limit. Ten minutes after that, Colleen poked her head out of the shield's protection. *Dale?*

I'm here, Colleen, I said. *I'm about an hour and a half out. Is this too close?*

No, she said. But I could feel the first edge of stress in her voice. *I can handle a little more.*

Let me know when it gets to be too much. What's going on?

It's probably nothing, she said. *But a week ago I had to drive back to Regina, and I thought I saw the man who'd been with Barringer when he first came to my house.*

I'd been on the road way longer than I should have, and between the fatigue and growing mental ache my eyelids were starting to droop. But that sudden jolt of adrenaline kick-started everything back to full attention. *The one he called Alex?*

Yes, she said. *I might be mistaken—I only got a quick glance— Did he see you?*

I don't think so, she said. *I was wearing a wig and too much makeup and just driving past. Even if he saw me I don't think he could have recognized me.*

Unless he recognized your SUV, I said grimly. We'd swapped vehicles for her a couple of times, burying the transactions as best we could. But there were always paper trails waiting to be dug out, and Barringer's collection of minions included a lot of men with shovels. *What do you want me to do?*

I don't know, she admitted. *I just . . . I didn't want to be alone.*

I'll be there soon, I promised. *Get back inside the shield and stay put until I get there. Maybe on the way I'll take a drive past your old house.*

What if he's still poking around?

Then we'll know how serious Barringer is about turning over every possible stone looking for you.

He's supposed to think I'm dead, Colleen said, her pain taking on a tinge of guilt. *After what you and Gordy went through . . . you think he knows I'm alive?*

I think he's the type who doesn't believe anything until he has proof in triplicate, I said. *Wait—I've got an idea.*

Reaching down, I ran my fingers through the keys dangling from the ignition. Car, house, mailbox, shed, storage unit—

There it was. *I've still got your house key. I'll go inside and see if that sparks a reaction.*

That sounds dangerous.

Shouldn't be, not in the middle of the day, I assured her. *If anyone calls me on it, I'll tell them I'm looking for your will.*

My will's with Scott.

I made a face. *I should have guessed. Barringer's people won't know that.*

Colleen was silent a moment. *All right,* she said reluctantly. *You said you're a hundred miles out?*

About that, yes.

I want to be with you when you go in, she said. *I'll pack the shields into the car and start driving. As long as I stay a hundred miles away from you, I should be safe.*

You sure you want to do that?

I want to be there with you, she repeated in a tone that left no room for argument.

Okay, sure, I said hastily. *I'll stop somewhere south of town and wait until you're planted.*

Thank you. I'll call again as soon as I can.

Just drive safe, I warned. *The last thing we want is for Barringer to pick you up from a traffic report.*

You, too. I'll talk to you in a bit.

The key Colleen had given me was to her back door, and I'd hoped that sneaking around to the rear of the house would let me slip inside with a little less fanfare than if I'd gone in the front. In actual practice, given the light dusting of snow that would announce my fresh footprints to the world at large, that hoped-for advantage turned out to be a wash.

Anything? Colleen asked.

It's cold and dark, I reported, making my way down the hallway to the living room. It was a bit lighter in there, the gauzy privacy curtains letting in a fair amount of the bright sunlight outside. *You forget to pay the power bill?*

It's Regina in the winter, and I've been dead, she said with a hint of dark humor.

Except that no one here knows that, I reminded her. *As far as anyone in Regina is concerned, you just walked off into the sunset and disappeared a couple of months ago.*

Unless Barringer told them.

I thought about that. I couldn't think of any reason why he

would give up such a useful bit of information, but that didn't mean he didn't have one. *I suppose that's possible. But until and unless we learn differently, we'll assume everyone but Barringer thinks you're alive and well and off on a secret mission somewhere.*

All right. Can you tell if anyone else has been in there?

I don't see anything obvious, I said, looking around. *Everything seems to be right where it was the last time I was here. Though I suppose Barringer could just have a lot of neat freaks on his payroll. Where are all your papers?*

File cabinet's in the bedroom. The key's hidden inside the packaging of the Casablanca *DVD.*

Got it.

The cabinet was tucked into a corner of the bedroom and disguised by a decorative silk covering cloth and a lamp, which was why I hadn't remembered seeing it there before. I opened the bedroom curtains to give myself more light, then found the proper DVD and dug out the key. I moved the cloth and lamp, unlocked the cabinet, and started searching through the files.

Or at least pretending to do so. I'd positioned myself so that I could see the windows out of the corner of my eye, and most of my attention was focused there.

But no one appeared, and no one got far enough inside my range to touch my mind. *As long as I'm here, are there any other files you want me to get for you?*

There's nothing I can't do without, she said. *Did anyone see you go in?*

Not as far as I—

I broke off. Had that been a knock at the front door? *Hang on a second,* I said, closing the drawer I was working on and going back into the hallway. *I may have company.*

I could feel the sudden spike in Colleen's tension. *Be careful.*

Bet on it.

The knock—if that was indeed what I'd heard—wasn't repeated. I crossed to the door and unlocked it, resisting the urge to peek out one of the sidelight windows first. Bracing myself, I turned the knob and pulled the door open.

There was no one there.

I made a quick visual sweep of the street, then focused on the walkway leading from the street to the house. There were fresh footprints there, one set each coming and going, both disappearing out of my sight around the decorative bushes on either side of the walkway.

From somewhere below me came a soft trill.

Apparently, they're not just neat but also shy, I told Colleen, focusing on the phone lying on the welcome mat.

Maybe you should just leave, Colleen said nervously.

If I do, we'll never know what they're up to. I gave the street one final visual sweep, then stooped and picked up the phone. *Listen carefully.*

I tapped the button and held it to my ear. "Who is this?"

"Good morning, Mr. Ravenhall," a calm male voice came. "My name is Alex. I don't suppose you'll remember me."

You were right—it's Alex. "I do," I said aloud, trying to match his tone. "You're one of Barringer's lackeys."

"I prefer the term *problem-solver*," he said. "But *lackey* will do if it's more convenient for you. Did you have a pleasant drive up from Des Moines?"

"You've spent too much time in LA," I said, a fresh shiver running through me. Had Barringer's people been tracking me the whole way? Or was he just keying off the known fact that I lived in Des Moines? "*Midwest winter* and *pleasant drive* aren't terms that go together. What do you want?"

"I think the question is rather what do *you* want?" he

countered. "A long way to drive just to break into the late Colleen Isaac's house." He paused. "Or *is* she the late Colleen Isaac?"

"I'm looking for her will," I said. "What's *your* excuse?"

He gave a small chuckle. "Really, Mr. Ravenhall. Regina's a beautiful city. Why do I need an excuse to visit?"

"Because you're from LA and it's four degrees below zero out there."

"It *is* a bit brisk for my tastes," he admitted. "But I understand Ms. Isaac's house is vacant and abandoned."

"Who told you that?"

"The city's electrical and water services, for starters," he said calmly. "No bills have been paid since December. I also understand the post office is holding her mail, which I'm told they sometimes do even without an official request."

"Awfully nice of them." *Colleen? Do they really do that for you?*

Sometimes, yes, she said. *Debbie knows I sometimes leave unexpectedly and keeps an eye on my box so that the mail doesn't pile up.*

"I'm also told the summer weather here is quite nice," Alex continued. "Once the taxes go fully into arrears and the house goes up for auction, I might consider buying it."

Tell him I'm leaving it to my doctor, Colleen put in.

"Sorry," I said. "Colleen told me once that her house was going to go to her doctor."

"Interesting," Alex said, sounding politely incredulous. "I didn't realize Dr. DuBois was that destitute."

I gripped the phone a little harder. So Barringer had been digging into Colleen's friends and acquaintances, too. Between that and his inquiries into the post office and city services, this was definitely not just a cursory drive-by. "It wouldn't be for her personally," I stalled. *Colleen? What do I say?*

Tell him she's talked about getting a place where patients' families can stay during surgery.

"It would be for hospital patients," I went on. "Their families, rather. Where they could stay during the patients' surgeries."

"Ah," Alex said. "Like the Ronald McDonald houses in the States."

"They've got some in Canada, too," I said. That one, at least, I knew. "Just nothing in Regina itself. Are we done with this conversation? I've got things to do, I'm cold, and like you said I had a long drive."

"I think we're done for now," Alex said. "Do keep the phone handy, in case I have other questions."

"I can't imagine any question of yours that I'd be interested in answering."

"One never knows," he said. "Let me know if you find Ms. Isaac's will. I may be able to expedite probate."

"Thanks, but I can handle it."

"I'm sure you can," he said. "Good-bye, Mr. Ravenhall."

I moved the phone away from my ear and keyed it off. One more quick look around the area, a brief but strong temptation to see how far into the street I could throw the phone, then I backed into the house and closed the door behind me. I thought about stomping my heel on the phone, like they did in the movies, but instead tossed it onto the couch. He was right, unfortunately—I might need to talk to him again. *Finished,* I told Colleen, fatigue tugging at my brain as this latest adrenaline rush subsided. *I suppose that went as well as could be expected.*

It went horribly, she said, her tone a mix of anger, chagrin, and guilt. *Whatever possessed me to come up with that ridiculous lie about leaving the house to Dr. DuBois?*

It's okay, I soothed. *Really. It's not* that *ridiculous. At least it got him off our backs.*

For now, she said, still sounding miserable. *But what happens when he or Barringer talk to Scott?*

What could they say to him that would be a problem?

It's not what they'll say, but what they'll ask. What if they want to know why my will hasn't gone to probate yet?

I winced. Of course Scott hadn't started that process yet—he knew Colleen was still alive. *Maybe he can't do that without a death certificate,* I said. *Can the coroner here issue one without a body?*

I don't know, she said, some of her panic subsiding. *You may be right. And if they all assume I just left town, they won't even be looking for a body.*

Right, I said. *We can check with Gordy later, but it sounded like the pitch he gave Barringer was that you went into the lake where it hadn't yet frozen over, as opposed to making a hole his people would be able to spot. The police barely glanced at the lake, and since there were no follow-up calls or missing person's report they didn't bother with an investigation. So as far as the rest of the world is concerned there's no reason for anyone to assume anything's in there at all.*

I suppose. Though once the spring thaw comes, Barringer will surely send in a dive team.

Probably. But that still gives us a couple of months.

Unless Barringer decides to try something sooner.

I winced. And if he did, it would probably be my unexpected arrival that would provide the necessary spark of suspicion. *He might,* I conceded. *We'll just have to try to outflank him. Okay. I told Alex I was looking for your will.*

Which he probably knows is a lie. It would likely be filed with an attorney, Scott or someone else.

A sudden thought struck me. *Unless there's a second will, one you threw together just before you supposedly went into the lake.*

Oh. Yes, that's interesting. You mean a—what's the term?

I searched my memory. *Holographic will?*

Right, she said. *If it was dated and signed after the one Scott has, that would be the real, legal will, wouldn't it?*

I think so, I said. *In which case, anything Barringer might have wormed out of Scott about his version of your will would be useless.*

I sensed her sigh. *Except that I* don't *have another will.*

Not yet, I said. *But who says we can't put one together?*

I suppose we could do that, she said slowly. *What would that gain us?*

Well . . . we could at least establish that Dr. DuBois gets the house.

Seems like a lot of work to go through for just that.

I scowled again as I opened the file drawer I'd been working on before Alex interrupted. Unfortunately, she was right. *It would also give me an excuse to go see her. Is there anything you need me to ask her?*

I can't think of anything, Colleen said. *I already have several pregnancy books.*

There's still nothing like talking to a professional. A violent shiver ran through me. *Nothing like working in a warm room, either,* I added, looking around the bedroom. Half visible beneath the bed was a small suitcase. *If you don't mind, I'm going to throw some of these files into your suitcase and go to a hotel where I can look through them in peace and quiet.*

Just make sure Alex doesn't see you or he'll break into your room later to find out what you've got . . .

She trailed off, her thoughts going suddenly odd. *Colleen?* I asked, pausing with the suitcase half open on the bed. *You okay?*

I don't know, she said. *You said you could talk to Dr. DuBois. Can you do it without Alex or anyone else knowing?*

I can try to be low-key about it, I said doubtfully. *Probably can't keep anyone from knowing unless I lie in wait for her in her house.*

That's not what I meant, she said. *I guess people can know you talked to her. Some people, not too many. But no one can know what you talked about.*

Okay. I pulled out a couple of thick files marked *Medical* and carried them over to the suitcase. *What exactly are she and I going to talk about?*

You said you were going to move the files where there would be peace and quiet. Maybe it's time for me to do the same.

Okay, I said, frowning. Was she talking about moving again? Someplace where Barringer couldn't find her?

Did such a place even exist? *Ah . . . are we going to tell Calvin and Gordy about this?*

Not now, she said, the oddness in her voice taking on a grim edge. *Maybe . . . I don't know. Maybe not ever.*

The sign on Dr. DuBois's clinic said that it closed at six o'clock on Fridays. But it was after six thirty when she finally emerged through the door into the reception area. "Thank you for waiting, Mr. Ravenhall," she said as she walked toward me. "I got your message two hours ago, but we've just been slammed today."

"Not a problem," I assured her. She was within reading range, but just barely, and there were a lot of other people broadcasting nearby. As she got closer, I'd be able to focus more accurately on her mind and thoughts.

"I hope you're bringing news about Colleen," she said. "I've been worried about her since she suddenly left town in December."

"Actually, I'm here on another matter," I said. She was almost in range . . .

And then, her thoughts hit me like a punch in the face. *Is she dead, Dale? Is she in the lake? Is that what the dive Monday is all about? Are they looking for her?*

A hand seemed to squeeze my heart. There was going to be a *dive?*

"Sort of a business matter," I floundered, trying to stall. *Colleen, they're going to search the lake on Monday.*

Oh, no, her horrified words cut through the mental cluster. *It has to be Barringer. Dale, when he doesn't find my body—*

Hold on, I cut her off. DuBois was thinking at me again—

If this is about Colleen and you need to talk privately, compliment my necklace.

"It's rather private, though," I continued aloud, trying to mentally juggle the two conversations. "I was hoping we could go somewhere and talk, if you're not too tired." I nodded toward her throat. "Interesting necklace. It reminds me of one of Colleen's. It was her mother's, I think."

Understood, DuBois said, her thoughts taking on a melancholy tinge. Clearly, she thought I was here to tell her that Colleen was dead.

And she was close enough now that I could read somewhat beneath the surface. If there was any duplicity there, any private deals with Alex or Barringer himself to worm information out of me, I couldn't find it.

"I *am* tired," she said, rubbing briefly at her forehead. "But as someone once said, we still have to eat. The dinner I was planning with a friend fell through, and I hate to waste a perfectly good reservation. If you don't mind talking over a meal, we could do that now."

"Actually, I'm at loose ends myself," I said. "Dinner sounds great."

She nodded. "All right," she said without much enthusiasm, Colleen's assumed death filling her mind with darkness. "I'll drive."

Basic tactics dictated that I not say or do anything provocative that might be picked up by anyone observing us. But her ache was pressing so hard against my mind that I couldn't help myself. "I hope this place is on the lake," I added. "I understand the scenery there is very nice."

A slight frown creased DuBois's forehead, her eyes locked on mine, her focused thoughts collapsing into a confused babble of competing threads and half thoughts. *The lake? But if Colleen—that's a horrible idea—you can't be serious—or are you saying?—but the lake—are you saying she's alive—if she's alive—*

And then, with what I could tell was a supreme effort, the clutter vanished into a single, laser-focused thought. *If she's alive, offer to pay for dinner.*

I hesitated. I'd made that comment hoping to assuage DuBois's sadness, but now that I'd put her on that track I belatedly realized I'd had no right to do that. This was Colleen's secret, and I was being asked to betray it.

It's all right, Dale, Colleen's thought came. *We need to trust her, and we need her to trust us. She might as well know now.*

Okay. Thank you. "Sounds good," I said aloud to DuBois. "But fair is fair. If you drive, I pay. Deal?"

Another flurry of emotions swept through her, a mix of surprise, relief, excitement, and dread. She was smart enough to know that a person didn't just disappear without a very good reason.

She also knew that, whatever was going on, she was likely being invited to step squarely into the middle of it. "If you insist," she said. A name flashed across her mind—*Gingold's Steakhouse*—

Colleen? I asked as DuBois and I headed toward the door behind me. *You know this place?*

Yes, it's in the north part of the city, Colleen said. *Do you think you can get her to drive to Qu'Appelle afterward? It's about sixty kilometers east. I can be there in an hour.*

You think that's wise?

I think it's necessary, she said, a quiet anxiety in her tone that warned me not to argue about it.

Okay, I said. *I'm going to need a little help, though, to keep Alex from following us. Calvin?*

I'm here, Calvin's thought came back.

I'm here, too, Gordy's voice put in.

I pushed back a flicker of surprise. I'd assumed Gordy was still in his self-imposed mental exile. *Good—I'm going to need both of you. Calvin, I need a rental car at Gingold's Steakhouse as soon as you can arrange to get one there.*

Are any rental places still open?

The ones at the airport should be, Colleen said.

Good. Okay, I'm on it.

What can I do? Gordy asked.

I'll need you to make an untraceable call, I said as DuBois and I stepped outside and headed toward the clinic staff parking area. Night had taken over the city, the darkness accompanied by bitterly cold air. Briefly, I wondered which of the parked cars out there Alex was shivering in. *Once Calvin's rental car is in place. I'll tell you when.*

I smiled tightly. *The doctor and I are going to need a diversion.*

To say my plan went off without a hitch would be a bit of an exaggeration. Certainly DuBois wasn't happy with the idea, and argued vehemently against it. But we were sitting in a booth with her in close-approach range, and even through her protests I could tell she reluctantly agreed it was our best bet.

We were in the middle of dessert when Calvin reported the rental had been delivered to the employee parking lot behind the restaurant, with the keys tucked above the visor. I cued Gordy, and two minutes later the dining room's quiet civility was replaced by controlled urgency as his phoned-in bomb threat emptied the place. I'd made sure DuBois and I were near the restrooms at the back before that happened and got us out the service entrance without being seen or stopped. I located our new car, got the doctor inside, and we were off into the night before the sirens and flashing lights arrived.

No one in Regina was going to be any happier about the incident than DuBois was, and I had no doubt the authorities would spend long hours with the nation's phone systems trying to track down the hoaxer. I wished them luck.

I also made sure to leave two hundred-dollar bills tucked under a napkin on the bar to cover our meal and the trouble. It seemed the least I could do.

"Where are we going?" DuBois asked as we left the city limits and headed east.

"Colleen's meeting us near Qu'Appelle," I said. "She wanted to talk to you, and with Barringer involved we don't dare trust phones or the internet."

"Are you talking to her now?"

I shook my head. "She has to bring the telepath shield with her to protect her and her baby."

"And you." Out of the corner of my eye I saw DuBois shiver. "It must be . . . very strange to live the way you do."

"Strange, limiting, and often depressing," I admitted. "And not just because we're permanently separated from each other. I don't know if you remember, but when the first of us popped up there was a huge slew of publicity, with some pundits screaming doom and the collapse of the Fifth Amendment—that's a U.S. thing—while others made glowing predictions of how we could help secure treaties or provide checks against government or corporate abuse."

"None of which happened."

"No, but not from lack of trying," I said. "The problem was that by the time anyone got around to testing any of these ideas our faces were too well known for the secrecy that was required for most of them. For a while governments and security specialists made sure to keep track of where all of us were, and even after that particular paranoia faded everyone knew better than to negotiate important treaties or contracts where one of us could be lurking behind a wall or one floor up within close range."

"Yes," she murmured.

I sighed. She wasn't saying it; but sitting right next to me, she didn't have to. "And then there's everyone else," I continued, replying to her unspoken thoughts. "Some of them hate us, and more of them are afraid of us. Thanks to all the idiot misinformation out there too many of them think we can pick their thoughts out of the general background noise a mile away. And that we would even want to."

"Whereas you can only do that when you're this close," DuBois said calmly.

"Yes," I said, frowning sideways at her. "I have to say, Doctor, that I'm impressed at how calm you are."

She gave a small shrug. "I'm sure you know how and why."

She was right. At this range, it was easy to pluck such things from the substrate of her thoughts. "Yes," I murmured.

Will you tell me? Just to make sure it wasn't just Colleen who could read me this way?

I felt a touch of old weariness. Worse even than the swirling of half-uninformed emotion were the constant demands for us to prove ourselves. As if that would quiet anyone's fear or hate. "You were Colleen's doctor before you realized who she was," I said. "You'd always been frustrated by people who misunderstood or belittled you, and wished there was someone who truly understood and accepted you, your skills, and your slightly lopsided way of thinking. Your own words."

My own words, her thoughts confirmed.

"By the time you learned the truth, you were comfortable enough with her that her ability didn't matter to you."

And then, the baby.

"And then Colleen got pregnant," I echoed her thought. "And your own maternal instincts kicked in. You really see yourself as a mama bear protecting her cubs?"

"Absolutely," DuBois said, a note of wry humor in her tone and thoughts. "Colleen and her baby both. I'm still wondering . . . do I really need to talk aloud to you?"

"It's helpful," I said. "Not just to help me sort out the main conversational line from the background, but also so you can stay clear on what you're actually saying as opposed to the side thoughts you're working on."

"Interesting," she murmured. "I didn't realize we were that complicated to read. It always seemed easier for Colleen."

"You two knew each other much better than you and I do," I reminded her. "One of us—his name was Amos—used to say it was like listening to someone with a thick foreign accent. The more you interacted, the better you got at sorting out the words and grammar and making sense of it all."

"Another reason people shouldn't be so afraid of you."

"Which we've tried to explain until we're blue in the face."

She was silent a moment. I tried to block out her thoughts to give her some privacy. It didn't work any better than it ever did. The analysis and speculation coalesced into a puzzlement— "So with all those limitations, why does Barringer still want Colleen's child?" she asked. "I assume all of this is about her child."

"It is," I confirmed. "And it's because Barringer hasn't really thought it through. He thinks that having an unknown, unidentified telepath will give him all the advantages government and corporate officials first thought we could give them."

"Won't it?"

I shrugged. "Maybe for a while," I said. "But sooner or later people would cotton on, and then he'd be right back where he started, with just another known telepath whom everyone of importance knows by sight."

"Assuming no one noticed the power when it first manifested," she pointed out. "Before Barringer could get hold of the child."

"There's that," I agreed. "When he reaches his teens—"

I broke off, my throat tightening as DuBois's thoughts took another, horrific turn.

"That also assumes the rest of you hadn't already blown the whistle on him—" DuBois stopped abruptly in turn. "Unless. . . ?"

"Unless he plans to kill all the rest of us once the baby's born," I finished for her.

I could feel her eyes on me. "Can he do that?"

My mind flashed back to that horrible day when Nelson flew his Piper Commanche straight toward me in an insane effort to kill both of us. If he'd made it just a few miles closer . . . "Oh, yes," I told DuBois quietly. "Killing us would be the easiest thing in the world."

Following Colleen's instructions, I pulled off the main road a few miles outside Qu'Appelle and drove onto a gravel lane that had once served a handful of now-abandoned buildings. At the end of the lane was a crumbling plant nursery, and I headed toward it.

Halfway there, DuBois's stream of thoughts suddenly vanished as we drove into range of the telepath shield.

Colleen's SUV was already parked behind the nursery. I settled my rental beside it and got out, ushering DuBois toward the back door and making a point of checking the SUV's hood as I passed. Colleen had estimated she would arrive fifteen to twenty minutes ahead of us, and from the engine heat it looked like her guess had been right.

We found her sitting in a dilapidated wicker chair in what had probably been the nursery's showroom, bundled to the eyelids against the cold. Her posture was stiff, her eyes focused toward the gloom around us as we made our way through the empty space toward her. Her shotgun was resting across her lap, her hands griping it tightly. Two more chairs had been arranged to form an equilateral triangle a few feet away from hers.

Beside her chair, nestled in the shadows, was the briefcase that held one of the telepath shields.

"It's okay, Colleen," I called softly. "It's us."

"Dale?" she called back, something in her voice twisting my heart. Tired, afraid, and worried.

"And Dr. DuBois," I said.

"Hello, Colleen," DuBois said, her own voice calm and professional. Fleetingly, uselessly, I wished I could see whether her thoughts matched her tone or if she was as stressed as Colleen. "It's good to see you again."

Even from twenty feet away I could hear Colleen's sigh of relief. "I'm glad to see you, too, Doctor," she said, and I saw her move her finger off the shotgun's trigger. "Thank you for coming. I know the invitation was . . . a bit crazy."

"Dale is very good at persuasion," DuBois said. "Also a decent enough traveling companion. How are you feeling?"

"I'm all right," Colleen said, her voice going a little hesitant. "How much did Dale tell you?"

"He told me about the telepath shield," DuBois said. "I'm

guessing from that and the fact you wanted to talk to me that you're still pregnant?"

"Yes," Colleen said. "And yes, the baby seems to be doing fine." She paused, and in the flickering light from the cars passing on the highway I could see the stiffness in her face. "I suppose the next question is whether you're planning to tell anyone."

"Absolutely not," DuBois said, a sort of quiet fierceness in her voice. "You're my patient, and everything related to you—*everything*—is strictly confidential."

"Thank you," Colleen said, her face smoothing a little. "Please; sit down."

"Thank you," DuBois said as she and I settled into the two chairs. "Tell me how I can help."

"First, I want to hear about this lake search Dale mentioned," Colleen said. "He said it was happening on Monday?"

"Yes," DuBois said, her eyes flicking to me. She had to know I'd pulled that information from her mind back in the clinic, and once again I wished I could tell what she was thinking about that unintended intrusion. "It's being listed as a cooperative training exercise for a private search/rescue group from California, with a side offer of free training for some of the locals if we want to take advantage of that. They apparently wanted to try a cold-water dive and settled on Regina as a good location."

"How convenient for someone," I muttered.

"Looking back at the timing, I agree," DuBois said. "But at the time, it seemed perfectly legitimate."

"Do you know who's behind it?" Colleen asked. "You said it was a private organization?"

"Yes, the Egiss Group," DuBois said. "At least, that's the name Mr. Winters gave Mayor Cassidy when he proposed the exercise."

"Has to be Barringer," I growled. "Probably buried under fifteen shell companies, but it's him."

"He knows Colleen's not dead?" DuBois asked.

"He must at least suspect," I said. "This is probably his way of proving it, one way or the other."

"Yes, that makes sense," DuBois said. "What exactly did you want to talk to me about, Colleen?"

Colleen took a deep breath. "I'm at a crossroads, Doctor," she said. "A decision I've known was coming since I first found out I was pregnant. The longer I try to stay off the grid, the more I realize I can't keep going this way. Not even until my baby is born; certainly not through the years it would take to raise her. I need a more permanent solution, and the sooner the better."

"Understood," DuBois said. "Have you any ideas?"

"I have one." Colleen hesitated. "Maybe it's crazy. I don't know. But I've been doing some on-line research, and I need you to tell me if it's even possible.

"I've been reading about a device called an *artificial womb*."

"Interesting," DuBois murmured thoughtfully after Colleen finished laying it all out. "I've heard of Dr. Ferrier and his work, and it seems promising. But I didn't realize it had progressed to the point where it might work for your particular situation."

"I don't know that it has," Colleen admitted. "But there's only so much I can learn from public web sites. I was hoping you could find out for me."

"Yes, probably," DuBois said. "Actually, now that I think about it . . ." She pulled out her phone and started scrolling through it. "Yes. Dr. Ferrier's going to be at a conference in Vancouver starting Monday and running through Thursday."

"*This* Monday?" I asked. "The day Alex's frogmen go into the drink?"

"Yes," DuBois said. "Maybe we could run over to the coast and talk to him."

"I can't leave right now," I warned. "They tracked me on the way from Des Moines, so we know they're watching me. We hopefully slipped Alex's leash tonight, but I can't count on doing it a second time."

"I was more talking about just Colleen and me going," DuBois said. "Colleen?"

"That's an awfully long drive," Colleen said hesitantly. "And I don't dare fly, not with the shields. I doubt they'd get through airport security."

DuBois looked at me. "Didn't you bring them in from the States?"

"Yes, but I was driving," I said. "Customs didn't care about strange-looking electronics—they just wanted to make sure I didn't have any contraband. Colleen's right. Airport X-rays of these things will look very weird."

"That's only if she flies commercial," DuBois said. "Maybe we can charter a private plane."

"Gordy's friend Jean Forster has one," Colleen offered. "Maybe she'd be willing."

"Can't hurt to ask," I said. "You want me to talk to Gordy when I get back to town?"

"I'll do it," Colleen said. "You know how he is these days."

"Yes," I said, still wishing I knew why he was that way. "Okay, you can call him once you're back home. Let me know if you want me in on the conversation."

"I will."

"One more thing," DuBois said hesitantly. "Whether this is possible, it's certainly highly experimental. At your baby's age, it might also be illegal."

Colleen shook her head. "I don't care about that."

"Neither do I, really," DuBois said. "The point I'm trying to make is that we'd be putting your baby at great risk."

Colleen looked at me, her face haunted. "I know," she said quietly. "But the alternative is to have a cloud hanging over her head the rest of her life."

I felt a sudden twitch. "That's the second time you've said *her* or *she*," I said carefully. "Are you saying you know for sure it's a girl?"

"I think so," Colleen said. "That's what the home test says, anyway."

"A girl," I repeated, trying out the sound of the word. Colleen's daughter. *My* daughter.

"Which leads to my next question," DuBois said. "The baby is also yours, Dale. You get a say in this, too."

I reached over and took Colleen's hand. "I hate the thought of putting our daughter in danger," I said. "But Colleen's right. She's already in danger. So is Colleen. If there's even a chance this will keep them both alive and safe . . . then yes, I'm good with it."

"I should also mention that waiting another month or two could also make a world of difference," DuBois persisted.

"We can't," Colleen said. "Not with Barringer back on the scene."

"I agree," I seconded. "We need to get this ball rolling as quickly as we can."

"All right." DuBois took a deep breath and huffed it out. "All right," she said again, all professional now. "No matter what Dr. Ferrier says, he's not likely to be able to do anything for at least a month. What are we going to do about Barringer until then?"

"For starters, I'm definitely sticking around Regina to keep an eye on Alex," I said.

"He'll also be keeping an eye on you," DuBois warned.

"That's fine," I said. "I think as long as I keep my reactions right that could work to our advantage."

"Your reactions?" Colleen asked, frowning.

"If I look like I don't care about the search, that'll tell him I know there's nothing to find," I said. "So I need to look and act worried."

"Worried about him finding her body," DuBois said, nodding understanding.

"*And* worried about what he's going to do when he finds it," I said. "If I can come up with a plausible assumption of what he's doing that's off on the wrong track, I may be able to lull him into false sense of security."

"Any idea how you're going to do that?" Colleen asked.

"Not yet," I said. "But I've got a couple of days to figure it out. I'll come up with something."

"Let me know if I can help," DuBois said, standing up. "In the meantime, we've probably been missed. Colleen, once you figure out how to get us to Vancouver, tell Dale and he can tell me. All right?"

"Yes," Colleen said. "Thank you, Doctor. You didn't need to stick your neck out this way for me. You still don't."

"You're my patient." DuBois gave me a half smile. "And as Dale will tell you, I'm a mama bear. Just let me know what you need me to do."

Earlier that evening, at my suggestion, DuBois had parked a discreet couple of blocks away from Gingold's Steakhouse. Now, freshly back from Qu'Appelle, I made sure to drive past her car a couple of times in case Alex or someone else was lying in wait for her. But if there were any sentries, they were being careful to stay out of range. I dropped her off beside the car, followed to make sure she got home safely, then went back to my hotel.

They hadn't been waiting for DuBois. They *were* waiting for me: two policemen, inside my room, feeling alert but not particularly nervous. If Alex had sicced them on me, he apparently hadn't bothered to mention the more infamous part of my identity.

I thought about walking past the room, going back to my car, and finding a different hotel. But it was late, the air outside had gotten even colder, and I wasn't in the mood for hide-and-seek.

Besides, my goal was to distract Alex away from what Colleen and DuBois were planning. I might as well see if I could turn whatever game he was playing back on him. I went to my door, waved the keycard at the lock, and unlatched it. "Good evening, gentlemen," I called as I opened the door. "How can I help you?"

They were in the process of standing up from their chairs as I came into view. The older of them—Sergeant Davis, I pulled out his name—was sharp enough to note the fact that I'd greeted them before I could actually see them. The second cop—Constable Ollion—reacted to his first look at my face as he belatedly realized the Dale Ravenhall they'd been sent to visit was in fact the well-known telepath.

"Good evening, Mr. Ravenhall," Davis said gravely, his surprise flashing as he, too, put the pieces together. "Apologies for the intrusion, but under the circumstances it was thought best that we wait for you in here."

"Yes, I'm sure someone thought that," I said. Davis had belatedly started running the kindergarten *ABC Song* through his mind, while Ollion was desperately working through the raucous lyrics of some rap tune. The tactic was one of many that had been used over the years to try to block our ability, and it worked exactly as badly as all the rest. "You want to explain these extraordinary circumstances that require two of Regina's Finest to lie in wait for me in my room?"

A muscle in Davis's cheek twitched. "Or you could just tell *us*."

I sighed theatrically. "You realize that trick doesn't work with people like me, right? The old he-knew-things-only-the-perp-would-know trap? Of course I know why you're here. Plus a whole lot more."

I nodded at Davis. "I could tell you your addresses if you wanted me to." I shifted my eyes to Ollion. "Or that the eight on your house number is upside down and you keep putting off fixing it."

I had the guilty satisfaction of watching both men's faces pale a little. What I'd done was little more than a parlor trick, just a matter of prompting them to bring information to the surface that I would otherwise have to dig for. But most people couldn't connect even such obvious dots, and the idea that their whole lives were laid bare before me was disconcerting at best and terrifying at worst.

Which was why I normally avoided such childish displays. But right now my job was to draw as much attention to myself as I could, and I knew from experience that nothing captured the imagination like nervous and resentful fear.

"But fine," I continued. "Your department got a tip—anonymous, no doubt, though I see they didn't share that tidbit with you—that I was the one who called in the bomb threat that ruined a lot of dinners at Gingold's Steakhouse this evening. Would you like to check my phone for outgoing calls?"

"I doubt you called it in personally," Davis said. "There's also this."

On cue, Ollion held up an evidence bag with the burner phone Alex had left at Colleen's house. "There's also the question of Dr. Renee DuBois's disappearance," Davis added.

"I think you'll find Dr. DuBois safe and sound back in her own house," I said.

"Yes, we got that news a few minutes ago," Davis confirmed.

"Lucky for you. Mind telling me where you two were for the past couple of hours?"

I raised my eyebrows a fraction. "Mind telling me why it's any of your business?"

"Dr. DuBois is Colleen Isaac's doctor," Davis said. "You're Ms. Isaac's friend and fellow telepath. Questions have been raised about the relationship between the three of you. Especially since Ms. Isaac seems to have disappeared."

This one was floating so high on Davis's thought stream that it might as well have been waving a flag at me. "Questions pertaining to Monday's so-called dive exercise in the lake?" I suggested.

Ollion muttered something under his breath. "We're asking the questions here, Mr. Ravenhall, if you don't mind," Davis said firmly. On the surface, he was calmer than his partner. Underneath, he was just as uncomfortable with my presence and supposed omniscience. "Where exactly did you and Dr. DuBois go after you left the restaurant?"

"We drove around for a while," I said. "Talked about Colleen."

"Did she mention the rumors that Ms. Isaac committed suicide in the lake?" Davis asked.

"They may have come up."

"You're her . . . colleague," Ollion said. "Have you heard from her since December?"

"We aren't continuously in each other's minds," I told him. "If Colleen wanted to go silent, she could easily do so. She wouldn't be the first of us to take a sabbatical."

"So you *haven't* heard from her?" Davis pressed.

"I think I'd like you to leave now," I said, stepping away from the door and gesturing to it. "Now that you know Dr. DuBois is fine, there's really no need for you to stay."

Davis waved a hand. "There's still the matter of the bomb threat," he reminded me.

"And we *would* like to check your phone," Ollion said. "You'd be amazed how many criminals get careless."

"Sure," I said, making no move to pull it out of my pocket. "I'll just take a peek at your warrant first."

Davis's lips compressed briefly. "Fine," he said. "Bring it along. The warrant should be ready by the time we reach the station."

So they were going to lock me up for the night. Not surprising, given that Barringer was pulling the strings. Briefly, I wondered if it would have been easier just to have stayed in my car and saved the price of a hotel room. "Then let's get to it," I said, backing to the door and opening it. "I assume you'll be driving?"

There were only two constables waiting when we arrived at the station. Either night desk duty ran on a skeleton crew, or else no one wanted to be around when the telepath was brought in.

They'd finished processing me, worrying and running their own useless versions of the *ABC Song* the whole time, and I'd been locked into a private cell for the night when Colleen finally surfaced. *Dale?*

I'm here, I confirmed, kicking off my shoes and stretching out on the cot. All things considered, it was reasonably comfortable. *Good news is that Dr. DuBois and I got back safely. Bad news is that Alex sicced the cops on me and I'm spending the night as a guest of the Saskatchewan government. Your turn.*

What? she said, sounding outraged. *That's crazy. On what grounds?*

Mostly on the grounds that Barringer doesn't like me, I said. *Plus everyone's a little freaked out at having a new telepath in town. But it's okay. I think they mostly don't want me looking over their shoulders while they search my room, phone, and car. Never mind that. You get through to Gordy?*

Yes, she did, Gordy's voice joined in. *Hello, Dale.*

Hello, Gordy, I said, trying to keep the surprise out of my voice.

Apparently, I didn't do a very good job of it. *Don't sound so shocked,* he admonished me. *Colleen's in danger. You didn't think I'd be right on board?*

Of course I did, I assured him. *So what's the word on Jean?*

She's ready, willing, and able to come get Colleen and Dr. DuBois, he said. *Plus she has a couple of, shall we say, alternate names she can come in under so she won't be as traceable. My chief concern is whether or not the doctor will be able to slip away without Alex and his triple-damned boss noticing.*

Definitely a concern, especially with her being freshly on their radar, I admitted. *That's one reason I'm playing along so nice with them, and why I'm going to start being mysterious and furtive once I'm back on the street. The more attention they have focused on me, the less they'll have to point elsewhere.*

Gordy gave a little grunt. *Let's hope it works. You said this polar bear dip is on Monday?*

Yes, assuming DuBois wasn't lied to. When's Jean coming in?

We haven't yet decided, Colleen said.

I'm thinking she gets there Sunday afternoon, picks up Colleen and DuBois, and deposits them in Vancouver before bedtime, Gordy said. *They crash the conference and have their chat with this Miles Ferrier guy Monday morning, and are back in Regina before Barringer finishes unchaining you from his dive site. I assume you're going to chain yourself to the site?*

I have something a bit different in mind, I said. *But yeah, it should provide Alex a headache or two. Colleen, how does Gordy's timing sound to you?*

It should work, she said. *I'm thinking Jean might want to fly into one of the airports near Moose Jaw instead of coming all the way to Regina. Dr. DuBois and I can drive ourselves individually there Sunday morning and wait for her.*

Gordy? I asked.

Shouldn't be a problem, he said. *I'll talk to Jean tomorrow and we'll figure out the best way to do this. Once we nail down the details, Colleen, I'll let you know.*

Sounds good, Colleen said. *Thank you, Gordon.*

No problem, Gordy said. *I was also thinking maybe I'd fly up to Vancouver and meet you there.*

I frowned. *Why?*

Because Colleen will have to stay inside the shield while she's talking to Ferrier, Gordy explained. *She won't be able to do the double-shield lie-down thing she does at home, which means she can't vet him while they talk. But if she sets the shield's edge properly, I can sit in the same room with her—or in the room next door if we don't want Ferrier to know about the shield—and listen in on the whole thing.*

I hissed out a soundless breath. It made sense. More than that, Colleen and I had pulled the same trick ourselves once or twice, so she knew how to set it up.

But the thought of Gordy instead of me being at Colleen's side for such a crucial conversation . . .

If you're willing, that would be wonderful, Colleen said. *Dale?*

I swallowed hard. But my sudden rush of frustrated jealousy aside—my quiet concerns about Gordy aside—it really was the logical way to proceed. Especially since I knew I had to stay here. *Sounds good,* I said, trying for an enthusiasm I didn't feel. *If you've got the time, Gordy, that would be great. I'd feel better— we'd all feel better—if someone could make sure Ferrier is on the up-and-up.*

Okay, Gordy said, sounding relieved. Maybe he'd expected more of an argument from me. *Once I'm in Vancouver I'll touch base with Jean, and we'll figure out when and where all of us can rendezvous.*

All right, Colleen said. *Anything else? Dale?*

No, I think we're good, I told her. *Gordy?*

Nope, that's all I had.

Okay, Colleen said. *We should probably all get some sleep now. Thank you, Gordon, and please thank Jean for me.*

I will. Sleep well.

And he was gone.

Dale? Colleen called. *You still there?*

Yes, I confirmed.

Are you all right with this? Me going off with Gordon, I mean.

I'm fine. It's definitely the smart move. I just wish I'd thought of it myself.

She was silent a moment. *Thank you,* she said. *I know that you . . . when this is all over, maybe we could take some time together. Just the two of us.*

I'd like that, I said. *You say where and when, and I'll be there.*

Thank you. Oh—one more thing. I was wondering if you should talk to Scott.

Way ahead of you, I said. *I've already got a list of legal things I want to float past him. Any idea when he's heading to Boise?*

He should already be on the way, Colleen said. *But he usually naps on late-night flights, so he may not be awake right now.*

Yes, I said, something unpleasant suddenly occurring to me. *Any idea when he's going home after his ski trip?*

No. Why?

Boise's only a few hundred miles from Vancouver, I pointed out. *If he's still there on Monday, he'll theoretically be able to eavesdrop on Gordy during your conversation with Dr. Ferrier. And he's working for Barringer.*

His firm is working for him, Colleen said, echoing Scott's own protest. But I could hear the fresh concern in her tone. *You don't think he would. . . ? No. Surely he wouldn't.*

I'd like to believe that. But he's a lawyer. Who knows where their loyalties ultimately lie?

"Hey! You! Ravenhall."

I opened my eyes. One of the night cops was standing a couple of feet outside my cell, a cordless phone in his hand. "Call for you," he said, leaning forward and down just far enough to slide the phone between the bars into the cell. "Slide it back out when you're done," he said. He backed up, his eyes and thoughts cringing a little, and hurried away.

Who's calling? Colleen asked.

Probably Alex, I said, getting off the cot and scooping up the phone. *Let's find out.* I held it to my ear. "Ravenhall."

"Ah, how the mighty have fallen," Alex's voice came, heavy with mock sorrow. "From media darling to a few nights in the drunk tank."

"Actually, it's quite peaceful in here," I told him. "And it'll be one night at the most. Don't worry, I'll be out in plenty of time for your underwater excursion on Monday. You going in with them? Or are you going to stand back from the hole and just watch?"

"I once heard someone say that the difference between a movie director and producer was that if the weather turned bad the producer could go back to the hotel," Alex said. "I'm the producer here. Why, were you hoping I might accidently drown?"

"That happy thought *had* crossed my mind," I said. "Doesn't matter. Dr. DuBois and I had a conversation this evening, and we've figured out what you're up to."

"Really," he said. "Care to share this revelation?"

"Since you can't stop us, why not?" I said darkly, glaring at the floor. Probably a waste of effort, but I'd been told once that the voice picked up cues from the face and I wanted Alex to think I was seething hard enough to say things I otherwise would be cagey enough to keep to myself. "Bottom line: we're not going to let you desecrate Colleen's body."

"Interesting," Alex murmured.

"What's interesting? That we're not ghouls like you and your boss?"

"No, not that," Alex said, still sounding thoughtful. Hopefully, the message he was taking away from my comments was that I genuinely believed Colleen had died a few weeks ago in the lake.

I knew better than to assume he would change any of his plans or actions on that belief, of course. Still, every bit of doubt I could plant would only help.

"And you're wrong if you think we're going to treat her body with anything except complete respect," he continued.

"Oh, I'm sure you won't *call* it desecration," I said, still glaring for all I was worth. "I'm sure you'll use words like *science* or *research*. Or *betterment of humanity*—that's a popular one these days. But it boils down to the same thing. Cutting her up, treating her remains like she was a lab rat."

"Methinks the gentleman doth protest too much," Alex said, his voice hardening to match mine. "Of course we intend to study Ms. Colleen's brain. But before you get all righteous on me, try replacing *betterment of humanity* with *betterment of Dale Ravenhall.*"

"And how exactly is this supposed to benefit me?"

He snorted. "Please. Try to at least *pretend* you're intellectually honest. Wouldn't you like to know the physiology behind your gift? Wouldn't you like to know how it works, maybe how to induce it in others? Wouldn't you especially like to know how it might be tweaked so you wouldn't have to spend the rest of your life trapped inside your private little bubble hundreds of miles from everyone you care for?"

I felt a sudden ache in my throat. Whatever else Alex was, he was really good at finding and pushing people's buttons. "We'll learn all of that in the proper time," I said. "*And* in the proper way."

"Fine," Alex said. "When you come up with a way to do that without using science, let me know. Until then, we'll proceed as planned. In fact, maybe a bit sooner than planned," he amended. "The dive team is nearly assembled. I may decide to start on Sunday instead of Monday. Unless you think you'll miss the show if I do."

"Hardly," I said casually, my mind racing. Was he really in a position to move up his timetable by a full day? Or was he just trying to get a reaction?

It didn't matter. My own preparations would only take a couple of hours and I should have all day Saturday to play with. Actually, with Colleen and DuBois scheduled to fly to Vancouver on Sunday, having Alex's full attention on the lake that day would work even better for our plans. "No, I'll be out by tomorrow," I said. "But do let me know what you decide. I really would hate to miss it."

"Absolutely," he said. "If only because I like knowing where you are."

"Oh, you'll know," I assured him. "Now, unless you have more pompous rationalizations to offload, it's been a busy day."

"Understood," he said. "One final question—nothing pompous, just idle curiosity. When you dream, do you dream your own dreams? Or do you dream Nelson's?" He paused. "Or Gordy's?"

I gripped the phone a little harder. He wasn't supposed to

even suspect that Gordy and I had had that close-approach encounter. The whole basis for the claim that Colleen had killed herself in the lake depended on no one knowing about that. "Everyone's dreams are their own," I said. "At least, ours are. Why, does Barringer assign dreams to his lackeys?"

Alex chuckled. "Sleep well, Mr. Ravenhall." There was a click, and the line went dead.

The cop had told me to set the phone back outside the cell. But I wasn't feeling all that cooperative at the moment. Rolling up onto my side, I lobbed the handset to land a few inches inside the bars. He could open the door to retrieve it or else work his fingers through the cage, I didn't care which. *Colleen?*

I'm here, she came back. *Do you think he knows what really happened in Los Angeles?*

No idea, I admitted. *He could be challenging me to deny it, or he could just be fishing. Either way, there's nothing to do but keep going.*

Yes. She was silent a moment, her sense that of someone who has something more to say but isn't sure she wants to say it. *We should probably get some sleep,* she said at last. *I'm going to start for Moose Jaw tomorrow, taking it nice and easy and staying to back roads. That way I'll be there and ready to go whenever Jean and Dr. DuBois arrive.*

So you'll be out of touch for most of the day, I said. *Got it. Please let me know when and where you stop for the night.*

I will. Sleep well, Dale.

You too. I hesitated. *I love you, Colleen.*

I love you, too.

With a sigh, I rolled over again. Sleeping was good. Sleeping was necessary.

But there would be no sleeping for me. Not yet.

Sometime in the next couple of hours Scott would wake up

from his nap as he came in for a landing in Boise. He and I needed to have a conversation before either of us finally settled down for the night.

As expected, I was ushered out of my cell just before noon the next day. My release was accompanied by some vague words about my equally vague threat having been resolved, along with a few private thoughts that conceded they really hadn't had any choice in the matter. They didn't have grounds to hold me, and they knew it.

The early-morning email barrage from the Canadian branch of Scott's law firm probably hadn't hurt.

None of the cops wanted to sit in a car with me long enough to take me back to my hotel, so I grabbed a cab. The driver didn't recognize me, which made the trip far less tense than it otherwise might have been. I showered, changed clothes, and headed out to shop.

Over the next few hours I hit several stores, buying small quantities of various materials that nevertheless slowly added up to fairly impressive amounts. I assumed the police were keeping track of my movements and purchases, and if they weren't then Alex certainly was.

Fortunately, most of what I needed was easily available. Even more fortunately, my shadowy stalkers would have no trouble recognizing my collection as being the ingredients of thermite.

I half expected my room to be invaded in the middle of the night, at which point I'd be hauled back to jail on some pretext. But Sunday morning dawned without intrusion, cloudy and a bit less frigid than the previous couple of days had been. I had a nice breakfast at the hotel, then took a leisurely drive around the lake. There was no sign of Alex or his dive team.

I was driving back to the hotel when I got the call from Gordy telling me that Jean and her passengers had left Moose Jaw and were safely on their way.

I spent most of the afternoon in my room, pretending I was mixing the ingredients I'd collected. My plan didn't require any actual thermite, but I needed the perceived threat of it to get Alex and the Regina government to move in the direction I wanted. The trick would be to leave the cops with the implication that I had something big in the works while at the same time not giving them an excuse to haul me back to jail.

Midway through the afternoon I spent half an hour in the hotel's business center printing out the most recent batch of Scott's emails. An hour before sundown, I took a second drive by the lake. Still no unusual activity. Alex's threat to move up his timetable had apparently been just talk.

I was getting ready for bed when Gordy once again contacted me, this time to confirm that Jean's plane had landed and that he was on his way to rendezvous with them.

With that comforting news, I was able to get to sleep quickly. Once again I wondered if I would get a police wake-up, but aside from some tense dreams my night's rest was untroubled. I got up with the sun, ate breakfast, put on all the warm clothing I had, and headed back to the lake.

From the way DuBois had talked I'd had the impression that the dive was supposed to be a low-key event, with maybe a few police or other first responders there to observe or participate. But yesterday's shopping trip had apparently rewritten the script. I arrived at the boat landing to find a police barricade had been set up fifty feet from the lake, manned by half a dozen Regina police officers. A couple dozen citizens were gathered outside the barricade, talking among themselves or on their phones and watching as the dive team sorted out their gear.

Standing near the dock, also watching the team, were three

more Regina constables and a half dozen men and women wearing the uniforms and shoulder flashes of the RCMP. Making sure the sheaf of papers tucked into my coat pocket was easily accessible, I headed in.

Sergeant Davis and Constable Ollion were on duty at the barricade. Neither looked happy to see me, but neither looked exactly surprised, either. "Mr. Ravenhall," Davis greeted me in a grave voice as I reached conversational range. "I'm sorry, but you can't come any closer."

"I think I can," I said. Pulling out the phone Alex had given me, I punched redial and set it on speaker. It rang twice—

"Ah—there you are," Alex's cheery voice came. "I was afraid you were going to miss the show. Please; join us."

I raised my eyebrows questioningly at Davis. He scowled, his thoughts dark and sullen, and gestured me through. I nodded my thanks and maneuvered through the narrow opening. It was probably a relief for both of us when I got out of range of his thoughts.

Alex was standing beside a middle-aged man and two of the Mounties a few steps back from the fresh hole that had been cut in the ice. "Mr. Ravenhall," Alex called in greeting. "No—stay there, please. I'm sure Mayor Cassidy has a few secrets he'd like to keep to himself."

"As do you, I imagine," I said, obediently stopping just short of the distance where I could pull clear thoughts from the overall clutter of the other minds around us. "I see you brought in reinforcements."

"Yes, thanks to you," Alex said, making a small gesture. Out of the corner of my eye I saw two Mounties detach themselves from their chunks of frozen ground and stride toward me. "You didn't really think we'd let you get close enough to Ms. Isaac's remains to incinerate them, did you?"

"To *incinerate* them?" I echoed, feigning surprise. "Oh—right. My little shopping trip."

"Indeed," Alex said. "Did you think we wouldn't figure out what you were making?"

"On the contrary," I said. "I was hoping you would so that I wouldn't have to go to the trouble of asking for all this extra security myself." The two Mounties came within range, their minds broadcasting calm professionalism. I raised my arms to the sides, just to show them I could be professional about this, too. "Let's get this out of the way and I'll explain."

The Mounties' hands were as professional as their minds, and it took them less than a minute to do their frisk. They stepped back, one holding my wallet, the other my sheaf of papers. "He's clean, sir," the first one confirmed. "No thermite or any other weapons."

"And those papers are for you," I added, nodding to the sheaf. "If you'd be so good to take them to him, officer?"

"What are they?" Alex asked, the texture of his mind taking on a hint of wariness.

"A whole bunch of legalese," I said. "The document states that if Ms. Isaac's body is found and retrieved, her will immediately kicks into action. It further outlines the provision that the will's executor will take immediate possession of any remains through his duly designated representative." I tapped my chest. "That's me."

"Interesting," Alex said, leafing quickly through the papers. "Of course, an attorney can write anything he wants. We'd need a legal ruling before I could accept this."

"Knock yourself out," I said. "While we wait, I'm sure whoever's in charge of these fine men and women will take the steps necessary to make sure no one unilaterally preempts that ruling."

"And you think all these people—" Alex waved his hand in

a wide gesture that encompassed both the police and Mounties "—are needed to make sure I comply?"

"Oh, I'm sure you'll be the epitome of cooperation," I said. "No, these people are needed so that they can surround the lake and make sure your divers don't poke a hole in the ice at the other end and sneak her body out."

Alex was pretty good at making his face do what he wanted. But even at my distance I could sense his sudden chagrin. Apparently, those had indeed been the divers' instructions.

"I assume, Mr. Mayor," I continued, "that you wouldn't want the city and province to suffer the public embarrassment that would ensue if something like that happened. Not to mention the potential legal ramifications."

The mayor was a couple of paces past Alex, and at that distance I couldn't read even the overall sense of his thoughts. But I didn't need to. Silently, he took the papers, gave them a quick skim and nodded. "Sergeant, you heard Mr. Ravenhall. Deploy your officers accordingly."

"Yes, sir," one of the Mounties said, flashing me an unreadable look as he pulled out his radio.

I was soaking in my hotel room bathtub, trying to drive away the day's chill when I finally got Colleen's call. *Dale?*

I'm here, I said. *Where are you?*

Back home, she said. Her voice sounded as tired as I felt. *Everyone's back.*

How did it go?

As well as could be expected. Dr. Ferrier started out disbelieving, aghast, and resistant. But eventually he came around to intrigued and reluctantly willing.

So he's going to do it?

Yes. Three weeks from tomorrow.

Sooner than DuBois expected. Interesting.

He said there was no point in putting it off any longer than we had to. He has his artificial womb setup in a private facility outside Winnipeg that's sufficiently isolated that we shouldn't be noticed.

A lot of Canada is like that, I hear.

Very much so. Jean's already agreed to fly me there. She hesitated. *Gordon said he'd like to come up, too.*

An unpleasant feeling ran up my back. *Why?*

You can ask him yourself. He wants to talk to you privately when we're finished here. Are we?

I winced. That last question had sounded more than half asleep. Clearly, the trip and conversation had drained her more than I'd realized.

That, plus the depressing ache of knowing that she was now looking at the beginning of the end. And possibly, given the risks of the procedure that DuBois had already pointed out, and Ferrier had undoubtedly emphasized, the loss of her baby. *Sure,* I said. *Get some rest. You sound like you need it.*

I do. Thank you, Dale. For everything.

You're welcome. Sleep well. I love you.

I love you, too.

And with that, she was gone.

And now, apparently, it was Gordy's turn.

I didn't want to talk to him. Not now. It was late, I was tired and hungry, and I was still carrying some low-level resentment that he'd gotten to spend time with Colleen in Vancouver and I hadn't.

But he was my friend and colleague. More than that, he was *Colleen's* friend and colleague. If I wanted to claim I loved her, it meant I needed to be willing to do whatever it took to make her life better and safer.

And part of that equation, unfortunately, was Gordy.

I took a deep breath. *Gordy? You there?*

I'm here, Dale. We need to talk about this plan of Colleen's.

You don't like it?

I like it fine. Or rather, I like it as well as I like anything about this mess.

I bristled. *You mean the mess of her being pregnant?*

No, of course not. You and she . . . never mind. No, the part I don't like is Barringer perpetually breathing down our collective neck.

No argument here, I agreed sourly. *The problem is how to fix it. We tried it once*—part of me wanted to say *you* tried it once, but that would be petty—*and it doesn't seem to have worked.*

Agreed, he said. *But that was then. This is now. Because now we've got a weapon he doesn't know about: you.*

I frowned. *Come again?*

Remember Oceanside, our close approach. Who was in the room with me?

Barringer and some of his thugs, I said, frowning a little harder. Where in blazes was he going with this?

Right. There they all were, in the room with a telepath.

Who was zonked out of his mind—

I broke off as I finally got it. *And who for a while was partially linked with* me.

Exactly, Gordy said with a kind of malicious satisfaction. *Like you said, I was too out of it to know what I was doing. But we were connected, which means that some of what makes Barringer the arrogant bastard he is must have seeped into your mind from mine.*

Maybe, I said cautiously, sifting through the weeks-old memories from that event. I had to admit it made a certain amount of sense.

But if there was anything of Barringer in there, I couldn't find it. *I don't know, Gordy. I don't see anything.*

Maybe it's tucked away in your subconscious. Maybe it's not full-blown thoughts, but just a sense of his mind and personality, a feeling for how he thinks.

I suppose that's possible. But if it's buried that deep I don't see how it'll help us.

It'll help us, he said, *because you and I are going to come up with a plan to get him off Colleen's back.*

I sighed. And all it would take for the plan to work would be my supposed knowledge of how Barringer thought.

But we had to do *something.* And Gordy was right—he and I were the only ones who'd gotten that close to the man. If anyone could pull this off, it was us. *Okay, I'm game,* I told him. *What did you have in mind?*

The strangest part was that the longer Gordy and I talked and planned, the more the vague impressions about Barringer began to surface from the dimness of my memories.

At first I thought it was just the power of suggestion, that maybe I was keying off the non-telepathic encounter I'd once had with Barringer, or else that I was extrapolating from my more recent interactions with Alex. But as Gordy and I continued to bat ideas back and forth I realized that they were, in fact, genuine images and voices that I'd picked up via Gordy's mind.

Somewhere along in there, I first noticed the woman.

She was seated to Gordy's right in the memories, as close to him as the four men I could see grouped in front of him. I hadn't noticed her at the time, but with the memories coming back I could see her now out of the corner of my eye. The corner of Gordy's eye, rather. She never spoke during the time Gordy and

I were melded together, but she was definitely there, and definitely involved.

So why wasn't she on the list of people who'd been caught with Gordy when the police raided the place shortly after he and I broke contact? Had Barringer made sure to get her out before they arrived? If so, did that make her unusually special to him?

I think this is going to work, Gordy commented into my musings. *Of course, it means we'll have to recruit another woman.*

I twitched, snapping my mind back to Gordy's current monologue. *Sorry?*

Another woman, he repeated, a hint of suspicion in his voice. *The plan I was just pitching. Are you falling asleep on me?*

Maybe, I said, trying to think back to where I'd lost his current train of thought.

No good. My mind had drifted away just as he was starting on this most recent proposal. *Sorry,* I apologized. *Tired, plus low blood sugar—haven't eaten since breakfast. Can you run through it again?*

I'm sorry, too, he said. *Forgot your day was as rough as ours. I'll give you the elevator pitch, then let you eat and sleep. Okay?*

Okay. Shoot.

We need a decoy to point Barringer in the wrong direction in case he finds Colleen before Dr. Ferrier's magic machine brings the baby to proper term. A fake uterine transplant would be just the thing to—

Wait, what? I interrupted. How sleepy was I that I'd missed something like *that? What's a uterine transplant?*

Just what it sounds like. You take the uterus from one woman and put it in another. It's usually done when the recipient's own equipment has been damaged but she wants to conceive.

And you're suggesting this for Colleen?

No, I'm suggesting we have this story ready to pitch as our diversion. We get a woman to play decoy, plant her somewhere far away from Colleen and Ferrier, and be ready to trot her out if we need to shake Barringer off our backs.

How are you going to find someone like that?

Don't worry, I'll handle that part, he said, a little evasively. *Maybe Dr. DuBois can help.*

I felt my stomach rumble, and not just from hunger. I knew little about Gordy's telepathic persuasion work on our would-be extortionist Ted Green except that Gordy steadfastly refused to talk about it. That, plus I could feel a distant darkness in his mind whenever anyone brought up the subject.

As far as I knew, Ted had never spoken again about the telepath shield. To anyone. Whatever Gordy had done, and whatever price he'd paid for doing it, it had apparently been effective.

All I need from you is to think about the plan and let me know if you see any flaws, Gordy continued. *Go eat and sleep, and we can come back to this tomorrow.*

Okay, I said. *A question. There was a woman sitting at your right in there. Any idea who she was?*

There was a short silence. *A woman?*

Yes, sitting right at your elbow. You don't remember her?

I don't even remember anyone being there, he said slowly. *You're sure you're not getting your wires crossed and remembering one of Barringer's goons?*

No, she wasn't a goon and she was definitely a woman. Nothing?

Nothing at all. Weird.

Not necessarily, I said. *The drugs probably screwed up your peripheral vision.*

And my peripheral brain?

It's okay, Gordy, I soothed. *My guess is that she was just there to take notes. A stenographer or something.*

Sure, he growled. *They've got things called digital recorders for that now, you know.*

Barringer strikes me as the old-school type, I said, trying one more time.

But the battle was already lost. My question had unintentionally put Gordy on edge, and recent experience had taught me that it would take him the rest of the night to climb back from that brink. *Doesn't matter,* I said *Whoever she is, she seems to have gone to ground right afterward. We can probably leave her out of our calculations.*

Maybe, Gordy said darkly. *Maybe not.* He paused again, and I could sense the effort as he pulled himself back together. *Got to go. Sleep well, Dale.*

You, too, Gordy.

For a few minutes afterward I lay on the bed, staring at the ceiling. Gordy's plan was about as off-the-wall as I would expect from a man who'd once allowed himself to be kidnapped by Barringer's men, leaving his own life—and Colleen's—hanging on whatever the rest of us could come up with on the fly. He seemed to have thought this one through a little better.

But there was the potential for a big hole in it. A hole that needed to be addressed.

And there was only one way I could think of to do that.

With a tired sigh, I dragged myself off the bed and put on my shoes. The last time Gordy had taken up that burden, it had affected him deeply . . . and the only way to keep him from going down that dark road again was to take the walk myself.

Gordy had made some terrible sacrifices for Colleen and me. This time, it was my turn.

Her name was Lainey, and she was sitting alone in a noisy sports bar when I met her.

Not that she was all that interested in the game. Her thoughts as I strolled casually past her booth were on her father, memories wrapped in ache and sadness. This had been his favorite watering hole, I saw, where he and his friends had watched the big-screen TVs and shouted or booed with the roller coaster ride that was the world of sports.

It was only as I brought my beer to the unoccupied table beside her booth that I picked up the final detail: her father wasn't dead, but was instead locked inside the living prison of Alzheimer's.

I sat down, took a small sip from my glass, and pulled up a list of memory-care nursing homes on my phone. I peered at it for a few minutes, scrolling and wincing, until I could tell I'd caught her attention. One final scowl—

"Excuse me," I said, looking over at her. "You wouldn't happen to have a calculator, would you?"

"There's one on your phone," she said.

"Oh." I peered at the phone, punched the *tools* key, and did some more scrolling. "Thanks," I added, pretending to still be searching.

"Here," she said, holding out her hand.

"Thanks," I said again, handing it over. Her eyes flicked over the apps that were still open, and I caught her reaction to the nursing home list. "It's right here." She pulled up the calculator and handed it back.

"Ah. Thanks." I punched in a few numbers and shook my head. "Damn, these places are expensive."

"Tell me about it," she said ruefully, a fresh wave of ache flowing across her mind. "My father's in one of them."

"Your father—?" I sent her a puzzled look, letting it clear away as I looked again at the phone. "Oh. Right. Memory-care places."

"Sorry—didn't mean to snoop," she apologized. "You'd left the app open and I just happened to notice it."

"That's okay," I assured her. "Actually, if you wouldn't mind, maybe you can help me sort through all these. I mean, since you've got some experience and all."

She hesitated, and I could see her desire to grieve her father in private warring with a loneliness she'd probably been denying—"I just want the best place for my mother," I added.

The loneliness won. "I understand," she said, beckoning me to the other side of her booth. "Let's start with where you live— you'll want to be close to her—and your price range."

I'd never done anything like this before. But it turned out to be frighteningly easy.

I knew all the right things to say before I said them. I knew all the right buttons to push, all the memories and emotions to evoke, all the buzz words and gestures and obscure but important connections to hit. I got into her mind, touching it, manipulating it, bending it to my will and purposes. In the end, as we lay together fully clothed on her bed, just sharing an hour of comfort in an effort to temporarily keep the loneliness at bay, I knew she would do exactly what I needed her to do, without ever knowing I was the one who had pulled the strings.

I hated every minute of it.

Nelson had done this at least once as part of his ice-blooded murder of Amos. I could visualize his smirk of triumph, his reveling in the power to manipulate the minds and actions of lesser beings. Gordy had done it with the far more principled motive of protecting Colleen and her baby.

Now, I'd done it too . . . and I knew that all the professed nobility in the universe couldn't keep me from feeling filthy clear through to the core of my being.

No wonder Gordy didn't want to talk about it.

Lainey's breathing was slow and steady as I eased away from her side and slipped silently out of the apartment. She would wake as refreshed as I had been able to arrange for her, with no memory of our encounter, no doubt wondering how much she'd had to drink that she'd made it home but fallen asleep still dressed.

More than once as I drove away I considered contacting Gordy and telling him what I'd done. But I didn't. Until the dirty feeling gripping me eased, I wouldn't feel like decent company for anyone.

But decent company or not, I still had to be in Winnipeg with Colleen for her upcoming procedure. Sometimes, I reflected, the telepath shield's ability to block our thoughts from each other was a welcome relief.

The procedure on Colleen, two weeks later, went off smoothly.

Or at least that was what they told me afterward. At Colleen's suggestion, DuBois and Gordy joined her and Dr. Ferrier in the operating room while I stayed outside the shield's range, roaming the building's perimeter, ready to check out anyone who came within range for any abnormal interest.

But Ferrier had been right about the facility being isolated, and he'd already sent away everyone except the couple of assistants he absolutely had to have. I roamed through the icy breeze and slushy snow for nothing and for no one.

Finally, it was over.

Colleen spent the next three days in a recovery room across from the room where Ferrier had performed the operation. DuBois stayed with her, handling all the doctor parts of her recovery while Gordy and I took over the basic nursing duties. When Colleen was able to travel, we got her into her SUV and drove her back to her wilderness cabin.

And with that, after weeks of fear, stress, and concern, Colleen was free of the small being that she'd carried inside her.

Now came the waiting.

* * *

The next months went by slowly. There was little for me to do except worry about Colleen and the baby and oversee Rob's still-futile efforts to replicate Amos's kernels. Early on, during one of my broodings about Barringer, another thought occurred to me. At the moment the eight D-cell batteries that powered each of the two shields were in individual sockets. It would be faster to change them out if they were instead packaged in a modular quick-swap casing. I turned the project over to Rob, who tackled it with an odd mix of enthusiasm and reluctance.

But the job only took him a couple of days, plus the long drive to deliver the new casings to Colleen. After that, it was back to our individual tasks, and our individual frustrations.

It was three months after Dr. Ferrier had finished his work, and I was driving up to see how Colleen was doing, when the storm we'd known was coming finally hit.

I'd finished a brief chat with Calvin, almost inevitably about the state of Gordy's mental health, when I rounded the last curve onto Colleen's property to find a large helicopter squatting on the ground beside the cabin. *Calvin!*

Too late. I was already within range of the telepath shield, and the world had shut down around me. I slammed on the brakes, but before I could do more than shift into reverse two large men with guns stepped out of the trees at my sides. One of them motioned ahead to the cabin; huffing out a sigh, I shifted back to drive and continued on.

Barringer had come outside the cabin as I parked and got out of the car. The briefcase containing the shield, I noted, was on the ground beside him. "Mr. Ravenhall," he greeted me. His voice was calm, but there was a tightness around his eyes. "This is a surprise."

"Likewise," I said, walking toward him. "I guess congratulations are in order."

"Congratulations?"

"You found this place," I said, waving my arm around me. "You found Colleen."

"So I did," he said. "Where's my baby?"

I blinked. "Excuse me?"

"My baby," he repeated, his voice going darker. "Where is it?"

"I assume still inside her mother," I said, frowning. "Are you saying Colleen's not home?"

For a moment he just studied my face. Then his lip twitched. "Alex?" he called. The cabin door behind him opened—

And Alex and Gordy walked out to join us.

My breath froze in my lungs. "*Gordy?*"

"Sorry, Dale," he apologized, his voice low and bitter. "Scott warned me a couple of days ago that Barringer might have located Colleen. I came up to help her pack and get out." He threw a sideways look at Barringer. "I guess I wasn't fast enough."

"I guess you weren't," I bit out. "Why didn't you tell me?"

"We thought—Colleen and I—that Barringer's goons might still be watching you and if you suddenly burned rubber away from Des Moines it would tip them off that we were on to them. Anyway, I could get here faster."

"Not that it helped." I looked back at Barringer. "Where's Colleen?"

"Inside," he said, nodding his head behind him. "In the bedroom. Don't worry, she's perfectly fine." He paused. "For the moment."

"What's that supposed to mean?"

"It means you've put me in a very awkward position, Mr. Ravenhall," Barringer said, his voice going a couple of shades darker. "My doctor has examined Miss Isaac, and tells me the baby is gone."

I let my eyes narrow, feeling some of the rush of adrenaline subsiding. The timing was unexpected, but this should get us back on track for Gordy's decoy plan. "Are you saying she had a miscarriage?"

"I'm saying the baby is *gone*," Barringer repeated. "Miss Isaac tells me she decided to end her pregnancy." He gave a little snort. "A pointless lie. Abortions don't leave three-month-old C-section scars behind."

"Wait a minute," I said. Yes; definitely on Gordy's track. "Three *months?*"

"My intention," Barringer continued, ignoring my question, "had been to take Miss Isaacs and this nicely intact telepath shield to a safe and comfortable location where she could bring her child to term. That plan has now gone by the wayside. Further complicating matters are the presence of Mr. Sears—" he nodded toward Gordy "—and now you."

"Yes," I said, trying to strike the proper balance between anger and thoughtfulness. "So suddenly you have three telepaths within close-approach distance and only one shield to keep them from instant mutual annihilation."

"Big deal," Gordy growled. "Once the baby was born you were planning to kill all of us anyway, weren't you?"

I winced. We'd reached that conclusion long ago, but I would never have thrown it into Barringer's face that bluntly.

Barringer took it in stride. "That's always an option," he said calmly. "But as you said, none of that would happen until the baby had been born and deemed healthy." He gave me a smile that didn't make it all the way to his eyes. "After all, if we needed to try again I'd want at least one male/female pair of you still alive."

I felt a hand close around my heart. *Selective breeding,* the old elitist phrase echoed through my mind.

"And to be honest," Barringer added, "I'm still hoping you'll all be reasonable enough that I won't have to take such actions at all."

"Reasonable, as in not telling anyone you have an unknown telepath tucked away in your lair?" Gordy demanded.

Barringer gave a theatrical sigh. "As I've already explained to Miss Isaac and Mr. Ravenhall, the baby stays with me or it goes to whichever government gets to it first. No matter what happens, there is zero chance Miss Isaac will be permitted to raise it herself. I submit that I'm still the lesser of those evils."

"I'd suggest that contemplating mass murder puts you farther down that list than you think," I pointed out.

"Of more immediate concern is the situation here and now," Barringer continued. "Much as I'd like to transport you all safely outside your mutual kill zone and be leave you to your own devices, I'm afraid I can't do that. At the moment you're all incommunicado, and I need to keep it that way until I've secured my baby. Something funny, Mr. Ravenhall?"

"Sorry," I said, wiping away my sudden and totally unanticipated smile. "I was just thinking that most people would consider holding three telepaths to be a winning hand. Problem is, this isn't poker. It's more like Go Fish."

"Hilarious," Gordy muttered.

"Yes," Barringer murmured. "Let's return to the question of my baby. I presume you'd prefer to do this the easy way?"

"What's in it for us?" Gordy asked.

"Your lives." Again, Barringer nodded at the cabin behind him. "And Miss Isaac's."

"I thought you wanted to hang onto some breeding stock," I said.

"Oh, I didn't mean I would kill her," Barringer said. "I meant she would be allowed to keep her life as she currently knows it. The freedom to walk free in the wind and sunshine, as opposed to an existence in a small room forever cut off from you and her other friends."

"You wouldn't get away with it," Gordy warned. "We'd find her. We'd get her back."

Barringer shrugged. "It's a big world, Mr. Sears. You'd be welcome to try."

"It would also be a waste of your resources," I said. "Feeding and housing her for no gain? That doesn't sound like the Lawrence Barringer we all know and hate."

"As you said: breeding stock."

For a long moment the only sound came from a light breeze rustling through the tree leaves. I found myself eyeing the shield, wondering suddenly if I could grab it before Barringer or Alex could stop me. If Gordy and I could get far enough from the cabin to get Colleen out from under its effect, she could call to Calvin—

"I may have failed to mention," Barringer said into my thoughts, "that as you arrived Dr. Vyas was in the process of sedating Miss Isaac. By now she'll be sound asleep."

I looked at Gordy questioningly. "I don't know," he said. "They were alone in the bedroom—Colleen, the doc, and a guard. I thought she was just doing an exam."

I nodded, the impromptu idea fading away. "All right. Brass tacks time. What happens to Gordy and me if you get the baby?"

"You live," Barringer said simply. "There's no need to kill any of you—"

"Not yet," Gordy said under his breath.

"—and certainly no desire on my part to do so," Barringer finished with a quick look at him. "As I said, once the baby is secured, you're welcome to scream all you like. You'll have no proof. You'll certainly not have the baby."

"And if we *don't* give her to you?" I asked.

"In that case, I'd have to settle for my consolation prize." Barringer tapped the briefcase with the toe of his shoe.

I frowned. "What in the world would you want with a telepath shield?"

"Please, Mr. Ravenhall," he said with another small smile. "Did you really think I was unaware that it can be reconfigured into a telepath finder?"

I felt a sudden hollowness in the pit of my stomach. How in the world had he learned that? Had Ted Green talked, after all? Or had one of the techs on Barringer's payroll somehow figured out the physics behind Amos' creation?

"Or maybe I won't have to wait that long," Barringer continued. "There are other female telepaths in the world. One of them might see my offer as a step up from her current life."

He shrugged. "Of course, if I have to leave here with just the shield, there would be no time to move the three of you to safety. But I'm sure Alex would pick a nice spot for your graves."

"The others will know it was you," Gordy warned.

"They'll *suspect* it was me," Barringer corrected. "That's a long way from knowing. It's an even longer way from proving."

My pulse was pounding in my ears. He could do it, too. With the shield having blocked all telepathic communications since the time he arrived, he could kill us and take the shield without any of the others knowing what happened. And there was nothing any of us could do about it.

"So now that you fully understand the situation, let me refine your options," Barringer said. "Tell me the truth, and all three of you live. Tell me a lie, and one of you dies. Tell me two lies—" He tapped the briefcase again.

"What about Colleen?" I asked.

"You've convinced me that she's more trouble than she's worth," he said. "Especially when a telepath finder will allow me to find other, more pliant telepaths, possibly even before the rest of the community is aware of them. No, I think I'll leave Miss Isaac here, alive, to wonder forever what happened to the two of you."

He turned to Gordy and raised his eyebrows. "You first, Mr. Sears. Where is my baby?"

Gordy hesitated, and I found myself holding my breath. I didn't know for sure if the decoy plan was properly set—he hadn't kept me fully in the loop on that. But even if it wasn't, Barringer would surely send someone to check on whatever we told him before he did anything irrevocable. That would take time, and at this point any time we could buy would be to our advantage.

Gordy seemed to wilt. "Okay," he said. "You don't need to—okay. She's in Winnipeg somewhere. I don't know exactly where."

I felt my jaw tighten, a sudden chill running up my back. *Winnipeg?* That wasn't the plan. We were supposed to point Barringer toward Sioux Falls, not Ferrier and his Winnipeg facility.

Had Gordy frozen up somehow? Had he forgotten his own damn plan?

"Explain," Barringer said coolly.

Gordy's tongue flicked over his lips. "A doctor named Miles Ferrier took the fetus out three months ago and put it in a sort of super-pre-natal pod he'd designed," he said. "He called it an artificial womb. Experimental—wasn't supposed to handle fetuses younger than sixteen weeks. He did some modifications, I guess, and it worked. It's somewhere near Winnipeg—that's all I know."

He looked at me, a deep sadness in his eyes. "I'm sorry, Dale. But he threatened Colleen. I couldn't . . ." He trailed off.

My heart seemed to wilt inside me. So there it was. No plan, no decoy, no planting of confusion. The whole truth, handed to Barringer on a silver platter.

"Ah, Mr. Sears," Barringer said, shaking his head in clear disappointment. "I'd hoped you would take me seriously." He motioned to Alex.

A gun appeared in Alex's hand, the muzzle pressed against Gordy's side. "I told you a lie would cost you a life," Barringer reminded him. "Whose life shall it be? Yours, or Mr. Ravenhall's?"

"Wait," I yelped. Barringer had gotten what he wanted. I knew it, he knew it, Gordy knew it. So why was there suddenly a gun in the mix?

What the *hell* was going on?

"You wish to go oh-for-two, Mr. Ravenhall?" Barringer asked, his voice like something from a graveyard.

"No," I said. "I don't . . ."

"*Where is my baby?*"

"Sioux Falls," the words tumbled reflexively from my mouth. The decoy—but Gordy had already told him the truth—but it was all I had left—

"There, now," Barringer said approvingly. The menace was gone from his voice, leaving only a darkly amused anticipation behind. "Was that so hard?"

I stared at him. "What—?"

"Really, Mr. Ravenhall," he said reproachfully. "Did you think we weren't paying attention? Alex, Mr. Ravenhall seems surprised. Explain it to him."

"Two days ago, Mr. Sears and Jean Forster flew to Regina," Alex said. "We think Mr. Lowell learned that Mr. Barringer had located this cabin and called to warn them."

"Which may earn Mr. Lowell a trip to the judicial review board," Barringer added. "Continue."

"They rented a car and drove up here," Alex said. "Ms. Forster left Mr. Sears with Ms. Isaac and took the car back. She then met with Dr. DuBois, who immediately left Regina and headed southeast in a great hurry."

"There were no medical, professional, or personal reasons in her schedule to warrant such a trip," Barringer said. "The obvious conclusion was that it involved my baby."

I looked back at Gordy. He was watching me closely, an edge of worry in his eyes. "All right," I said, for lack of anything better to say. "So why. . . ?"

"Why are we playing Russian roulette with your lives?" Barringer shrugged. "We knew Dr. DuBois headed southeast, but we lost track of her shortly after she crossed into the States. We simply needed her destination."

"Oh," I murmured.

"I'm surprised at you," Barringer chided, all calmness now. "Surprised at both of you. Did you really think I could be fooled so easily?"

"I . . . don't . . ."

"We knew Miss Isaac and Mr. Sears met with Dr. Ferrier in Vancouver last January," he said. "We also knew of Dr. Ferrier's work and this most impressive artificial womb of his."

He raised his eyebrows. "Unfortunately for you and your pathetic cover story, we also dug deeply enough into his resume to learn of his proficiency with uterine transplants."

I felt my eyes go wide. The decoy Gordy had pitched to us had included a uterine transplant as part of the story. But he'd never mentioned that Dr. Ferrier had any expertise in that field.

Why *hadn't* he mentioned it? Why hadn't Colleen?

Unless what they'd told me was the decoy plan wasn't a decoy at all.

The whole scenario flashed back across my mind, hitting me with the force of a gut punch. Gordy and Colleen meeting privately with Dr. Ferrier, with no way for me to independently corroborate their account of the discussion. The two of them further making sure I was outside the operating room when the time came, where again I was told the fetus had been transferred to the artificial womb. The other door, two down the hall from Colleen's recovery room, a door I'd spotted Ferrier going through furtively a couple of times. The room where Colleen's transplant surrogate was likewise recovering?

And now Gordy's far-too-quick revelation that the baby was in Winnipeg.

Had they lied to me? Had they *all* lied? Was Sioux Falls the baby's actual location, and Winnipeg the diversion?

Because if it was, my side project with Lainey—the job I'd quietly taken on to spare Gordy from the additional pain, the project I likewise hadn't told *them* about—was about to blow up in our faces.

And unless I could come up with some way to fix this, Colleen was going to lose her baby.

"Please, Mr. Ravenhall," Barringer admonished me. "Your histrionics notwithstanding—" He broke off, staring closely at my face. "They didn't tell you, did they? They let you truly believe that my baby was locked away in some mechanical monstrosity that was impossible to move and therefore open to discovery and attack."

I took a careful breath. Decoy or reality, it didn't matter. All that mattered was our daughter. "You won't find her," I told Barringer. "Sioux Falls may not be LA, but it's big enough. You'll never find her."

"Oh, I think we will." Barringer gestured toward the helicopter. "Just leave your phone there on the ground, Mr. Ravenhall. We'll be going to Sioux Falls together.

"To get my baby."

We left Colleen sleeping peacefully on her bed, were herded into the helicopter, and headed southeast toward the Dakotas.

The fact that Barringer left Colleen alive and unharmed struck me as a bad sign. Inside the telepath shield, she wouldn't have known I was coming, and she'd been in the cabin the whole time I'd been there. That meant she wouldn't be able to so much as point a finger at Barringer if I disappeared, and he knew it.

For that matter, she might not know Barringer was involved at all. It was entirely possible she'd only seen a couple of his goons as they burst into the cabin and was immediately taken to the bedroom for the doctor's examination. If that was the case, all she'd be able to say was that there'd been a break-in and that Gordy had disappeared. Once they disposed of my car, there wouldn't be any evidence that anyone else had ever been there.

Which left only two loose ends: Gordy and me. And I would be the easiest one to dispose of.

Alex had put me in one of the helicopter's window seats, and over the next four hours I experienced a panoramic view of the Canadian countryside, a colorful sunset, and a night sky dark enough to offer an impressive array of stars. I barely noticed any of it. My thoughts were on Colleen and Gordy, wondering if I'd screwed up their plan, wondering even more why they hadn't told me the truth, trying to come up with a new plan.

Somewhere over North Dakota, all that fear and simmering anger settled into something hard and deadly and ruthless.

If Colleen had lied to me, she must have had a good reason for it. I could accept that. Not happily, but I *could* accept it.

What I could not and would not accept was Barringer in possession of our baby. If it came to that, if there was no other way, then I would kill the baby myself. All of us: the baby, Gordy, and me. Quickly, efficiently, and with no chance for second thoughts.

I had my Plan B.

"Got it."

I turned from my contemplation of death to focus on the seats across from us. Alex, sitting between Barringer and a stone-faced bodyguard, was holding up his phone. "We have her, sir," he announced to his boss. "Dr. DuBois is in a small clinic called Saint Anne's near McKennan Hospital. William has found an empty lot nearby big enough for us to land in. Bruno will work the clearances and meet us there with the van."

"Is the baby there?" Barringer asked.

"William thinks so," Alex said. "He didn't want to risk going in and possibly spooking them. He also said there seemed to be an unusual amount of activity going on in that part of the clinic. They may be getting ready to run."

"For all the good it will do them," Barringer said grimly. "How long until we're there?"

"Including the van ride, should be about twenty minutes."

"You have fifteen."

"Yes, sir." Alex nodded and put his phone back to his ear.

Barringer focused on me. "Almost there, Mr. Ravenhall," he said. "Ready to meet your child?"

"Thank you," I said.

He gave a small shrug. "It's the least I could do."

"No, I meant thank you for calling her *my* child."

Barringer raised his eyebrows. "And *I* meant it was the least I could do, since it will only be yours for a few minutes."

I felt my stomach knot up. "Sometimes a few minutes is all you need."

"A very mature attitude." Barringer's eyes shifted to my side. "Though not one I believe Mr. Sears shares."

I turned to look at Gordy. On the surface, his face was calm enough. But beneath the veneer I could see the steel-spring tension there. Like me, he was contemplating the future.

Maybe also like me, he was wondering if there was one.

Sixteen minutes later, we pulled into the Saint Anne's parking lot.

From Alex's use of the word *small*, I'd envisioned a quaint, one-story building that would hold maybe a couple of examination rooms and a dozen or so beds for recovering patients. To my mild surprise the place was three stories high, covered a quarter of a block, and faced a decent-sized municipal parking lot about a quarter full of cars and minivans. Barringer was out the door and heading for the clinic almost before our van came to a halt, the shield briefcase gripped in his hand, his two bodyguards at his sides and the doctor trailing a couple of steps behind them. One of the guards was lugging a large case I'd seen the doctor fiddling with throughout the flight. Alex and the driver, Bruno, got Gordy and me out of the van and followed only a little more slowly. We caught up with the others at a service elevator where another of Barringer's thugs was holding the door open, and we all headed up.

"Security?" Barringer asked.

"Nothing obvious, sir," the door thug said. "There were a couple of nurses earlier, but right now DuBois and the other woman are in the room alone."

"They're *alone?*" Barringer asked, frowning.

"Yes, sir."

"And the activity William reported?"

"It seems to have stopped."

"I see," Barringer murmured, his voice gone grim. "Alex, you're on point. Secure the room, make sure there aren't any surprises hiding behind closed doors. Doctor, you're with me."

A few seconds later the elevator ground to a halt and the doors wheezed open. Alex strode out, Bruno and the door thug forming up on either side of him like a flying wedge, and headed toward a lighted door halfway down the corridor. One of Barringer's bodyguards caught my upper arm in a solid grip, and the rest of us followed. Alex flung open the door and went inside, his sudden appearance eliciting a startled gasp and a flurry of outraged words. I recognized Dr. DuBois's voice—

"Sir?" Alex called tightly. "Sir, you need to see this."

Barringer broke into a jog and disappeared through the doorway. My pulse thudding in my throat, I hurried to join them. I entered the room—

And stopped dead in my tracks.

In the center of the room was a young woman, her eyes closed, dressed in a hospital gown and stretched out on a half-propped up rolling bed. Dr. DuBois was standing at the foot of the bed, her face drawn, her own eyes half closed with weariness. A gurney holding a wrapped blanket stood in front of her. Barringer and his men had gathered around DuBois and the gurney, frozen into statues.

And mostly hidden within the blanket's folds, was the top of a tiny head, as motionless as the men around it.

"Dale."

I tore my eyes from the gurney. DuBois was looking at me, the weariness in her eyes deepening. "I'm sorry," she said, her voice soft and aching. "She was stillborn. There was nothing I could do."

My knees felt shaky. My stomach wanted to be sick. "Stillborn," I repeated, my voice sounding like it was coming from a well.

"I'm sorry," DuBois said again. She looked at Barringer. "I'm sorry, gentlemen, but under the circumstances, I must ask you to leave. I had to sedate Ms. Oliver, but—"

"A moment," Barringer said. His voice was quiet, but the initial shock of the grim discovery had worn off. "Dr. Vyas first has a test to perform."

The doctor started forward. DuBois was faster, slipping quickly around the side of the gurney and stepping into the other woman's path. "No," she said. "This patient is under my care—"

She broke off as Alex took her arm. Angrily, she twisted it away. "Dale, she can't just—"

"It's all right, Doctor," I said. "There's nothing we can do to stop them. No point getting yourself hurt."

"Mr. Ravenhall is correct," Barringer said. "Please step aside."

Swallowing visibly, DuBois obeyed. "Thank you," Barringer said. "Dr. Vyas?"

The doctor nodded and continued forward. By the time she reached the gurney the bodyguard with the big case had set it beside the folded blanket and opened the top and front. It was some kind of medical machine, I saw, but not of any sort I'd seen before.

"This will only take a few minutes," Barringer said into the brittle silence as Vyas pulled a slender syringe from the case and eased it beneath the blanket. "I just want to confirm that this is, in fact, Miss Isaac's baby. Did you assist in the transplant procedure, Dr. DuBois?"

"I don't know what you're talking about," DuBois said, a hard edge coming into her voice. "If you're asking about this baby—*Ms. Oliver's* baby—yes, I delivered her."

"And you came all the way from Regina to do so?" Barringer said, clearly not believing it.

"She contacted me a few weeks ago," DuBois said. "She was facing a difficult pregnancy and said a friend had recommended me to her."

"Of course," Barringer said, watching as Vyas injected her sample into a port in the machine. "Did she mention her uterine transplant?"

DuBois's lip twitched. "I don't know what you're talking about. Ms. Oliver hasn't had any surgery of any sort, let alone something so dramatic."

"Dramatic and dangerous both, I have no doubt," Barringer said. He was toying with her, I knew, the cat letting the mouse prattle on while knowing full well there was nowhere the mouse could escape to. "Fortunately, you had Dr. Ferrier to handle the difficult part."

DuBois flicked a look at me, then one at Gordy, then turned back to Barringer. "I have no idea what you're talking about."

The machine gave a soft beep and a strip of paper started feeding out of a slot. Vyas waited until it was finished, then tore it off and ran her eyes over it.

"Well?" Barringer prompted, his voice a mixture of anticipation and dread.

"Yes," the doctor said, her own voice a little sad. "It was Ms. Isaac's baby."

Barringer huffed out a breath. The anticipation was gone from his face, leaving only darkness behind. "You're certain?"

"Their DNA samples are a match," Vyas said, offering him the paper. She turned her head to look at the sleeping woman. "I've never heard of a uterine transplanted with an embryo already inside. I wonder how they talked her into letting them do that."

"You'd be surprised how good these people are at persuasion," Barringer said. He studied the paper a moment, his face hardening. "I'd hoped you were lying, Dr. DuBois. I'd hoped all of you were lying. But . . ."

He left the sentence unfinished. For another moment he gazed at the paper, as if sheer willpower could change what was printed there. Then, with quiet viciousness, he crumpled it into his fist. "Pack up your gear, Doctor. Bruno, Michael, escort her back to the van—we'll be leaving for the helicopter shortly. Alex, stay with me. The rest of you, secure our exit route." His eyes drifted back to the wrapped blanket.

I looked at Gordy. He was staring at the blanket, too, his body sagging, his face drained of everything but weariness. "What about us?" I asked.

Barringer stirred, coming out of whatever dark thoughts he'd wrapped himself in. "I told you back at the cabin," he said. "One lie, one death. You told me the truth. Mr. Sears lied. The path seems clear."

I looked back at Gordy. He'd saved Colleen's life once at the risk of his own. He'd suffered a close-approach with me, at the risk of his sanity.

And he loved Colleen. He'd admitted that out loud, back when he thought he was about to die.

So what had I done for her?

Gotten her pregnant, which had put her life in terrible danger. Brought Barringer into the open, which had put all the rest of us in danger along with her. Colleen probably hated me for screwing up her life so badly.

And now the child who'd been at the heart of all this was dead. If Colleen didn't hate me already, she certainly would. Maybe as much as I hated myself.

So what, really did I have to live for?

I took a deep breath and turned back to Barringer. "Actually—"

"All right," Gordy interrupted. "I'll do it. And I'll do it in a way that doesn't implicate you, Barringer. But there are conditions."

Barringer eyed him coolly. "I'm listening."

"I'm guessing Dr. DuBois has stuff in her bag that will kill quickly if you overdose on it," Gordy said. His voice was as glacially cool as Barringer's face. "I'll take a hypo of the stuff out to the parking lot, inject myself and die. Once I'm dead, you and your people can take your damn consolation prize—the shield—and leave without hurting Dale. So far so good?"

"So far," Barringer agreed. "I assume you're next going to try to persuade me that Mr. Ravenhall and his colleagues won't be able to make trouble for me."

"Like you said earlier, they can scream all they want," Gordy said. "But Dale and Colleen will both be alive. *And* you'll keep it that way. That's the deal. Take it, or create a situation that the cops *will* investigate."

Barringer looked at DuBois. "Doctor?"

"No," DuBois said flatly. "I can't be a party to—"

"Do you have such drugs, or don't you?" Barringer interrupted. "Because the alternative is for me to shut down the shield and let Mr. Sears and Mr. Ravenhall both die, right here, right now, and I'll take my chances with Mr. Sears' police investigation."

"Let me also point out that the investigation won't be the worst of it," Gordy warned. "You kill us that way, and the world will figure out that you have a telepath shield. So far, you and Dr. DuBois have been able to keep that a secret. You know as well as I do that once people know something is possible they'll figure out how to duplicate it. There'll be a hundred of the things out there before the end of the year."

Barringer's lips briefly compressed into a thin line. His whole plan to find an undiscovered telepath relied on him being the only one with Amos's locator. "Alex, check Dr. DuBois's bag," he said. "Find some morphine or something equally deadly. Give it to Mr. Sears and escort him to the door. Be sure to stay clear of the outside security cameras."

"Yes, sir," Alex said, walking over to a doctor's bag sitting on a back table. "You want me to make sure he takes it? I can do that from the door."

"No need," Barringer said, checking his watch. "In exactly five minutes I'm going to turn off the shield. If Mr. Sears has some duplicity planned, he and Mr. Ravenhall can still die together."

I looked back at Gordy. "Gordy—"

"It's okay, Dale," he said quietly. "I've been ready to die since—" his eyes flicked to Barringer "—since the day his mind pushed in on mine. Say goodbye to Colleen and the others for me, will you?"

For a moment my mind spun in a hurricane of ideas, options, alternative plans. But none of them landed. None of them would work. Either Gordy died, or we both did.

And sooner rather than later, all the rest of us would. Barringer would have no choice but to shut us up. "I will," I said. "I'm sorry, Gordy. For everything."

"It's okay. Really." He turned to Alex, who was now holding a syringe. "That's it?"

"That's it," Alex confirmed, handing it gingerly to Gordy. "Should do the job about a minute after you inject it."

"Thanks." Gordy nodded to him, nodded to me, and looked at Barringer. "You leave Colleen and the others alone. I mean that."

"Of course."

For a second he and Gordy locked eyes, and I had the sense that Gordy was wondering if he should try to deliver a final punch to that casually evil face. But the moment passed, and Gordy merely gave him a thin smile. Without another word he strode out the door, Alex close behind him.

Barringer looked at his watch. "Five minutes, Mr. Ravenhall."

I nodded silently. At this point I didn't dare speak.

The minutes ticked by. I could tell that the two bodyguards standing their silent vigil by the door were watching me closely, but neither made any move. Once, Dr. DuBois checked the sleeping woman, but I had the feeling it was less concern for her condition than it was just trying to fill the tense silence with something. I looked at that sleeping face, the doctor's comment echoing through my mind: *I wonder how they talked her into letting them do that.*

There was movement at the door, and I looked over to see Alex slip back into the room. "Well?" Barringer asked.

"He took the shot and collapsed onto the pavement," Alex said.

"Cameras?"

"I watched from inside the clinic door," Alex assured him. "No problem."

"Good. Have you spoken to Gene?"

"Yes, sir," Alex said. "The chopper's fueled, and he's back at the lot."

"Excellent." Barringer held out the case. "Do it."

"Wait a second," I protested. "You said five minutes. It's only been four."

"It's all right, Dale," DuBois murmured. "He's gone."

There didn't seem to be anything more to say. I watched silently as Alex opened the case, revealing the intricate electronics wrapped around the three kernels that Amos had worked so hard to create. At the front of the case, the edge with the briefcase's handle, was the modular casing Rob had built to hold the rack of eleven D-cell batteries. "I'm thinking you just pull that battery array loose from its connectors," Barringer said, pointing to the contacts at the edge of the casing. "Quick and brief."

"Yes, sir." Visibly bracing himself, Alex popped out the casing.

And for the first time in hours, a chorus of minds flooded in on me.

That one brief flash was all I got. Half a second later, Alex popped the pack back in place and the world once again went dark. "Did it work?" he asked.

"Yes," Barringer confirmed. "I could see it in his face. He was back to full power." He smiled faintly at me. "And obviously, he didn't die."

"Did he get anything from you?" Alex asked, turning suspicious eyes on me.

"I don't think so," Barringer said. "There wasn't time for him to get anything important. And I was also focusing on the dinner I'm planning for later tonight."

"So now what?" I asked. "You made a deal, you know."

"A deal I intend to keep," he said with all the sincerity I would expect from a cold-blooded murderer. "None of the rest of you are a genuine threat to me."

"Not even if we testify about today's events?" DuBois asked.

Barringer shrugged. "My lawyers can keep any testimony tied up in challenges, continuances, and a dozen other legal thorn hedges. You'll have a better chance of dying of old age than you will of taking the stand against me. *Any* stand."

He took the case back from Alex. "In the meantime, I'll have someone reconfigure this back into its telepath finder mode. Your child may be lost to me, Mr. Ravenhall, but there will be others."

He gestured to the two bodyguards. "We're leaving now," he said. "I suggest you wait until we're gone before you and Dr. DuBois try to leave." His eyes flicked briefly to the sleeping woman. "A pity Miss Oliver wasn't a stronger surrogate mother. Good evening."

He left, the bodyguards crowding out into the hall in front of him. Alex lingered another moment, probably expecting some final desperate act on my part. But I stayed where I was, and so did DuBois, and with a final look Alex was gone.

I took a deep breath, let out a long shaking sigh. "Doctor?" I asked, gesturing toward Ms. Oliver.

"It's all right," DuBois said. "I just gave her a sedative. Another doctor and nurse are standing by to bring her out of it and get her home."

I frowned. "Just like that? What about the baby. It *was* a C-Section, wasn't it?"

"Yes, but not on her," DuBois said. "She was just a friend I asked to help us set the stage. The real mother—" A flash of deep sadness crossed her face. "She miscarried earlier this morning."

"Oh," I said, my mind skidding sideways as I fought to make sense of everything that had just happened. "Sorry, but I'm lost."

"I know," she said. "Gordy and Colleen . . . we needed your reactions to look real, Dale. And after all you're the one who warned us that Barringer was the suspicious type who double- and triple-checked everything."

"Okay," I said, eyeing her closely. That *was* some of what Gordy and I had sifted out of my second-hand mental contact with Barringer. "So?"

She took a deep breath. "Three days ago, when I knew the baby's mother was about to miscarry, I alerted Gordy that the timing was finally right. He told Scott, who slipped Barringer's people enough information to let them find Colleen."

"And added that bit about uterine transplants to Dr. Ferrier's resume?"

She nodded. "That was done back in January, but yes, that was also Scott's handiwork. So Gordy flew into Regina—"

"And talked to you, and sent you rushing down here," I interrupted, the pieces finally starting to fit together. "Knowing that Barringer was watching and would figure you were heading to the baby."

"Yes," DuBois said. "It really *was* the decoy plan you and Gordy worked out, just with a few extra wrinkles added."

I braced myself. "And Gordy?"

"In a minute," she said. "Let me make sure Teresa is all right first."

She crossed to the desk, picked up the phone, and punched in a number. "It's clear," she announced. "You can come back in."

Three minutes later, one of the doors at the back of the room opened and two women in scrubs came in. "Doctor," DuBois greeted the older woman. "Can you take it from here?"

"Yes, of course," the older woman said, throwing me a speculative look as she walked to the bed. She leaned over the sleeping woman, took her pulse, then pulled a syringe from her pocket. The other woman went to the gurney and began gently rewrapping the blanket.

"How's the mother?" I murmured to DuBois.

"Hurting," DuBois murmured back. "Agonizing. But she's back home, and among family." She sighed. "That's really all that can be done for her right now. She'll have to do most of the healing by herself."

We waited silently until the sleeping woman floated her way back to consciousness. DuBois went over to the bed and held a brief and quiet conversation with her. The two women gripped hands, and then DuBois retraced her steps to me.

"She's fine," she assured me. "She said to tell you she was glad she could help." DuBois smiled faintly. "With whatever it was we did here tonight. I promised I'd tell her all about it someday."

She gestured to the door. "We need to go. Barringer must be far away by now. And I imagine Gordy is freezing."

We found him lying on the pavement beside DuBois's car. "Gordy?" DuBois called softly. "Rise and shine."

He half opened his eyes. "About time," he said, standing up and brushing off his jacket and trousers. "That pavement is *cold*."

"Sorry," DuBois apologized. "Come on, we need to get on the road."

"I assume Barringer took the shield," Gordy said as DuBois unlocked the car. "The *other* shield, anyway."

"Yes," she said, her eyes flicking to her car's trunk. "A good thing they didn't know you had two of them."

"Yeah," Gordy said. "I guess we'll just have to hope he isn't able to convert the one he's got back to a telepath detector. I don't like the idea of him finding the next one of us before we do."

"Won't be a problem," I assured him. "I always figured that however this worked out he'd be taking one of the shields. Luckily, Colleen knew which one to give him. Did you hear their helicopter take off?"

"Yeah, about half an hour ago," Gordy confirmed. "I didn't want to move until you showed up in case he'd left someone behind to watch me."

"No, I think he figured you were adequately dead," I said. "Which way did it go? Toward California?"

"Also toward most of the United States and parts of Mexico," Gordy said dryly. "South-west. But you're right, he's probably scampering straight home with his new toy. I wonder who he bribed in the local control towers to let him take off and land in the middle of town that way."

"Probably had his doctor spin some medical excuse," I said. Half an hour at the speed that helicopter could make . . .

"She made my skin crawl," DuBois said as we all got into the car. "So cold and detached. I still don't know how you all gimmicked the DNA test."

"Yeah, I wasn't expecting that," Gordy agreed. "I was standing on eggs the whole time. I never knew you could make a DNA tester that small and that fast."

"I did," I said. "I've had Rob keep track of Barringer's companies and the stuff his R&D departments were coming up with for the past few months."

"Ah," Gordy said. "So it wasn't just a mistake or misread?"

"No," I said, shivering with the memory. "Not exactly, anyway. And really, Dr. DuBois, you're being a little unfair. Lainey's not such a bad person when you get to know her."

We all closed our doors and DuBois started the car. "One other question," Gordy said as DuBois headed toward the parking lot exit. "You mentioned Colleen giving Barringer the right shield. I looked inside the shield case I brought down from Colleen's to give to Dr. DuBois, and it had *eight* batteries."

"*Eight?*" DuBois asked, frowning in the mirror at me. "The one Barringer took had eleven."

"No, his still only has eight," I said. "The three middle ones are a bonus I had Rob put in. Like I said, I expected him to walk off with it. Doctor, can I borrow your phone?"

"You wanted extra batteries for this one?" Gordy asked, frowning as DuBois handed her phone over the seat. "What, for more range or stamina?"

"No, the shield's the same as the other one," I said. "The extra three in Barringer's just look like batteries. The middle one's a cell phone receiver, and the two on either side of it are . . . something else."

"What are you going to do?" DuBois asked as I started punching in a number on her phone. "Are you going to listen in on them?"

"I wish I could," I said. "Their upcoming conversation would probably be highly entertaining." I finished entering the proper number, waited a few seconds for the phone to connect to the briefcase, then keyed in the coded command. "No, like I said, it was a bonus feature." I shut off the phone and handed it back to her. "I just thought it would be a shame to waste all that thermite material I collected in Regina."

Four months later, with Dr. DuBois in attendance and the rest of us watching from afar, Dr. Ferrier's gloriously horrendous artificial womb gave birth.

So what's the latest? Gordy asked. *Have the new parents picked her up yet?*

Yes, three days ago, Colleen said. *They're all home now, and Rachel tells me her daughters absolutely love having a new baby sister.*

I hope you're not contacting her directly, I warned. *Barringer's still out there, and I doubt he's cooled off any since we wrecked his telepath finder.*

No, we've got a secure system, Colleen assured me. *And Scott says there's no way the adoption paperwork can be traced.*

I hope not, Calvin said. *I can't help thinking that if Scott can slip information about your whereabouts into Barringer's data network, it's not impossible for Barringer to pull information out of ours.*

It's safe, Scott said. *The only reason I could do that was because the firm already had connections to his people. Barringer doesn't and won't have any such access.*

In that case, you be sure to watch your back, too, Gordy warned. *He has to suspect that the information—or at least the timing—was all you.*

I have safeguards in place, Scott said. *I'm more concerned that he'll figure out you aren't dead.*

Not a chance, Gordy assured him. *I'm in a very peaceful place at the back edge of nowhere, and I can stay here as long as I need to. Anyway, with probate finished there's no reason for anyone to even want to look for me.*

Though it could have been awkward if your insurance company's suicide clause hadn't still been in effect, Scott pointed out. *But no insurance payout means no fraud they can hit you with down the line.*

As I of course planned from the very start, Gordy said, a hint of slyness to his thoughts. *Just because you're the only lawyer in the group doesn't mean the rest of us can't think that way when we have to.*

Ooh—quiet, everyone, Colleen interrupted, her tone a mix of excitement and wistfulness. *Can you hear her?*

I strained. Right at the edge of my limit . . .

There it was. A tiny mind, brimming with unreadable thoughts and feelings, vaguely aware of everything in the world around her but with no words to attach to any of it.

She just woke up, Colleen said. *I think she's hungry.*

Right on cue, I felt the sudden shift of emotion.

I'm too far away, Scott said. *What's happening?*

I think she's crying, I said.

Yes, Colleen confirmed, the wistfulness going a little deeper. *But . . . there. Rachel's there. The bottle . . . there, she's got it.*

Sounds like Rachel's right on top of things, Scott commented.

Well, she does *have two other daughters,* Gordy reminded him. *She's probably pretty good at anticipation by now.*

Are you all right, Colleen? Calvin asked gently. *I know this isn't how you wanted it.*

I sensed Colleen take a deep breath. *But it was always how it had to be,* she said, the darkness of her mood easing a bit. *Barringer was right: I was never going to be able to raise her myself. This way, at least she gets to grow up free.*

With a loving mother and an ex-military cop father, Gordy added. *Definitely the best and safest of all possible worlds.*

I winced. The best of all possible worlds. For people like us, that was sadly the case.

I get to watch her grow up, Colleen reminded us. *And maybe someday, when she's older, I can dig the telepath shield out of hiding and visit her in person.*

One step at a time, Calvin said. *And speaking of steps, we should probably let you go. You have a baby girl to watch.*

I sensed Colleen's smile. *If that's all right,* she said. *I'll talk to you all later. And thank you again for everything you all did for us.*

You're welcome, I said for all of us. *Gordy, can I have a word?*

Sure, he said. *Good night, everyone.*

We all said our good-byes, and I felt Colleen, Calvin, and Scott vanish.

Gordy got in the first word. *I don't think I've apologized properly for taking you down the garden path with Barringer,* he said. *It wasn't that we didn't trust you. It was just . . .*

That you thought I was a rotten actor, I finished the sentence for him. *And you were right. I am. If I'd known that wasn't Colleen's baby, I don't think I'd have been able to pull it off.*

I'm still sorry, Gordy said. *But I'm glad you understand—it's been bugging me this whole time. So what did you want to talk to me about?*

I hesitated. But this question had been bugging me, too. *During our close-approach with Barringer, I think I got some of your ability to plan and your bulldog attitude toward problem-solving.*

Yeah, that sounds about right. And that's a problem?

No, not at all. My question was . . . what did you get from me? And why did it make you so . . .

Morose? Depressed?

Yeah. All of that.

I sensed him sigh. *What I got from you was a reality check.*

I frowned. *Come again?*

I know you know that I—how I feel about Colleen, he said, the words coming reluctantly. *I'd sometimes fantasized . . . and then we had our close-approach, and I saw how it had been when you and Colleen were together inside the shield. Not* that *part of it,* he hastened to add. *Just the whole . . .*

He paused. I waited silently, watching him trying to pick out the proper words. *We're telepaths, Dale,* he said. *We don't get to live like ordinary people. I saw how it was with you, and it threw me for a loop. A big loop. And then I got to see for myself, in Vancouver. But because I'd already seen it through your eyes and had had time to work it through, I was ready for it.*

I nodded, understanding now. *You can have Colleen's smile, her voice, her face, and her body,* I said. *Or you can have* her. *Her heart, her mind, her soul.* Her.

Yes, Gordy said soberly. *I'm sorry for you, my friend. I really wish it could be otherwise.*

Thank you, I said. *But it can't. And given that choice . . . yes. I'll take Colleen any day. All of her.*

Agreed, Gordy said. *It's funny, you know. I keep thinking about that old song, "The Impossible Dream."*

I smiled sadly. *"To love, pure and chaste, from afar."*

That's the one, he said. *An impossible dream for some. A way of life for us.*

For a moment neither of us spoke. Then, I felt his mind stirring away from that depressing thought. *Anyway, you sound tired. Good-night, Dale. Sleep well.*

You, too, Gordy.

And then he was gone.

I stretched once, working some of the tension out of my body. Yes, I was tired; and yes, I would sleep.

But not quite yet. Baby Miriam was still eating, but she'd be drifting back to sleep when she was finished.

Like all good parents, I would wait to sleep when my child did.

ABOUT THE AUTHOR

Timothy Zahn is the *New York Times*–bestselling science fiction author of more than forty novels, as well as many novellas and short stories. Best known for his contributions to the expanded Star Wars universe of books, including the Thrawn trilogy, Zahn also wrote the Cobra series and the young adult Dragonback series—the first novel of which, *Dragon and Thief*, was an ALA Best Book for Young Adults. Zahn currently resides in Oregon with his family.

TIMOTHY ZAHN

FROM OPEN ROAD MEDIA

OPEN ROAD

INTEGRATED MEDIA

OPEN ROAD

INTEGRATED MEDIA

Find a full list of our authors and
titles at www.openroadmedia.com

FOLLOW US
@OpenRoadMedia